D0443923

FROM WHERE
I WATCH YOU

FROM WHERE I WATCH YOU

SHANNON GROGAN

Published in the United States by Soho Teen
an imprint of
Soho Press, Inc.
853 Broadway
New York, NY 10003

Library of Congress Cataloging-in-Publication Data

Grogan, Shannon.
From where I watch you / Shannon Grogan.

ISBN 978-1-61695-554-0
eISBN 978-1-61695-555-7
1. Stalking—Fiction. 2. Sisters—Fiction. 3. High schools—Fiction.
4. Schools—Fiction. 5. Baking—Fiction. 6. Family problems—Fiction.
I. Title.
PZ7.1.G76Fro 2015
[Fic]—dc23   2015001669

Interior design by Janine Agro, Soho Press, Inc.

Printed in the United States of America

10 9 8 7 6 5 4 3 2 1

For my sister.
I'll always watch out for you.

SNOWFLAKE SUGAR'S 15TH ANNUAL VALENTINE COOKIE BAKE-OFF

Congratulations, Kara! You've been selected by your high school culinary arts instructor to compete in Snowflake Sugar's annual Cookie Bake-off!

Saturday, February 6, 2016
Hyatt Grand Regency, San Francisco, California

FIRST PLACE PRIZE
Full Scholarship to La Patisserie Pastry School!

SECOND PLACE PRIZE
$1,000 college scholarship

Contestants will be given a four-hour time window and be judged on creativity in using the Valentine theme, appearance, and taste. Good Luck!

P.O. Box 123
San Francisco, CA

Kara McKinley
Queen Anne High School
123 Upper Queen Anne
Seattle, WA 98109

STEP 1:

Beat until pale and fluffy.

1. *Mix.*

· ·

We can all smell when someone's getting an F. Right now that F smells like burnt sugar, and there's a lot of noise coming from the other side of the room where someone is actually failing home ec.

I try to ignore it and keep stirring, but my sister Kellen's knee bobs up and down, up and down, threatening to knock my mixing bowl to the floor. I wonder if she can tell it's ticking me off. Once upon a time, I would've tried to smack her. Maybe.

"Kara." The teacher spooks me from behind, oblivious to the panic across the room and to my sister sitting there, now kicking her legs back and forth.

Mr. King balances a stack of catalogs and paper, topped off with a half-eaten apple fritter. He pulls out a shiny postcard and waves it in the air. Kellen keeps kicking.

"Read this after class. And, I have something else for you in here," he says, rummaging through his stack, "I know it's here somewhere . . ."

Kellen's gone.

Poof.

While Mr. King keeps digging, I drop the postcard into my backpack without looking at it. But my stomach knots because I locate the "something else" before he does.

He swears under his breath, which is usually funny to me,

but not now, not when I see a familiar blue-gray envelope with bloody red fibers poking out of his pile.

"Here it is!" he exclaims. He smiles as he hands it to me. "Found this on my desk this morning. I—" His smile sags into a frown. "Kara?"

Different sounds spin through the air: the creak of an oven door, the hum of mixers, and the throbbing in my head. My teacher's voice registers somewhere in the midst of it all. I stare at the envelope he offers while I point to the counter, hoping he'll stick it there because I don't want to touch it.

"Kara? Are you feeling okay?" He sets the envelope down. "You look pale."

"I'm fine."

"Okay. Hey, make sure you don't read that postcard in class."

I nod. My hand shakes. I hope he doesn't notice as I pull the sealed envelope through the flour spill on the counter. The tracks remind me of when Kellen and I were kids, and she would pull the sled, running with it just ahead of me so I couldn't get on.

"Go on, dumbshit, get in!" she'd say.

I'd put my hands down to climb on and off she'd go—pulling it away, unable to contain her laughter as I fell on my face, eating snow.

My hand is still shaking when I stuff the unopened envelope into my backpack, as if hiding it from my sight will make me forget about it.

MR. KING THINKS I'VE come down with the flu so when he sends me to the office, I sneak out early. I don't usually cut class, but I needed distraction from that *thing* in my backpack. Now I'm hiding, sitting on an old root at the bottom of my favorite tree, at my old house. I'm pretty sure no one can see me. I pinch a joint tight between two fingers—because I tend to drop lit joints—while I doodle a cookie design in my notebook.

I suck in a long drag, trying hard not to cough this time. The weed is probably expensive so I don't want to waste it. As if I would know the going rate. Kellen would know. But she's not here anymore. She's not here to teach me how to be a girl who cuts class to smoke weed.

The third-story attic used to be my room. Kellen had the room below mine. I stare at my sister's old window and try blowing a big puff of smoke toward it, but I end up coughing.

This is the third time I've tried to properly smoke one of her buried treasures. I found her stash rolled up in a kitchen towel decorated with cherries, stuffed into a Playtex tampon box, inside one of the boxes her roommate packed up. Before I found it I'd never smoked even a cigarette. I'm doing it all wrong, I'm sure.

November wind carries the faint horn of a ferryboat. On my old front porch, a pile of U-Haul boxes sag from the damp Seattle weather. The boxes haven't budged since the new family moved into my house, so there's no room on the porch for a nine-year-old to sit and paint her toenails while her Barbies watch. No room to pretend to do homework while wishing for her crush to ride by on his bike, or to watch a summer thunderstorm and wonder if she should tell her best friends about that terrible secret she's keeping.

On second thought, there is no wondering. She'll never tell.

I'm ready for another puff when the bushes next to me move.

Branches snap and leaves pull back and fly in the opposite direction like arrows. In a panic I try to get to my feet but my toe catches the underside of a root. My notebook lies in the dirt. I drop the joint and fall backward on my ass, landing in the cove of moss and muck between tree roots.

Tiny wisps of smoke swirl and tuck, swirl and tuck, over and over as the joint rolls down the slope. I stare at it, keeping still and holding my breath, which is really hard because leftover weed smoke tickles my throat, just daring me to cough. But I have to keep quiet because the noise in the bushes might be *him*—the one who sent the note Mr. King gave me. The note that prompted me to cut class and sit here like the idiot that I am.

The new family's dog appears out of the bushes. He sniffs through the dead grass and dandelions infesting Mom's flowerbeds. I puff out my cheeks, meaning to exhale slowly, but I cough yet again. The stone angel I gave Mom when I was ten reaches above the tops of the weeds, begging to be saved. The dog lifts his leg and pisses on her wing.

Edges curl inward on the leaves covering the ground, and my little joint sits on top of one, still smoldering like a trooper after all that rolling downhill. I grab it and snuff it out.

I would absolutely kill for a Twinkie right now.

The damn dog finds me, poking its head through the bushes. When he growls, I grab my backpack and haul ass before he tries to pee on me, too.

MY BEST AND ONLY friend, Noelle, is sitting at our table when I push through the door to my mom's café. She glares as if I'm the biggest bitch on the Hill, probably because I'm so late.

"*Kar*-a!" Mom sings. She skips around from behind the counter. The woman does this every day, like she totally forgot she saw me that morning. "Was your day blessed, sweetheart? Did you make good with the breath God gave you today? Why are you so late? Is everything okay?"

My face is in her hands, my cheeks squishing against my eyeballs so everything is a blur. It's fine because I can't see the people in the café watch Mom embarrass herself.

"Mom, I have homework," I mumble into her neck, hoping she doesn't smell weed. She kisses my forehead and whirls off to handle a customer. Emergency gum-chewing worked, I guess.

"*Kar*-a," Noelle sings, mimicking my mother. "Did you make

good with the mouth God gave you? Did you make Hayden's dream come true? Bet he'd leave his girlfriend!"

I ignore this as I scoot into the booth and drop my bag. Noelle must not smell me, either; otherwise she'd be clawing her way into my backpack for my joint. I frown at her. She has new highlights. So this is the reason I was alone at lunch. Sometimes Noelle forgets that her Mini has two seats and that I have no friends. But I don't mention it.

"You're late, and—" Noelle cracks her gum, pointing her head and thumb in the same direction. "Hayden's here, by the way."

I already know that, but I act cool when I turn toward a group of college kids in a booth, all hunched around laptops and laughing like dorks. Except for Hayden; he catches me looking and smiles. I blush.

Hayden's a college junior, so kind of too old for me. Noelle disagrees. She hopes I'm lucky enough to lose my virginity to a college guy soon, and she agrees that Hayden's hot, but she also thinks he's disturbed and a dork because he plays trombone in the marching band. I don't think that's so dorky when you're out of high school. At least he doesn't wear eyeliner, like *her* boyfriend.

They're laughing at something on Hayden's computer. On the rare occasion he's by himself, he'll usually try to get me to watch something funny on YouTube.

Noelle twists a freshly colored lock of hair around her finger. "You really should give up on that trom-*bone* player, Kar. You know he's a *boner*, right? Yeah, he likes to play the *bone*, you do realize that, don't you?"

"You're gross. Hayden's nice to me."

Hayden's disgusting girlfriend, Babe, sucks on his neck. I'm pretty sure her real name isn't "Babe." but that's what Hayden always calls her. And I don't really give a crap what her real name is because by next week there will be a new "Babe" and it won't be me.

There's no way in hell Hayden will ever be into me, which is probably the reason I can actually talk to him without throwing up. But still, I often fantasize about delivering my cookies to him, all bundled in a white box and tied with a red ribbon. He would smile while Babe shot me eye-daggers, and after he finished a cookie he'd sweep across the room, pull me out of the booth and kiss me—right there in the middle of Mom's holy café.

I smile when Hayden unleeches Babe from his neck. Maybe he's also remembering last time Mom kicked them out:

"The Lord and I are not amused by your lewd behavior in this establishment, where miracles occur daily. When you're ready to check your Godless groping at the door and prepared to order food instead of nursing Cokes all day, then you have my blessing to come back!"

It was a glimpse of my old, badass Mom. The Mom I had before Kellen died, before she vanished inside herself and twirled back into the world six months later with Jesus on her arm. My mom thinks she had a near-death experience and that when she was dead, she saw Kellen, who told her to sell our house, open a café, and heal everyone on the Hill with her pea soup.

My mom is crazy, and it's Kellen's fault.

A dish shatters in the kitchen. I flinch. Noelle raises an eyebrow at me. I reach for the postcard in my backpack so she won't hassle me about why I'm jumpy. When I grab it I can't help but see the blue-gray envelope wedged between the pages of my math book. That will have to wait. I haven't told Noelle about the notes I'm getting. I haven't told anyone about them. About *him.*

"What's this?" Noelle asks, grabbing the card from me. Her eyes narrow, zooming in on the Snowflake Sugar logo.

"Uh, it's a baking contest in San Francisco that Mr. King wants me to enter."

She reads it and sighs. "Snowflake Sugar Cookie Bake-Off. Wow."

"Shut up," I whisper. "I don't want my mom to know, okay? And yeah, *wow*, the prize is a full scholarship to La Patisserie Pastry School—far away from here."

After I graduate from La Patisserie I'll go live in France and take more pastry classes and eat lots of cheese and baguettes. And I'll force myself to drink wine, which I don't like. I'll make myself like it because I won't want to stick out as the dumb American who doesn't like wine. Then I'll open my own bakery somewhere on the California coast. Or maybe on the East Coast. Or maybe I'll love France and I'll stay there and find a guy to teach me French and other things.

Mom keeps telling me La Patisserie is out of the question because it's out of state. Yeah, like that will stop me. My whole future lies in winning this contest. If I don't, I'll be stuck here forever with Mom and bad memories.

Noelle sighs. "Uh, hey, Genius? You'll need a plane ticket to get there and that requires actual money, which you don't have. So how can you get there without telling your mom? Unless you're planning on asking Officer Frank?"

The ceramic mug warms my fingers. I ignore her reference to my father. "I'm going to start working at Crockett's." I stare into the mug at the latte foam, swirled into a perfect brown creamy spiral. "The guy called me yesterday and said I got the job. I'll earn enough money." I look across the table. "And seriously, don't tell anyone. I don't want your mom telling mine."

Noelle's cell chimes. She looks at it and laughs before texting something back, probably to her boyfriend, Mason.

"What's so funny?" I ask her.

"Sorry, your eyes are just too young for this." She sets the cell on the table and raises her eyebrows. "Hey, Mason's parents are going to Vegas for the weekend."

"Is he having a party?"

She cracks her knuckles. That sound always makes me sick.

"Nope. Well, just with me . . ." Her eyes drift from mine. They fix on a spot behind me and her face lights up. "Hey!"

"Ladies." Mason, Noelle's boyfriend of two years, the guy who wears black eyeliner, slides in next to her.

"Hey." I sip my latte.

They kiss and I become wallpaper.

Noelle hasn't always been my friend. She moved up here from California in sixth grade, and for some reason being from California gave her instant fame, even though she was a bitch to everyone, including me.

But once we started high school, she talked to me when my best friends Jen Creighton and Gaby Navarro stopped. Something happened during that summer between middle school and high school. Horrible secrets have a funny way of erasing friends from your life.

Mason is texting and Noelle has her head on his shoulder. They both laugh and I assume they're making fun of me because of the looks I'm getting. I hate that Mason's black eyeliner looks really good. His skin is the color of Dove soap. But it is weird when Noelle drags us into Sephora and I catch Mason checking out the products.

He sets his phone down. "McKinley, what's up? You look almost happy." He smiles and rests his elbows on the table.

"Aww." Noelle grabs Mason's arm and pulls him into her. "Our girl's growing up, honey. She's going to fly herself off to a big baking contest in Frisco and make all her dreams come true!"

Mason smiles. "Hey, that's awesome. Is it like a contest-contest, like on uh . . . you know, like *Iron Chef* or some shit like that?"

"Yeah," I say. "Something like that, except not on TV." God, I hope it's not on TV. I flick my eyes to Noelle. Her face oozes condescension. Her eyes are wide, blinking at me and nodding like she's fixated on every word I say.

Then she's back to texting. I scoot out of the booth, grabbing my bag. "I gotta get to work. Call me later, 'kay?"

"Like 'frosting cookies' work?"

Taking a deep breath, I turn without a reply because when Mason is around, Noelle's even snarkier than usual. I hear them giggling. But I still have to smile. They are all I have.

FOURTEEN-YEAR-OLD CARROT

I stop. Jen stares at me from the end of my bank of lockers. It's the first day of our freshman year. The last time we were in school together, she was one of my best friends. Jen gives me a half-smile, looking like she wants to say something.

It's September and I haven't talked to her since June. Not since the end of eighth grade.

Her expression is like an open door for me, and I remember all the times, all summer when she called or came over and I ignored her because I just couldn't talk about it. Gaby called once, and then gave up on being my friend. But not Jen—she kept it up all the way through August.

Closing my locker, I walk toward her.

I'm ready to tell her my secret.

I'm finally going to tell her what happened way back in June—after I left her and Gaby at the pool.

But I'm not ready to tell Gaby. I just can't. She'd say it was my fault. But Jen will understand. She always does.

Then Gaby comes from around the corner and stops before I can say anything. Her eyes flick from me to Jen and she leans over to whisper in Jen's ear, her eyes resting on me. Jen nods and lets Gaby pull her away.

So I eat lunch alone.

Alone on my first day of high school.

Alone with my secret.

My sister Kellen is the only person who knows. Now she's a freshman, too, a college freshman—far away, across the mountains at Washington State University and I don't talk to her anymore.

She only has a month and a half left to live.

But I don't know that, and neither does anyone else.

2. *First, pick cut-outs or drops.*

· ·

I open the old four-paneled door marked PRIVATE and drop my backpack on the bottom step, deciding to take a walk instead of going upstairs to the tiny apartment I share with Mom.

We couldn't stay in the house once my dad left. He wasted no time sticking around after Kellen died.

When I was little and hated dinner, I'd swipe bits of food into my napkin every time eyes were off me, so each time someone looked there was less food on the plate. I think of my dad and how he started leaving us in the same way, bit by bit.

Pieces of him fell away—or were swiped away—long before my sister died, with every shift change, every new case.

But I really noticed Dad's departure when Kellen would talk about college, and he'd find a way to leave the room. As the time got closer, he went out on more calls.

Swipe.

And then he'd pick more fights with Mom and always leave the house. Where did he go?

Swipe.

Kellen went off to college, and I don't think he or Mom even knew I'd entered high school. He started taking phone calls in the garage, and in the bathroom.

Swipe.

The chores Kellen used to do were left to me, including

laundry. Hard not to notice that distinctly not-Mom smell on Dad's shirts. Mom was allergic to all perfume.

Swipe.

By the time Kellen died, he was all but gone. A few pieces of him were left, but all of them were too sad to stay in a house of memories. Mom didn't care. She was already lost inside herself, not seeing the last bit of him slip away. My dad couldn't even stand the memories of being on this side of the state, so he moved three hundred miles east to Spokane and I have to spend summers with him. Until I turn eighteen.

I walk down to my favorite store because it always makes me happy. This is how I fool myself into pretending I don't have another note, unread and burning a hole in my backpack.

Wind gusts up from Puget Sound, stinging my face. It delivers the aroma of the bagels and coffee and grilled meat. I pull up the hood on my jacket and tighten the drawstrings under my chin.

On Queen Anne Avenue—"the Ave"—I pass five people, each holding the leash of a big-ass dog in one hand and a latte in the other. The Hill is very coffee-addicted and very dog-friendly. I'm sure if all the coffee shops found a way to sell dog water, everyone on the Hill would buy it. All the shops set out water dishes for the dogs, year-round. The Moon Bar's water dish is frozen and yellow, with two dead flies and a cigarette butt in it. They're just putting on an act.

The pet shop where Noelle works has three dishes out front, all clean with fresh water. I slow down enough to peek through the window to look for Noelle, even though I know she's with Mason in my mom's café; it's a reflex. It's hard to see around the display of organic, vegan dog treats. I'm pretty sure dogs would rather eat meat.

On the next block, I pause at the display window of Hill Kitchen. It's only November but cookie cutters dangle from a twinkly Christmas tree; sprinkle jars with bows on top sit underneath. This is my favorite store. I collect cookie cutters and sprinkles like other girls collect makeup or shoes. But this time I can't have them. I have a plane ticket to save for.

Something catches the corner of my eye and when I turn, I see my former friend Jen. She stands a couple doors down, in front of Queen Anne Pizza, her backpack slung over one shoulder. She's by herself, so the disgust I sometimes see on her face when she looks at me is only half there.

I'm used to odd looks from people; I've been putting up with it for almost two years. Because I'm *her*, the daughter of that crazy lady who used to be an ass-kicking lawyer and now sells sandwiches and Jesus soup on the Ave. I'm *her*, the sister of that dead girl, Kellen McKinley, who spent her time mouthing off to teachers, cutting class, and basically blazing a trail of shit and splattering it all over the faculty—making them hate any future McKinleys who might walk through the door.

Jen disappears into the pizza shop and I turn back toward the window. More people pass behind me, their reflections in the storefront window distracting enough to make me notice.

A boy wearing a Mariners ball cap stops to look at the Christmas tree. He meets my eyes in the reflection, holding them for a moment before he walks away. I think I've seen him at school with Noelle before.

I shiver and walk toward home. I'm freezing and I don't like the way that boy looked at me.

And I have another note to read.

JUNE: THIRTEEN-YEAR-OLD CARROT'S SUMMER FUN BEFORE HIGH SCHOOL

Kellen sits on the bathroom counter, watching me.

Mom has finally started letting me use makeup. I begged her to let me buy some with my allowance so I could become a pro at putting it on over the summer. A week ago Mom took me to Bartell's to pick out my own stuff. I've given up on waiting for her to show me how to put it on.

"You're such a baby, Carrot. I was wearing makeup to school when I was eleven. You should've snuck it to school like I did. Mom never knew."

Focused on not poking my eye out, I don't say anything. She's right. I'm thirteen. I'm wearing makeup and growing boobs and Kellen still calls me that dumb baby name.

On the day I was born, my sister learned two new things— one she hated right away and the other she learned to hate later. At the hospital, Grandma made her eat cooked carrots for the first time. A few hours after that, Kellen was introduced to me. She confused "carrots" and "Kara," which Mom and Dad thought was so adorable that they never corrected her.

"Hey, dumbass, you're supposed to put the eye shadow on first, then the mascara. And you stretch out your face. Like this." Kellen opens her eyes and mouth wide. "So you don't get mascara all over."

I pretend to ignore her, but really I don't because she's showing me and I want to learn. But I'm sunburned and it hurts the top of my cheeks to stretch out my face.

Kellen pulls her legs up on the counter and sits cross-legged. She smells like aloe vera lotion. "Why do you wanna wear makeup anyway? Are you hot for someone? Hmm, Carrot?" She smiles wide and her eyes almost pop out as she reaches in front of me, almost making me stab my eye out with the mascara wand.

"Stop it," I whisper.

"Speaking of hot for someone . . ." She grabs her makeup bag. "Almost forgot it!" She makes a big show of taking out her birth control pills.

I only know what they are because she's told me at least a hundred times. She punches one through the foil, pops it in her mouth, and chases it with a swig from her Bud Light. She sets down the beer and smiles as she opens the pill case again. Then she snaps it shut, opening it, shutting it—in my face, practically clipping my sunburnt nose.

"You know, Carrot, you're going to need a lot of makeup if you ever want the chance to use these."

I blink hard and get mascara under my lower lid.

3. *Remove from heat before it melts.*

. . . .

KARA,
ALWAYS WATCHING YOU. ALWAYS WAITING.

My name, printed in careful handwriting, always has the same
monstrous K that looks as if it's trying to eat the rest of my name.
And like the other notes, the paper is folded twice and tucked
into a matching envelope.

Tired hardwood planks groan under my feet when I cross
the room. The old floor makes different sounds depending on
where you tread, warning me anytime Mom's approaching my
room. And since I started getting the notes, I've memorized
where in the apartment each creak originates.

Warm air thaws my cheeks, but I still wrap a quilt around my
shoulders. My hands shake. I read the note again and then stuff
it back into my backpack.

This ancient house, like many others on the Ave, has a shop on
the bottom floor and an apartment on the top. Our apartment has
a window seat where I sit now, staring blankly at the vine maple that
grows out of the sidewalk below. The top branch reaches a few feet
above the window and has shed most of its fiery leaves for winter.

Pigeons stare in, framed by branches and puffs of gray cloud
against a darkening sky. I wonder if *he* can see me up in this
window, because in another week, when the rest of the leaves
fall, the tree will barely hide it.

Who could get into the classroom and leave me a note without Mr. King noticing?

An hour passes and I've moved to my bed, to the sofa and back to the window, trying to get comfortable. I can't. Each time a note shows up I run through a list of possible suspects, but I come up with nothing.

Every note has come from school.

Before the notes, I was starting to relax because with each new gossip-worthy scandal, the spotlight moved off me, little by little, until I was back in the dark. High school used to be just an annoying thing to slog through. Now I can't even feel safe there.

WHEN I COME DOWNSTAIRS I smell coffee and celery and something brown and meaty. But the first thing I notice is Hayden. He sits by himself at his usual table. He's concentrating on his laptop screen, his eyes narrowed like he's angry about what he sees. Or maybe he needs glasses. I think he'd be adorable in glasses. The baseball cap he always wears is turned backward and pieces of his dark blond hair stick out through the backside. I don't want to bother him because he's probably studying. Even so, I slow down when I pass his table, my heart sinking when he doesn't say anything.

Something grabs the back of my hoodie, making me jump.

"I see how you are, sneaking by without a hello," he says impishly.

Of course I act like I never saw him. I whip my head around and say, "Oh! Hayden, hi, how's it going?" I'm a little too cheerful.

He smiles, playful and confident. I guess that's the difference between high school boys and college men.

"Better now." He turns his cap the right way around. "Are you baking? I could stick around and eat the broken cookies for you."

Now he watches me from under the frayed bill. Hayden has

this way of staring at me, like his eyes could suck out all my secrets. When he does this I have a hard time talking; I mean, I have a hard time talking anyway, but especially now.

He reaches his arms up and clasps his hands behind his head. "You okay?" he asks, the smile returning.

I fidget with my fingers behind my back. "Um, I've, uh, had a lot of caffeine today."

He nods.

Nice. I'm boring him because I have nothing better to say. Because I have no life that would be interesting to someone who's already escaped high school.

I don't even have time to think before Hayden's up and out of the booth, towering over me so that my eyes are inches from his Seattle Pacific University Falcons sweatshirt. It looks like it would be soft if I touched it. He smells of wood smoke and a faded scent of cologne or deodorant.

Hayden's arm circles part way around my back but he doesn't touch me, though I wish he would. And maybe if he didn't have a skanky girlfriend around I might lean back into his arm a little. He says, "Maybe you should lay off the caffeine."

I nod and then shake my head before I pivot and walk toward the kitchen because I can't conjure up a grown-up college girl response. I'm such a dork. The noise Hayden makes behind me—shoving papers and books into his backpack—seems amplified.

My hands are still shaky when I pull sugar cookie dough out of the walk-in fridge. After flouring up the board, I roll the dough out as thin as possible and press into it with a turkey cookie cutter. I should be decorating hearts because the contest has a Valentine cookie theme. But who can get in the mood for Valentine's Day in November?

While the cookies bake, I mix up royal icing and imagine I'm in my own bakery, far from here. Mom and I have a deal. I get this little corner of her kitchen to make up for losing the gourmet kitchen in our old house. In return I let her sell my cookies. It's doubly nice because I'm blocked off from Mom's business by the dishwashing area, so I can avoid her and the cook.

My corner smells of warm, buttery sugar. By the time the cookies have cooled, I have three piping bags full of icing in shades of chocolate, pumpkin orange, and gold. During the contest we'll have a time limit so I need to practice tinting the icing a little faster.

I outline the edge of my first turkey in chocolate icing, making a dam, before outlining the feathers. Then I flood random feathers inside the dams so the icing doesn't escape the edge of the cookie. Then I do the same with the other colors. An idea has me up on a chair, sifting through my collection of sprinkle jars . . . until I reach too far.

I teeter and catch myself but my other hand accidentally knocks three jars to the floor. Broken glass and sprinkles surge out onto the dirty floor, in between the holes of the black rubber mat.

"Shit!" There's no way I'm fishing those out. I see the dirt and crap that would wind up under my nails. I'd probably end up with a flesh-eating disease.

"Whoa!" a voice shouts.

I hop off the chair as a boy emerges from the dishwashing area. Mom said she hired a new dishwasher. But I had no idea it would be Charlie Norton.

"Sprinkles?" he asks, staring at the floor.

I ignore him and mourn the colored gems, pooled and sparkling inside the mat holes.

"Kara McKinley," he continues. "I wondered when I'd finally see the daughter of the famous pea soup lady."

I haven't seen Charlie since he left town our freshman year.

What the hell?

Why is he back?

"You are Kara McKinley, right? Or should I call you Sprinkles?"

The difference between the skinny freshman arms I remember

and the ones now crossed over his chest is a lot of physical labor out in the sunshine. His dark hair is shorter than it used to be, close cropped everywhere except the top, where it's sticking up. A few strands fall over part of his forehead because of his cowlick, reaching toward his coffee-colored eyes.

"Aw come on, Sprinkles, you've forgotten me? You've known me since we cut each other's bangs in kindergarten. But since I'm a gentleman I'll reintroduce myself: after all, it's been a while." He bows before offering me his hand. "Charles Norton the Third, at your dishwashing service."

"I remember," I manage, turning back toward my cookies.

My jitters show again when I pick up the piping bag, and my icing dam results in a loopy mess that I'll have to wipe off before it hardens. A shadow grows over my left shoulder.

"Hey do those turkey cookies taste like real turkey?" Charlie asks.

"Don't you have some pans to scrape?" I hear myself snap. I don't want him to leave. Even though he already smells a little like bleach.

"Just checkin' to make sure you're okay, Sprinkles. I know when I'm not wanted. If you get lonely, I'll be around the corner—"

"Playing with your bubbles, I'm sure."

He says nothing, and I wait until he walks away before I turn and look. I'm so dumb. I'm sixteen going on ten when it comes to Charlie Norton!

From around the corner I hear him above the tinny buzz of water hitting a stainless steel sink. "Hey, Sprinkles!" he yells. "If you need help with the giblets, let me know!"

I rearrange shelves until my hands are steady enough to pipe straight lines again. Charlie's whistling rises above the noise of clinking dishes and the pinging spray hose, and a whole half hour passes before I think about weird notes and being watched.

ELEVEN-YEAR-OLD CARROT

I hate PE, and I especially hate dodgeball day.

Mr. Scott has blown the whistle because I'm on the floor.

"Sorry about that, Kara McKinley."

It's skinny but athletic superstar Charlie Norton. He holds out his hand. He always calls me by my first and last name. Sometimes I like it. Sometimes it ticks me off. Always it embarrasses me.

I rub the scraping burn on my cheek where he nailed me with the ball. He pulls me up so I'm standing and I don't want him to let go of my hand. We're eye to eye and I stare at the soft brown freckles dotted across his cheeks and nose.

"Here you go." He hands me the ball like my hands could break. "You get me back."

He walks away, and I know that I love him. I hear giggling along the perimeter. I try to sneak off the floor, pretending I'm hit, but Sara Nguyen calls me out, threatening to tell Mr. Scott.

I throw the ball as hard as I can and Charlie steps into it, taking it in the chest when he very easily could've caught it and brought back one of his teammates. He winks at me as he crumples to the floor. Everyone is laughing. I think I might crumple to the floor, too.

4. *Space three inches apart.*

. . . .

The next day at school, I look for Charlie. Not in an obvious way or anything because I don't need Noelle giving me crap about it. There were rumors about why Charlie left freshman year, but I wasn't sure anyone knew the truth. He hung with my crowd, sort of. Even when I had a crowd to hang with, I was still the quiet one. So I pretty much never talked to Charlie. I just stared at him a lot. Everyone loved him. Even the seniors invited him to their parties.

Why does he have to work at my mom's café?

Why haven't I noticed him back at school?

When did he move back?

"Hey, sista," Noelle says, slamming her shoulder into mine.

"Hey!" I sidestep to keep my balance as a rush of adrenaline takes me out of my own head. "You scared me."

"Why? What, were you picturing yourself under Hayden again? I called your name like two times down the hall." She flings her backpack over her other shoulder.

"*No.* Nothing. Just thinking about plane ticket money. Wanna give me some? I really don't want to work at Crockett's."

She smirks. "American Express, dear one. My parents didn't notice the jeans I bought you, but I don't think even they are stupid enough not to notice a plane ticket on their bill."

"I know. Guess I'll have to schlep bags of food after all."

"Maybe accidentally sneak some Trojans into your purse for me, too? Really hate paying for those suckers."

Some people turn to look at us in the crammed hallway. I stare at the floor because if I say anything back about condoms it will lead to yet another discussion about my virginity. No thanks.

A pair of too-skinny legs in too-big leather boots stop in front of us. Jen Creighton offers a paper to Noelle. "Since I don't have your number, here you go." Jen's eyes flick to me, only for a second. "Of course, Kara's invited, too."

That's bullshit and she knows it. She'd never give me an invite if Noelle wasn't around. Her eyes tell me she knows it's bullshit, too. Her eyes tell me that she might even be doing this on purpose, to set me up somehow.

"Gee, thanks," I reply.

But then Jen does that eyelid flick thing she used to do when she was nervous. Back when we were friends.

"I'll consider it," Noelle tells Jen. "On second thought . . ."

Noelle takes her gum out of her mouth, real slow, and sticks it in the middle of the flyer, squishing it in for extra emphasis. Then she folds and unfolds it to see the pink wad stretch from both sides of the paper. She hands the little flyer gum package to Jen. "Thanks, but I don't think I can make it."

I hate that I feel a little bad for Jen. She totally deserves that. But I know her and I know right now she's mortified. Of the three of us—me, Gaby, and Jen—Jen wanted the attention, the popularity. So I know she's lying awake at night obsessing about her party and who might show and who won't. I know she spent hours making her little flyer perfect with just the right wording so people won't think she's too desperate, even though I think a fancy flyer says it all.

Jen gapes at the paper mess. And then down at her big boots. Gaby always teased her about not having calves or a butt. Part of me still wants to put my arm around her shoulder; that little part of me who remembers spending the night in the bathroom, feeding her Kleenex and Junior Mints because her crush didn't show up to her seventh grade swimming party.

Noelle grabs my arm. "We're late for third period."

I know she doesn't care about being late for class. People stare now as we walk. Everyone stares when I walk through school with Noelle. She doesn't give a crap about anyone here but Mason and me. And Mr. Hoyt. When she fights with Mason she flirts heavily with Mr. Hoyt, who is only one year out of college.

Mason comes up behind Noelle and winks at me.

"Hey! Asshole!" Noelle whirls around and fake punches him before stripper-pole hugging him.

"See you guys later," I say.

They're already making out.

MY SIXTH PERIOD CLASS is at the back corner of the campus in the Arts building. I step outside and the wind stings my face with a mix of rain and snow. There's not a single person with me in the small courtyard. Before I started getting notes, I never noticed the bushes everywhere; thick evergreens, holly bushes, and rhododendrons that never lose their leaves.

Hiding places.

I can't walk through this part of school without wondering if the note writer is watching.

I exhale and feel my anxiety vanish when I get through the Arts building entrance. When I reach for the door, I turn. I feel like I'm being watched. At first I think I'm being paranoid, but then I see that boy from the kitchen shop window the other day, the one wearing the Mariners cap. I know him, don't I? It'll drive me crazy for the rest of the day because he seems familiar but not because of school.

He turns and saunters off down the hall.

Mr. King smiles at me as I walk in. "So, will your parents let you enter?"

Today he wears the tie with tiny bottles of Jack Daniels. The man must have a tie for every bottle of liquor ever invented.

You'd think the school administration would have something to say about his choices in neckwear.

"My Dad has no say in my life until summer, and I haven't asked my mom yet."

"Kara, you need to ask her, since you aren't eighteen. You're driven and talented and you could win. You could get your-self into La Patisserie, plus the prize money. Become a famous pastry chef," he says with a wink, "and give all the credit to your favorite teacher."

"I started sketching designs." I feel the same sudden high I feel every time I talk or think about cookie baking. It's a sugar rush without eating actual sugar.

"Good for you, maybe you can show them to me when you're ready. And I trust you'll take care of the permission part soon." He pats me on the back before heading to the front of class.

When I turn toward my station, Kellen is there.

I blink twice and look around the room. Everyone's already at work.

When I turn back Kellen is still there, her green eyes spar-kling, clearer than I have ever seen her since she died. Granted, this has been happening for a few weeks now. But every time she visits, she becomes more real. I *see* her. Her black hair is pulled into a tight ponytail. She wears a crimson Washington State Uni-versity hoodie and those stupid brown and pink monkey pants she lived in. She kicks her legs back and forth. The dirty pink Uggs she relentlessly begged our father to buy her pound the cabinets, yet make no sound. I peek down at my own battered Ugg knockoffs from Target.

I don't want to look up, because I know she'll make fun of me.

I'm a skinnier version of my dead sister. Where she had boobs and curves, I have flat and flatter. If Kellen had starved herself and shrank half a foot then I'd be looking up at myself right now. Except that my hair is a duller shade of black, and she always tanned.

Why can't she bug me in math? I live for this class and my dead sister always harasses me *here*.

I wonder if I'm going crazy like Mom. Without a word, I run to the bathroom, hoping she'll be gone when I get back. For five minutes I stand in a stall facing the latest gossip, etched into industrial gray paint. Below an unidentifiable smear, I read about Noelle and all the horrible things she's doing all over school. Man, she's busy. I wonder if she knows what she's doing in an alternate bathroom-stall universe. If she comes to this stall, she must.

WHEN I GET BACK to class Kellen is gone. I pour sugar over the two sticks of butter in my bowl. Granules accumulate on the top and spill off the sides like icy snow. Butter, sugar, and vanilla. Butter at the right temperature makes the perfect cookie dough. Screw up the butter, and you have to start over. Or expect less.

Mr. King lets me in before first period on dough-making days. He knows I like to get the butter out so it's at room temperature by the time I work with it later. For everyone else he tells them to microwave it.

Heather Greenwood studies my bowl, as if our assignment is a chemistry test. She does this every day, but never asks me a thing. She used to talk to me. Now it's habit and I wonder if she remembers why she stopped talking to me in the first place.

After my sister died, no one knew what to say. It's not like I was paying a lot of attention—I was ignoring *everyone* when school started, that month before she died. But I do remember how they would look away if I made eye contact. Looking away meant they didn't have to deal with me, and I didn't have to tell anyone what happened. I could keep my secret.

Or maybe they remembered me from a few months before—June of eighth grade, when I still talked and still had friends. When I told them every lunch hour about how much I hated my sister and how horrible she was and how I wished she would die. And then *voilà*, in October, four months later, my wish came true.

My sister died and I became the freak who made her sister die by wishing it. Or at least that was the rumor Katy Morgan started.

While I mix dough, a tiny part of me misses her.

What I miss is the sister that used Ted Ryan's baseball bat to smear dog poop on his bike seat. It was the night after he told everyone I was gay because I wouldn't French-kiss him. His mom obviously never told *him* not to leave his toys out in the front yard.

Now my sister is gone and still causing me misery, and when I think of what she did to me, I don't miss any part of her.

JUNE: THIRTEEN-YEAR-OLD CARROT'S SUMMER FUN BEFORE HIGH SCHOOL

I finish my mascara and sneak out of the house before I run into Kellen again. Ten minutes later I'm in the locker room of Hillside Pool to meet my best friends, Gaby Navarro and Jen Creighton. School's just let out and we have lots planned. There's no freaking way Mom and Dad can send me to summer camp! I'm sure Kellen is lying about overhearing them say it.

The crowd in the locker room makes me wish I'd changed into my one-piece at home. I hate the locker room. The reek of chlorine burns my nose. Wet swimsuits worn too long smell like Fritos to me, so the whole locker room stinks of chemicals and corn chips.

Jen and Gaby were supposed to meet me in here. I see Gaby's yellow flip-flops. I only know they're hers because the daisy on the left one is half-chewed off, thanks to her dog, Tinker.

When I walk out to the pool I see them. Gaby's fake butterfly tramp stamp rises above her bikini bottoms as she sits on the edge of the pool with her legs dangling in the water. Gaby and her sisters give each other fake tats in areas they can't reach. You couldn't pay me a million bucks to get that close to my sister's butt crack. Jen kicks her legs back and forth, her curly hair piled up on top of her head. The concrete burns my feet so I walk in the wet spots that haven't dried up yet. This grosses me out because who likes walking in other people's wet spots?

I sneak up behind my friends and push their shoulders.

"Ouch! Sunburned! Watch it!" Gaby hollers as she turns around. "Oh hey, Kar!"

"Hey yourself, scoot over." I bump her so I can sit in the corner, sticking one foot at a time into the water. "Thanks for waiting for me in the locker room."

"Sorry but we had to get out here," Jen says. "We saw Nate in line ahead of us at the cash register."

"Yeah, Kar," Gaby adds, "you know we can't miss the first bone dive of summer."

I have to laugh. We noticed last summer that some of the boys on the diving board have boners. We don't know why. Gaby won't ask her sisters because she likes to pretend she knows everything in the universe, so she dared Jen to ask her lab partner, but Jen chickened out. We even Googled it, but Jen's mom came into her room at that exact moment.

Nate Hansen has the longest boner of all the boys that get up on the diving board. We always have our sunglasses on so it's not obvious we're staring.

"I wish I could just see what it looks like, sans swim trunks." Gaby whispers. *Sans* is Gaby's new word. It's really annoying.

"Eww, Gabs," Jen hisses. "You're such a pig."

"Shh," I whisper. "There he goes!"

Nate steps out onto the board. At school, we never pay any attention to Nate because he's kind of boring and geeky, but he's nice. So I feel bad when we talk about him.

There it is—the front of his swim trunks looks like a sideways tent. All three of us hold our breath at the same time. Gaby sits way back, popping her gum while she smiles, watching him.

5. *Squeeze with both hands.*

. . . .

My first day on the job at Crockett's Market has me seriously reconsidering Mom's offer to work for her. She pinned me in a booth before I left for my first shift.

"Kara, why would you want to work *there* when you could work here with me doing the Lord's work?"

I left out the main reason why I needed money. I wasn't ready to tell her about the contest yet. Maybe when I get on the plane.

"Mom, I'm sixteen. Don't you think I should get some experience working for someone else? In the real world your mom is not your boss."

"You'll not gain any favor with God working at Crockett's, Kara. That place is Satan's handiwork. Everything is organic or handcrafted or whatever heathen label they can stick on it to defend their ungodly prices."

I bumped against her but she wouldn't budge. "Mom! Let me out! I don't want to be late for my first day."

She clasped her hands together and bounced them off her lips for a second, *boing, boing, boing* before scooting out. "Fine. Be home right after. I'll be watching the clock."

Now I'm bagging groceries, taking them out to cars, and hauling ass back into the store as soon as I'm done because "walking" is forbidden. A Crockett's bagger must run. Every time I take carts outside, my boss stands in the doorway, arms folded, sniffing. The checkers are all bitches, and the customers all bring their reusable bags lined with dollops of nasty, oozing crap with hair stuck in it.

I just need to focus on why I'm here: to get to the contest, to get out of here, to get away from memories and keep my secrets hidden forever.

"Honey," a customer says to me. "Stick the tomatoes on top please? If I'd wanted them pureed I'd-a-bought them canned."

"Sorry." I mumble. She embarrasses me, so when she opens the passenger door to put her purse inside, I drop the bag with the eggs in it hard onto the pavement. Really hard.

I ride the cart on my way back into the store, smiling over tiny victories. Then I jump. Kellen peeks out from behind one of the trees.

When I look again, she's gone.

I don't remember ever seeing Kellen outside before. And she disappeared so fast.

Later I see Hayden across the street outside the smoothie bar. I act like I don't see him because of the dorky apron and bow tie that I'm wearing. When his skanky girlfriend walks out carrying two large smoothies, I feel a tiny stab of approval for her. Maybe Babe actually cares about his health. They start walking down the Ave, and Hayden turns and smiles. Or maybe it's just a laugh over my uniform.

WHEN MY SHIFT ENDS, my body hurts. But I have to say one good thing about Crockett's—they have a kick-ass selection of sprinkles, so I reward myself for a hard day's work by buying a jar that I destroyed earlier: cerulean blue sanding sugar. The head cashier frowns at me, probably because I stare at the jar as if it were filled with diamonds.

I tuck it into my coat pocket as I head outside. Smoky gray clouds sail above the Olympic Mountains, and the wind off the bay lashes my face. It feels like the temperature has dropped twenty degrees since I was last out.

Halfway home, I see Charlie Norton.

Charlie walks with purpose down the Ave instead of crossing the street to Soul Soup, so I follow him for two more blocks before he disappears into the old, brick Catholic church.

For some reason this depresses the hell out of me. He's going to church in the middle of the week. Who does that? Oh yeah, Mom does. Nice.

I walk faster because the Ave seems too quiet and the words on the last note are ticking across my mind.

ALWAYS WATCHING YOU.

THAT NIGHT. I HAVE nightmares. One hundred cans of organic pork and beans roll down the Crockett's checkout conveyor belt. They spill out onto the floor, I run out of bags, and then I fall, naked, into a gargantuan shopping bag covered in cat hair and oozing crap. Mom and Charlie yell at me to repent. Hayden peeks into the sack and gives me a thumbs-up.

I better make enough money for that plane ticket soon.

FOÜRTEEN-YEAR-OLD ~~CARROT~~ KARA

I pass Katy Morgan's locker, and a *Playgirl* magazine falls at my feet. "Kar-a McKin-ley!" Katy squeals, looking around the entire hallway. She points at the magazine and then wags a finger at me. "Who knew she was such a perv!"

It's the first week of high school and I ignore her because I always ignore Katy.

But when I look up, there they are. My friends. I expect them to put Katy in her place, or at least stand next to me, or something. But both of them act like they don't even know me. Gaby stares right at my face, and Jen stares at the floor and neither of them does anything about Katy and her friends laughing at me.

And then I hear a voice behind me.

"You're such a bitch, Katy."

Noelle Butler is an even bigger bitch than Katy. Me and Jen and Gaby always thought so, and Gaby was always coming up with new rumors to spread about her.

Noelle picks up the magazine, sticking it in Katy's face.

Katy backs up, flinching, while Noelle runs her finger in circles around the guy's crotch on the cover. "Kara doesn't even wear lip gloss. And, Katy, why the fuck are you carrying this around? I thought you were into girls."

Noelle sticks the magazine into her backpack and strolls away, leaving Katy pale-faced and everyone's mouths hanging open.

Noelle didn't talk to me again until December. Things changed when I skipped class to go to the mall and saw her cram a T-shirt from Hot Topic into her purse. Two days later

I caught her smoking weed in the bathroom on the far end of campus, where I went for privacy.

"God, you're like my ugly shadow these days." She inhaled long and slow, keeping her eyes on me. Then she blew a cloud of smoke in my face. "Get the fuck out of here."

The next day I saw her waiting for the school counselor. She stared at me as I sat down and tried to focus on one of the stupid posters in the office.

"Why are you in here?" She asked. "Does *your* Mom always have her mouth on a bottle or a dick that doesn't belong to your father, too?"

I said nothing, because she's gross, so I waited quietly for my turn with Ms. Phillipe. She replaced the old counselor in November and it was December and I guess she'd gotten to the *M* section in her case file reading. Damn.

"Oh, I know. Your sister's death is fucking you up right? I've heard. Don't sweat it. We're only stuck here a few years and as long as we can party it's all good."

I still said nothing.

"Kara?"

Pretty Ms. Phillipe looked like she just graduated from college and smiled way too much to be working in an urban public high school. I hated her already.

"Hmm, says in your file that the last counselor was quite concerned about you, and how you're dealing with your sister's death, or rather, how you aren't dealing with it."

I wish I could've seen my notes from the last counselor—from here they looked endless, even though we didn't talk very much. I'll bet it said I was at risk, cutting, eating disorders, suicide . . .

"I hated my sister. She was horrible."

"Well that's an unusual reaction to someone dying."

"Do they teach you that in counselor school? No one handles death the same way. Maybe you were absent the day they covered that." I looked down, staring at my fingernails because I didn't usually talk to authority that way. I tried to make up for it. "My sister wasn't normal and you don't know how horrible she was to me."

Ms. Phillipe adjusted her scarf and I saw the flush of red at the base of her neck. "It's just that—"

The phone rang, cutting her off. She answered and told whoever was on the other line that she was "Melanie Phillipe, School Counselor" and she sounded so proud saying it, I wonder if it was her first time using the school phone.

Her eyes locked on me, and even though she's puny, I sensed trouble.

"Oh. I'll send her right out." She hung up. "That was your mother. She's here to pick you up for your, um, appointment with the gynecologist." Ms. Phillipe looked at me as though maybe I wasn't just dealing with Kellen's death but maybe I was a slut, too. Her face was red and she looked away.

When I got outside, I knew for damn sure Mom was not taking me to the gyno. And she wasn't in the office.

"Kara, dear," the secretary called out to me. "Your mom is outside in the car. Please tell her next time to come in and sign you out. That's school policy but I'll let it slide this time."

When I walked out to the front, Noelle stood there.

"Let's get coffee? It's right next to your gynecologist's office."

She smiled, just a quick flash, and then it was gone, and I stood there wondering if I should go back to math class or to Ms. Phillipe.

Then I saw Gaby walking and she stared at me like she didn't recognize the best friend she ditched.

I nodded. "Yeah let's go."

We spent the rest of the school day drinking lattes and

gorging on donuts and making fun of Ms. Phillipe and the other faculty we hated. We never said one word about my sister and it was the best day I'd had in a really long time. I made it back in time to get the bus and she disappeared with some guy into the smoker woods.

6. *Glaze and add sprinkles.*

· ·

Charlie Norton walks by, smiling at me as he heads back to the kitchen. I'm hoping he didn't see me follow him to church.

I only notice Noelle has come back from the bathroom when I get a Snowflake Sugar packet in the eye. One of her eyebrows is arched. I catch her sideways smile. I'm caught.

"Well, well. Such a smile there, Miss McKinley. Is that who I think it is? Is that uh . . ." she taps the table with three fingers. "What's his name? Charles Norton the Third? Charlie? The guy who fell off the Hill freshman year?"

"Uh huh, yeah, it is. He's my mom's new dishwasher."

Noelle is ready to interrogate. "So why are you red, Kar? Ahh, you still want to lose it to Charlie Norton, don't cha?"

"Bite me, Noelle. God, you're worse than a guy. Do you think about anything else besides sex?"

She shrugs. Fortunately we're both distracted by a woman sniffing and holding a tissue to her eyes. She latches onto Mom and lets out a big sob. My mother's arms wrap around her, a weird stranger, like she's family. Mom says something about *the glory of God* and all that crap she likes to serve up as a free side dish these days.

Before my sister died, my mom was a straightlaced, no-nonsense, black-and-white, successful defense lawyer. Today she's a full-fledged Holy Roller and we're practically poor.

Mom dances over. "See how the Savior blesses us with all this *good* we are doing?" She kisses my cheek and Noelle's forehead before disappearing into the kitchen.

I hear a loud "Praise, Jesus!" from behind the kitchen door. The "Hallelujah!" that follows sounds like Charlie's voice.

I roll my eyes while Noelle smiles.

"I love your mom, Kar."

I stretch my hands out in front of me. My cuticles are stained with three different shades of food coloring. I tear open the sugar packet Noelle threw at me and sprinkle it on the table.

"Okay, back to Charlie." Noelle props an elbow on the table and rests her chin on her palm. "You want him. Your face is red and your eyes have that lusty, glazed look."

I use the edge of the packet to push my tiny sugar pile into a neat line while I try to ignore Noelle. "Shut up, No."

She cracks her knuckles. "Such a crab today, Kara. Maybe you need to eat some sprinkles, too. I know you want Charlie Norton, Kar. You've been saving yourself for him for years."

"Why do you have to be a bitch about everything?"

"Can a day ever pass without you calling me a bitch, Kar? I'm just trying to help you get some. Mason and Charlie used to be friends. I'll find out if he's seeing anyone."

I pick up my bag. "Are we ten years old? Why don't you pass him a check-the-box note, too."

"Okay, okay. I'm sorry. Hey, come and visit me at work? Mason's working tonight." She takes a sip of her latte.

I stand up without a word and walk to the apartment door.

"Just trying to help!" I hear Noelle call out after me.

UPSTAIRS. I PULL BOOKS out of my bag and stack them on the bed. My math book misses the pile, sliding off the bed and crashing to the floor, and suddenly I see the purple droplets and bloody-red flecks on an envelope poking out from under the book. Breath catches in my throat. Carefully I use two fingers to push the book aside, revealing the whole envelope.

I scoot back up to my bed, my fingers digging into the quilt until they hurt. Did the envelope slip out of my math book or did *he* leave it here?

Mom keeps her keys on a hook in her kitchen office that's open to everyone who might wander back there. Suddenly I'm certain. *He* was here. He came into my room.

I leave everything on the floor and go back to the front door. Maybe if I re-enter and focus I'll notice something off. The Oriental rug covers half of the scuffed wood planks in the living room. The tiny coffee table holds a half-dead candle and Mom's coffee mug from this morning. The tiny kitchen has dishes drying in the bamboo rack, and the tile counter is wiped clean like always. The bathroom and Mom's room look untouched.

Back in my room, my hands shake as I pluck the envelope off the floor.

I look around at my room through a stranger's eyes. A few dirty clothes on the floor, a bowl with ice cream residue in it from last week. Did I leave the closet door open? I never do; a childhood habit born of fear. I rush to the closet. Everything seems normal and untouched. One of Kellen's dorm boxes sits on the floor.

I rip open the envelope and sit down on the bed. This note is only one word:

COMPETITION?

So he knows about the contest, but how could he? I'm being stupid; of course he knows. He's watching. I can't breathe. I have to get out of here.

I run downstairs, wondering whether I should tell Mom he was in our apartment. I'm standing in the doorway, practically out of breath with my heart pounding, watching Mom flutter around the café, complimenting this person, touching that person, smiling constantly.

Why is she like this? These people are strangers!

She's so weird and she's making a fool of herself.

But she looks happy.

She twirls by me with a plate of food. Tilting her head to the side, she smiles and stares at me in that way she has, waiting for me to say something.

Just like I had to wait for her to speak to me, all those times I caught her staring out the window. Staring but not seeing the pumpkins rotting on the neighbor's porch. Not seeing the living daughter waiting for her mom to acknowledge the fact that she still breathed and needed her.

"Just a minute, sweetie, I'll be right back. Looks like you need to tell me something." Mom raises one eyebrow at me, and then she's off, parking the sandwich plate in front of an old guy. Mom leans down to him, pinching and then kissing his cheek. She's beaming when she gets up and heads back behind the counter.

I should tell her about the notes. I should tell her about everything.

I can't tell her.

I can't handle her getting upset ever again.

I won't worry her with any of it because she can't handle it. She'd make me quit my job and my leash would get even shorter—she'd probably make sure I have a chaperone walking me to school and then it would be goodbye contest for sure. It's better to keep her in the dark and deal with it on my own. So I leave. Outside, the Ave crawls with college students from Seattle Pacific University. The crowd suffocates me and my eyes flick to every face that passes, looking for eye contact that holds more meaning than it should.

A FEW MINUTES LATER I'm sitting across the street at The Teakettle, drinking one of their overpriced tea lattes. Here, the tables are full of college kids with laptops and teapots and tea cozies and mismatched cups and saucers. Most of the customers are girls, which makes me feel safer.

Halfway through my tea I'm calm enough to sift through my notebook full of design ideas for the contest. I can't stop thinking that he was in my room and I don't know what to do about it. Maybe I should tell Noelle. But I know I won't.

COOKIE DECORATING IS AN art, even though people have always teased me about it. I think Noelle understands, but she never misses an opportunity to give me shit over it.

He was in my room.

I sketch a cookie and try to focus. My drawing takes the shape of a fabulous high heel shoe I saw in a store window last week. Since I won't wear them, I turn them into cookie art. I take inspiration from everything—clothes, nature, people, and pop culture. Holidays, too.

Mom sold out of my last holiday cookie, my glittery silver skulls. When I showed her she gasped and said they were Satanic and grabbed a napkin to cover them up. Not fast enough though. One of her customers saw it and ordered three dozen for her kid's Halloween party and Mom made an extra trip to church afterward.

Did he see my private things? Did he take anything?

My intention was to work on contest designs—Valentines—but I end up sketching the daisy-adorned teapot sitting at the end of the counter. The baking part and design comes easily. The problem is getting to San Francisco. Plane tickets cost serious money. I could ask Dad for it, like Noelle suggested, but then I'd have to talk to him, and I really don't want to waste my breath. Besides, I need to stockpile stuff all year so that when summer comes I'll have a big supply of short answers to his questions. I'd rather earn money at Crockett's.

I turn the page in my notebook and see two old notes. The very first and second.

WEAR MORE GREEN, IT BRINGS OUT YOUR EYES.

Back then, I didn't know the notes would be a regular thing.

HMM, LEAVING THE TOP BUTTON OF YOUR BLOUSE
UNDONE FOR ME?

After that one I made sure all of my shirts had high necks.

A reflection in the window startles me.

"Sprinkles," Charlie says, sitting down next to me with a smile.

I sip my tea quickly.

"Just got off and saw you head over here," he says. "No cooking today?"

I hear the snark in his voice and I'm not sure if he's intentionally trying to piss me off. "Baking. I am a baker, not a cook," I tell him.

"You're not avoiding me are you, Sprinkles? You kind of ignored me back there."

"I didn't see you," I lie. "I think you better get back. I can smell those crusty dishes from here."

Charlie laughs, but I still keep my eyes on my notebook. My right hand is on the page with the shoe cookie because I don't want Charlie to see it. I want to disappear because I can feel my face burning up. But a big part of me wants to ask him where he's been today.

"I'm off, Sprinkles." He grabs the contest postcard poking out of my notebook. "What's this?"

I try to grab it back but he holds it just out of my reach until I give up, unwilling to make a spectacle of myself. Charlie reads it in silence and then hands it back. "So you're sneaking off to California to compete in a baking contest, huh?"

"I'm not sneaking anywhere. I can do what I want." What the hell? I know it will come to that, because Mom won't let me go, but how does he know I won't tell her?

Charlie sits back down on the stool next to me. Another quarter inch and his knee would touch mine. "Sure you can." He pauses. "What time does the bus drop you off?"

"Huh?"

"The bus? After school?"

"Um, I don't know. Around three."

"Right. I can tell you that every afternoon around three o'clock, your mom starts asking all of us questions. If we've seen you come in yet. By the time you actually show up, she's asked me probably five times. So I'm betting you haven't told her about this contest, have you?"

I stay silent.

"You don't think she'll let you go?" he asks.

I say nothing.

"Why so secretive?" he prods.

I pull the notebook closer and rest my arms on it before I look at him. "How about you, Charlie? You're the secretive one." I'm pushing him away but I feel this pull inside, wanting him here next to me. When he doesn't answer, I keep going. "What happened? You left freshman year, loved by everyone with an XX chromosome, and possibly an XY chromosome—I mean we do live in the city. Then one day—poof! You disappear?"

Charlie turns and looks out the window.

I continue. "What? *Now* you can't talk?"

"Maybe when we get to know each other better, I'll fill you in," he says.

"Don't bother," I say, yet I still hold the promise in his words.

"You've changed, Kara. I guess it's hard not to, I mean with what happened. Your mom seems . . . she's, uh, taking things well. She's nicer than I remember."

He throws this out so casually, like the fact that Mom is different is a good thing. What does he know about anything? I turn away from him and dig into my bag, hoping he'll just leave. "I have homework."

As he slides off the stool I feel bad, and wish I could say something to keep him there, but I can't. I sit there, cookie designs forgotten, chewing on a red pencil and staring out the window.

A trolleybus passes by and the overhead wire shoots out sparks. Passengers stare out the window or bury their heads in books. One guy's asleep with his head against the window and his mouth hanging open.

A boy I don't know strolls past, stopping to read the cluster of garage band posters stuck on the glass, but I see him eyeing me. His eyes flick back to the posters and mine go back to my sketches. When I peek again, his eyes meet mine and he moves on. It's nothing. I'm being paranoid.

ALWAYS WATCHING YOU.

JUNE: THIRTEEN-YEAR-OLD CARROTS
SUMMER ~~FUN~~ BEFORE HIGH SCHOOL

Splash.

"Don't you wonder if his dick hurts when it hits the water?" Gaby asks.

She says this a little too loud. One of the lifeguards is walking by. An older high school boy. He smiles at us. Gaby's the only one of us with the nerve to blow him a kiss.

"You're really gross, Gaby," I say.

"Hey don't lez out on me, you guys. Am I the only one who appreciates dick around here? I need new friends."

With that, Jen grabs her hand and I kiss her cheek because she's always accusing us of being gay anyway.

"Eww, get off me, psychos! You two better enjoy this because it's the only dick you'll see until you're twenty, I'm sure!"

We are all laughing now and I hop into the water and dive under and when I come up for air, Nate Hansen is right there, smiling at me. My eye stings from the mascara. The sun makes it worse and I have to squint even more.

I start laughing because I'm a royal idiot and I'm nervous because we just ogled his junk. At school I would never be nervous talking to him—in fact, at school, he'd probably be too nervous to talk to me. But like the dork that I am I swim away and hope he never knows we were watching him.

When I pop up again, Jen and Gaby are pointing and laughing.

I cover my chest with both hands. "Am I nipping out?" I hear my voice come out a little higher pitched than normal.

"No stupid, your face!" Jen hollers.

"Raccoon much, Kar?" Gaby asks.

I wipe my eyes like I always do when I come out of the water but this time mascara comes off on my palms. My friends bust up laughing again, pointing and whispering.

"I don't see what's so hilarious!" I yell.

"Kara, you're such a babycakes," Gaby says.

"Yeah, Kar. And you need waterproof mascara, duh!" Jen adds.

They both laugh again and I grab the edge of the pool, watching the water slide back under the ledge. It gets sucked into that unknown place where pool water goes, and I want to get sucked in with it.

"Kara, baby, come over and I'll teach you how to do makeup. We've been doing it a little longer, you know?"

I'm so sick of them calling me that and pointing out the fact that they are older and practically a grade ahead of me.

At that moment, Trevor Dall stops by and squats behind Gaby and Jen. He balances himself by resting a forearm on each of their shoulders. I know they are both dying because they both have it bad for Trevor.

I can't hear what Trevor says but he smiles, giving my friends equal attention while they hang on every word, and look years older than me with their painted nails, perfect makeup, and lip gloss. Gaby and her sisters foil each other's hair. Both of my friends have been to the tanning bed a few times before school let out.

I look down at my own one-piece and pale skin spotted with random splotchy sunburns. My stringy, wet hair squeaks as I pull my fingers through it. Cold drips trickle down my back. The pool is full of kids, swimming and having fun. My friends have traded in Marco Polo and playing dolphins, for bikinis, boys, and fake tans.

No one notices as I climb out of the pool. Even when I'm walking home in my sundress, my flip-flops squeaking and farting from the water, I think I'll hear Jen or Gaby yelling for me.

But I don't.

Well, I'll show them and Kellen I'm not the baby they think I am. I just have to figure out how.

7. *The cookie monster waits.*

· ·

A bone-shaped copper cookie cutter with a red ribbon tied around it waits at my counter, and I smile until I see the blue-gray envelope stuck through it. My breath rattles as I pull it out and rip it open.

Do you ever wonder why?

I watch the note float to the dirty floor. Around the corner the dishwasher roars and swishes, the noise not helping the throbbing in my head. Raul and Charlie aren't around so I check the bathroom, the supply closet, and the fridge. All empty.

Picking up the note off the floor, I jam it into my pocket, forcing myself not to open the doors to the café to see if any psycho is out there, eating Mom's Jesus soup. I take a breath and walk calmly through the doors, and see Noelle at our table. Her back is to me and she's texting. I can't tell her about the notes because I'm afraid she won't believe me, and she'll spin it into some big joke—Kara and her secret admirer. I can't trust her or anyone with secrets.

Not this one, or the other one. Not ever again.

Mom stops me at the same time two ladies stop her.

"Oh, Meg—"

This is how it always starts, *"Oh, Meg, my gout is gone because of your soup!"* or *"Oh, Meg, I found Jesus in your soup . . ."*

Oh, barf.

My mother, the touchy-feely, born-again loony, of *course*, throws her arms around them. I think they all would've liked my old mom better. *That* mom didn't pay me a lot of attention but at least she was normal.

I slip away.

"Kara, where are you going?" Mom asks, her chin on the crying lady's shoulder.

"I have to *pee*, Mom."

Someone sitting at the counter catches my eye, and when I pass by he swivels around, like he's trying not to let me see him. And even though his Mariners cap is pulled down low over his face, I'm pretty sure it's that guy I've caught checking me out at school.

I feel a tug on my shirt and when I turn around, Hayden gestures to me.

"C'mere, got one for you. Check it out." He pats the seat next to him so I sit, but that makes me even more jittery.

He rubs his hands together, elbowing me in the shoulder a little. "You're gonna love this one. Watch." He presses a key on his laptop.

Some guy tries to Chippendale dance for his girlfriend. I'm embarrassed for the guy, and maybe a little for Hayden, too, for his glee. I'm also afraid to look and check around for Mom because I know she wouldn't approve of the video in her café. The guy takes off his pants and twirls around. His girlfriend bursts out laughing because Mr. Chippendale has a big hole in his underwear.

The video ends as I'm waiting for something funnier to happen. Hayden laughs.

I laugh a little, just watching him laugh. When he shows me this stuff I barely pay attention. Usually I'm overly focused on sitting so close to him and making sure I don't look or say something stupid.

"Nice, Hayden. Don't you have, like, tons of homework? Do your parents know you waste so much study time on YouTube?" I never know when it's time to get up and leave; I don't know if he wants me to stay there or get lost. Of course I always want to stay.

He reaches back and his sleeve touches my cheek. The sweatshirt smells like the fabric softener Mom buys, like it came right from the dryer. I think it's kind of cute that he cares enough to use fabric softener when he obviously has to do his own laundry, since he lives on campus. For the weirdest reason it makes me want to do his laundry. What the hell? I can't even stand to do my *own* laundry.

Hayden shakes his head. "*Fun*, Kara. It's all about balancing fun with the work. Don't you like to have fun? Don't you want to have a break from the serious stuff in your life? I watch funny shit on YouTube. How about you? What do *you* like doing for fun?" His breath is warm on my face; his lips are so close to mine. For a moment we stare at each other. He looks at my eyes and then my mouth and back again.

"I bake." It comes out as a whisper. Because of the way he looks at me now.

Hayden keeps silent while he stares at me for what feels like five minutes. "So dedicated. I love that about you, Kara. But that's not *fun*. That sounds like work. What do you do to cut loose?"

I'm about to answer but Hayden's eyes flick across the room and back to mine. He sits up straighter and ruffles my hair like I'm his pet dog. My head tingles until I feel two finger jabs in my shoulder. When I look up I face a giant stink eye, rimmed in overdone kohl.

"Hey, babe," Hayden says. "What took you so long?"

I slide out of the booth before Babe hexes me with voodoo or something. "See ya, Kara," he calls behind me. I feel like his little sister.

Noelle will likely give me crap for sitting with Hayden, even with her back to me. But I see she's on her cell so I duck into the kitchen. The tinny spray of water in the sink along with Charlie's whistling makes me smile. Maybe he's not pissed at me over our last conversation. Or maybe he thinks nothing of it because he doesn't waste time thinking of me at all.

Instead of walking around the corner to check, I chicken out and sneak out the service door.

THE NEXT DAY I stand in front of the bank with my first paycheck from Crockett's.

I had to wait twenty minutes after my shift ended for my sniffing dickhead boss to get it out of the safe for me. I waited while he showed Jason, the new guy who started this week, how to use the intercom. Jason's a college senior and kisses the boss's ass, and every customer's ass, too. I've been here longer than him and I haven't been taught how to use the intercom. Even though talking really isn't my thing, it still ticks me off.

Noelle blows out a smoke ring, drops her cigarette, and grinds it into the sidewalk. God I hate when she smokes; I don't want to be near the stink of it.

"Let me see that." She grabs the check out of my hand. Her eyes bug out and she laughs out loud. "Holy shit, Kar! Just quit. Quit Crockett's right now and take off everything but your apron and I'll drop you off at Mr. Peeper's. You'll have ticket money by morning."

Before we walk into the bank I see Charlie down the street, heading toward that church again.

When I hesitate, Noelle pulls me into the lobby and hands over my two weeks of hell on paper to the teller. The euphoria of getting paid fades fast as I slink out the door.

"A few more checks and I'll be good."

Noelle squeezes my arm, reeking of stale smoke. "If I could sneak you some cash I would, you know it, right? I only work to get away from my parents but it would take me a lot of paychecks to afford a plane ticket. Speaking of, I gotta go. Come keep me company? For a little while? Mason might stop by later."

Luckily for Noelle, the owner leaves before she works the shift at the pet shop. Only she could find a job that lets her make out with her boyfriend on the clock. "Um, okay." I start across the street so she can't see my face, watching for Charlie.

She hops in front of me, blocking my path. "*Who* are you checking on?"

I wave her off. Charlie is out of sight anyway.

Suddenly it dawns on her. "Oh, ohh, Charlie," she moans, closing her eyes and shoving her hips back and forth.

"You're a psychotic pig."

"I know, but still, you love me. Oh!" She screeches, crouching down to a puppy that's stopped at her feet.

There are too many dogs around here.

The owner smiles and patiently holds the leash with two white-knuckled hands while the dog slobbers all over Noelle's face. I am forgotten so I melt away cross the street.

TWILIGHT NEARS AS I sit on the trampoline in the backyard of my old house. My frozen fingertips trace the rough-edged holes made from Kellen's cigarettes. In my lap sits the unread note that waited for me in math today.

I used to love the trampoline. *My* trampoline. It was a gift for *my* eighth birthday from Mom and Dad. Usually I'd jump and then take a break to read or play Barbies. Until Kellen and her friends took it over as we got older.

Now I sit and watch the back door. I'm determined to master Kellen's remaining stash, determined to get at least halfway down a toke without coughing. The weed burns all the way down my throat so maybe I'm doing it right—maybe I'll feel the effects this time. It would be nice to really forget life for a while. I won't read the note until I feel better.

Even though it's been a long time, these are the nights I miss my old friends. If Gaby wasn't trying to sneak us into a party, then we'd have a sleepover and watch horror movies and order pizza.

Noelle never wants to be home. And my apartment is already too crowded with just me and Mom. Sleepovers are out.

I puff again. So far, going through Kellen's stuff, I haven't found anything as interesting as the weed, though there's one more box to look through. When she died, she took my secret with her. It's ironic how I now have all of *her* secret things because the task of emptying her room fell to me. Of course it did. Back then Mom couldn't even get out of bed.

I snuff out the joint. Carefully I roll it and the lighter into the towel and stick it back into the Playtex box. The trampoline creaks as I shove the box into my bag. Dead leaves crunch under my feet when I slide off the trampoline. I suck in a breath and wait. The air feels wet and frosty but still smells of dead foliage and mud.

Dark and dead things are all around me. My heart starts to pound a little because I'm away from the safety of the trampoline.

Is he here, watching me? I scramble along the edge of the house, hoping the new owners don't pop out with a shotgun.

The sidewalks are old and cracked, bulging from the tree roots underneath. A person could wind up with a concussion if they didn't know where they were going in the dark. I'm thinking about this as I start to run. When I reach the Ave I have a seriously bad craving for ice cream. Maybe the pot did work a little. The sign above the ice cream shop is suddenly hilarious and I burst into laughter.

When I calm down, I see the place is packed so I keep walking, and giggling. I giggle with the sweet aroma of sugar cones tagging along with me.

The whole Ave is lined with sparkly trees sprinkled with white lights, and couples holding hands. Some of them walk dogs. More dogs! Slobbering over dog-lovers like Noelle! The Hill is one big sparkly, twinkly, dog-loving place! The whole thing makes me giggle even more, and as a horn honks I double over like an idiot, consumed with laughter. A bus roars past me, and now I'm wheezing and my eyes are watering and I'm out of control. My chest hurts and I don't want to laugh at all but I can't stop . . .

Charlie steps into my path. "Sprinkles?"

JUNE: THIRTEEN-YEAR-OLD CARROT'S
SUMMER ~~FUN~~ BEFORE HIGH SCHOOL

When I get home from the pool, Mom's car is gone so I know she and Dad have left for their anniversary weekend trip to Victoria. Kellen told me she thinks they will get divorced and this trip is supposed to save their marriage. I think my sister is full of it.

Kellen's boyfriend Tad's car sits in the driveway, but when I walk in the house all I hear is the hum of the refrigerator. Maybe they went for a walk.

I wait and listen for the sounds I've heard before. Sounds that will make me turn the TV up loud or else I'll barf. When I don't hear them, I switch off the Mr. Coffee that's been turned on by Dad for the third time today to reheat the morning dregs.

Mom left money by the coffee pot with a sticky note attached that says *Pizza*. Now through the screen on the sliding door I hear laughter coming from the backyard.

"Hey, Carrot!" my sister yells.

I peek out and see ten beer bottles on the deck railing. Kellen sits cross-legged on my trampoline, with Tad, and his best friend, Nick. They're all laughing at something.

"Carrot! C'mere!" Kellen yells again.

I walk into the laundry room, drop my swim bag and head back to the kitchen door to listen. Droplets of water from inside my swimsuit drizzle down the back of my leg as I try to hide in the doorjamb. But then Kellen's face is smashed up against the screen.

"Hey, I thought you were going to the pool," she says, opening the screen and stepping inside.

She seems like she's in a better mood than earlier. "I did," I say, biting my nail.

"Well." She grabs the pizza money off the counter. "I'm hungry and Mom left us money so let's go!" She's already down the deck stairs.

My hair is still wet and my sundress is damp. "Kellen, I need to change. I don't look—"

She stomps back up the stairs. "Come on, Kar! No one cares what you look like and I don't want to wait an hour for you to put your mascara back on. If you want pizza get your ass out here now!" She slides open the screen and pulls me through it.

"C'mon, boys, if you want a piece you better follow me!"

I don't look at them but I hear the trampoline creak as they jump down. Kellen starts running and Tad jogs up behind her, grabbing her butt. It's so gross when he does that. If they start making out I think I might puke. Tad wears flip flops and jeans and no shirt, and Kellen beats her fists against his back as he pulls her up and tosses her over his shoulder.

Nick walks behind them and I walk behind him. I don't want to be with any of them and I'll be so happy when Mom decides I'm old enough to not have Kellen babysit me. Jen and Gaby can go anywhere by themselves, even to the Ave. I don't know what Mom's problem is.

Nick stuffs his hands in his pockets and seems to be ignoring Tad and Kellen as much as I am. He looks like he stepped off the golf course with his polo shirt and Bermuda shorts and his legs are really tan and not too hairy. Even when Tad and Kellen are being jerks, Nick is usually sweet to me. If I were Kellen I'd go for Nick over Tad any day.

8. *Bake until golden.*

. . . .

Charlie looks so serious. Tears are running down my cheeks because of the crazy laughing. My cheeks feel cold. For some reason, that makes me giggle again. I can't stop. I blow out a shaky breath.

He wrinkles his nose. "You smell like weed."

I'll probably pee myself if I keep this up. "Uh . . . It's just gum," I whisper. God, what is wrong with me?

"Sure it is," Charlie replies, his mouth twisting up into a smile. "Okay." He grabs my elbow and steers me two doors down to El Diablo Coffee.

Charlie practically drags me to a table between the fireplace and the window. When I look at the window I see the fireplace reflected behind me. Little flames are lined up like perfect little demon soldiers, and they all dance on top of my head. I giggle because my head is on fire.

Charlie pulls his chair next to mine, watching me laugh because now his head is on fire, too. The steamer spray pings against metal pitchers and baristas yell out the drinks ready for pickup, and every other drink is hemp or rice because on the Hill, people forget that real milk comes from a cow.

He pats my shoulder. "I'll be right back."

I turn back around to the windows. Now the fire on my head isn't as funny, thank God. But in the reflection I see Charlie, talking with a blond barista with a fake red flower above her ear. He smiles and she laughs too much.

I consider leaving, but change my mind when I see the only escape route, crammed with college people. Charlie made me come here, and now he's flirting with other girls. But I don't care, so I take out my notebook.

Charlie lowers a mug in front of me and sits down with his black coffee.

"Diary?"

"No," I reply, staring at my mug of whipped cream perfection, topped with crimson sprinkles. "Baking stuff."

"So you're writing about baking stuff while you're baked?" He smiles at his little joke and I try not to smile back. "What were you doing out there in the dark, by yourself, laughing at the moon?"

My face flushes.

"You're not much of a talker are you, Sprinkles?"

"Not when you call me that."

"How's the job at Crockett's going? Doesn't seem like your type of place."

"Why do you say that? You don't really know me." I sigh because I can't seem to get a word out that doesn't sound bitchy. "I just need money."

"To get to San Francisco."

I want to say "duh" but again, I'm trying hard to be nice so I sip cocoa and get whipped cream on the end of my nose.

Charlie laughs. "I asked the barista to put extra on it."

I stare at his reflection and the sweatshirt he wears.

"Why are you wearing a Kennedy shirt?" I ask.

"I go to school there, Kara." His voice is dry, puzzled.

I don't know why it shocks me, but it does. He dropped out of sight freshman year, and now he's back, only in private school. "But why? Why there?"

"Just needed a change." He turns away and swirls the coffee around in his mug. "When I came back."

All of a sudden I want to know everything about him because there are secrets behind his eyes. I want to know *him*.

"Where were you?"

He studies his cup for a moment. "California, Sprinkles. Wanted to learn how to surf. Isn't that why anyone moves to California? Surfing or becoming famous? Or baking, in your case."

"You're lying."

One corner of his mouth curls up into a smile and he shakes his head, running a hand through his hair. "So, are you going to San Francisco by yourself?"

"I don't need anyone else."

"Hmm, a girl, traveling alone."

I exhale slowly. The "alone" in his sentence makes me think of the notes, and I wonder if whoever wrote them is watching us right now. I also think of Mom, the former defense lawyer, and the arguments I'm going to need so she'll let me go. "I'm a big girl, thanks, and I've pretty much grown up in a city. I can handle it."

"So what are you going to do with your big winnings?"

"Um, I'm going to La Patisserie. Pastry School."

Charlie sets his mug down and leans back, smiling at me in a way that warms me like the cocoa does. Maybe I could tell him about the notes. For some reason, telling someone I don't know very well seems like it might be easier than telling Mom or Noelle.

"Okay. Sounds kind of French and snobby. That doesn't really sound like you at all, Sprinkles."

Why is he laughing? He thinks it's all a joke and I'm not sure why my dreams are so funny to other people. Words simmer inside of me, so I'm careful before I speak again. "If I want to have any credibility as a baker I have to go to a good school. I'm going to open my own bakery someday, maybe go to Paris and learn with the best. Anything to get me out of here."

"It isn't so much better once you do get out of here, you know? Your problems still follow you."

My dad told me once that when the coffee beans come from the farmers, ready for roasting, the sacks have trash and cigarette butts inside because they are spread out on the street to dry before their journey to America. My insides twist and my eyes sting as I watch Charlie, with his permanent smile and half-full attitude toward life. Anger stirs inside me. "What do *you* know about problems, Charlie? Try having your whole life dumped upside down because your sister wasn't there when you needed her and screwed up so badly she got herself killed. Try having your mom go from catatonic to crazy and drive away your prick of a dad. You don't know anything about problems."

I take a huge swallow of cocoa so I can't talk anymore.

He looks down at his cup again. I look around to see people at the next table staring. I want to yell at them and I try to think of what Noelle, or Kellen, would say in my shoes. But I come up with nothing. Part of me wants to thank Charlie for the cocoa, but I can't get the words out so I jump up and push my way out into the night.

Once outside I almost run into Jason. It figures. He's just another loser out on the Ave. But I keep my head down so he doesn't see me. I don't want to say a word to him, even an insult, because he's not worth my breath right now. I lean against a wall, deciding if I should go back in because I've been such a bitch and Charlie's been nothing but kind to me. But really, what *does* he know about problems? I mean, his parents always had money, and if they can afford Kennedy then he definitely still has it. If I had his money I'd move far from here and find a way to get into La Patisserie. And even if I didn't get in, I'd go to France and live cheap and clean bidets in exchange for pastry lessons and baguettes. I would forget about notes and my crazy mother, who only needs Jesus and her Jesus-loving customers. I'd get fat on café au lait and chocolate and French cheese, but I wouldn't care. I'd be happy, and I'd find a French guy who likes curvy American girls.

I'd forget about the guy who is watching me.

I take the envelope out of my pocket.

WHAT SCARES YOU?

My breath forms an icy cloud as I exhale. Home is only a block away and I can see the light Mom always leaves on behind the counter. Above, in the apartment, it's dark so she must be asleep.

Passing the Moon Bar, muffled drunken laughter pours out into the air. A shiver ripples through me because I'm so cold. I look around. Jason is gone; everyone is gone. I can't remember a time I've been out on the Ave and it's been so deserted.

A trolleybus rumbles by, sending sparks shooting off the power line, lighting the night. Shadows creep behind me and I think I hear footsteps, but I'm not sure. I walk faster, wanting to get home but not wanting to look like a paranoid idiot. I breathe icy puffs in front of my face. Maybe the pot is making my pulse go crazy.

Every shadow, every noise is the one who wrote the notes waiting to get me. When I get to the café my hand trembles so badly, the key pokes and scratches and I can't get it into the lock.

The chalkboard outside the café lifts and bangs against the wall with the wind:

MEG'S SOUL SOUP CAFÉ: OUR MIRACULOUS PEA SOUP WILL ANSWER YOUR PRAYERS AND MAKE ALL YOUR DREAMS COME TRUE!

Mom tricked me into painting clouds and stars and other *heavenly* things on her chalkboard. She fooled me into believing she'd post daily specials on it. She never told me she'd fill it with crazy.

I use both my hands to steady the key. Finally I get the door unlocked, and then I'm inside and my breathing slows a bit and so does my heartbeat. I feel stupid to have been so scared, and then my foot slides across something on the floor.

I can't see the color, but I know the shapes of bloody droplets and the careful writing of my name. Two in one day.

We walk to the pizza parlor because it's only a few blocks away.
Kellen gets away from Tad. She slows down to grab my hand,
which is weird for her. But she's being nice to me so no com-
plaints. Tad and Nick walk in front of us.

The summer sun still burns, but a breeze blows up from Puget
Sound every few minutes, giving a bit more relief. Everything's
going fine, we order pizza and eat outside, watching people
walk by and enjoying the summer evening. Nick is pulling a slice
from the second pizza when trouble starts.

"Tad, you're such a fucking pig," Kellen says a little too loud.

I look up from picking olives off my pizza to see what's up.
People stare at my sister. My face turns red even though I should
be used to her embarrassing me. Nick hunches over his plate,
suddenly very interested in chewing. Tad's staring down the
sidewalk. I see a girl walking with super high heel sandals and a
sundress that barely covers her ass.

"What?" Tad asks, still looking down the street.

"I'm right here, you know."

"So." Tad glares at her. "I can look."

"No. You can't!"

"Whatever, we're not married. I can look all I want." He turns
to Nick. "Can't I, Nick?"

Before Nick speaks, Kellen turns and looks between the two
of them. "You guys are both pervs."

Nick drops his pizza, palms up. "What did I do? Don't bring
me into it."

Kellen folds her arms down and scowls at him. "Well, gee,

kinda hard not to when you are *always* around!" She turns back to Tad. "Did you ever stop to think that maybe I have feelings? Can you go one fucking minute without checking out some other girl's ass?"

Tad leans back and takes another huge bite of pizza. Kellen huffs and scowls at me, which makes me slink into my chair a little farther.

"You'd probably hook up with my own sister if you had the chance," Kellen declares.

I almost choke on my pizza.

"Hey, Kel," Nick chimes in. "Leave Kara out of this. What's the matter with you? She's only twelve!"

"Thirteen," I correct.

"Yeah, thirteen. Just a baby," Nick adds.

"Too bad." Tad leans into Nick and lowers his voice, but I can still hear him. "Shit, she's Kellen's clone, only smaller and without the big mouth."

He chuckles and I want to run away.

Kellen chucks a slice of pizza and it skims Tad's shoulder, leaving a smear of sauce. When I look at how red my sister's face is I really want to run away.

"You're a fucking asshole, Tad. But hey, wait around a year or two and you can have her!"

9. *Add sugar.*

. . . .

SMELLS LIKE BETRAYAL. I LIKE HOW YOU THINK
YOU CAN JUST WANDER THE STREETS AT NIGHT.

My name is Kara McKinley, and I'm being stalked.

During homeroom this morning we had to go around the room and introduce ourselves to Cassie, the new girl from Oregon. We had to tell Cassie one sentence to sum ourselves up. This is what I wanted to say but I didn't.

On my way to lunch I passed Ms. Phillipe, the school psych, or counselor, or whatever title the school gives her depending on their budget for the year. Today was the second time I ever wanted to talk to her. Not about Kellen—I never wanted to talk about Kellen.

The first time was in October. Noelle and Mason dragged me to a football game, and after the first quarter they disappeared, during which time Ms. Phillipe planted her skinny ass right next to me in the bleachers. I wanted to tell her to go sit with the old people. But then it was okay, because she didn't seem like her regular school self.

Her hair was up in a ponytail; she wore jeans and a hoodie and ate nachos like she was actually one of us. And I'd had a fight with Mom earlier, plus a note—the second one. It wasn't a pattern yet, but somehow I sensed it would be. I wanted to tell Ms. Phillipe. But I didn't. Plus it was too loud anyway.

Today I *really* wanted to tell her.

But when she smiled that smile, that pathetic *I'm-here-whenever-you're-ready-Kara* smile, her words came back to me from last year, when she *was* her regular school self.

I used to meet with her as an excuse to get out of PE. She talked about my grades and my attitude toward school and how it could all be blamed on my not dealing with grief. She told me that people who don't work through their grief inflict *tremendous* harm on themselves—whether they planned to or not. So she'd probably decide I'm writing myself the notes as a way of dealing with the grief I don't feel.

Not to mention, Ms. Phillipe has a reputation for breaking the rules of confidentiality. She'd tell the principal and he'd probably call Mom.

No way. I can handle it on my own.

When I was little, I used to stand in the doorway to my room and estimate the spot on the floor I needed to jump from to get on my bed without the imaginary monster grabbing my ankles and pulling me into his giant maw under the bed. Now there is a real monster, and he waits for me around every dark corner.

How's that, Ms. Phillipe?

FOR THE REST OF the day I try to focus on the contest and cookie designs. I'm supposed to come up with a Valentine's cookie but all I can think of is a variation on my Halloween skull cookies: Black icing, with bloody, slimy red eye sockets, and broken, bloody teeth.

When it's time for my shift at Crockett's I actually look forward to it.

There's a new checkout girl.

She smiles, with her too pink lipstick and her wine-colored hair tightened into a French twist. "What's your name, sweetie?"

"Kara."

"Well nice to meet you, Kara! I'm Justine—named after my dad, except with an *e*."

I decide immediately that I like her. When I'm too slow bagging groceries, she leans over to help without making me feel like a shitty failure. "Here, hon, let me help you."

Justine talks a lot, and I love that she ignores the customers to talk to me.

A HALF-HOUR INTO MY shift, the boss appears, scowling. "Kara, I don't pay you to talk and gossip. Get on with it," he says, pointing at the pile of groceries on the belt.

Jason stands with him, his shadow, smirking at me.

What did I do? I can't even manage to open my mouth in time to defend myself.

Justine smiles sweetly and flicks her hand at him. "Oh shoot, Mr. Stewart, it was my fault. I was asking Kara if she knew the code for bananas. She's innocent."

Before the two of them slither away, Dickhead sniffs and Jason looks at Justine's boobs.

I turn to her, frowning.

"Jason's just a little boy," she says with a wink, as if reading my mind.

JUSTINE AND I BOTH get off at the same time so I sit with her while she waits for the Metro.

"How long have you been here?" I ask. I nibble on a Snickers and she takes a drag from her cigarette. I think about Kellen's weed and how maybe Justine could teach me to inhale correctly. She's just a few years older, but in terms of worldliness, she's got decades on me.

"Oh," she starts, before exhaling a toxic cloud. "I suppose I been here about three months now, followed my ex up here when he landed himself a job with the electric company, working on power poles and stuff." She pauses, studying and frowning at her perfect fingernails. "He was gonna take care of me, we were gonna get married, start a family, all the things I wanted. Then the fucker cheated on me with some *ugly*-ass waitress at the Moon Bar, so I hope he goes ahead and singes his nuts on them wires."

I giggle because it's funny, even though her face is dead serious.

"I'm sorry," I tell her.

"Aww, it's okay. I'm over him." She blinks a few times, so I guess this isn't true. Plus she stops talking. In the few hours I've known Justine, I've discovered that talking for her is like breathing.

"So . . ." I start. "Why didn't you go back to Texas?"

Justine takes another drag and exhales. "I like it up here. I love that I can see the mountains and the ocean—right here." She gestures with her cigarette and smoldering ash falls to the sidewalk. "And I don't need my mom givin' me shit and telling me 'I told you so.' How about you? I'll bet you lived here all your life, huh?"

"Yeah."

Justine nods, dropping the cigarette and smashing it with the scuffed toe of her high heel.

"You don't talk a lot, do you, Kara?"

"Sorry."

"Don't apologize for being the way God made you."

The mention of God triggers my automatic eye roll.

The bus rumbles up to the curb. Justine hops up from the bench. I want her to stay. I want to tell her about the notes and my stalker and my dead sister. But instead I watch her fan away the exhaust fumes and cough, before she grabs my hand and squeezes it.

"You're a sweetheart, Kara. Thanks for making my first day special."

♡   ♡   ♡

AN HOUR AFTER I say good-bye to Justine, there's a loud bang at the door that separates our apartment from the café. It's Noelle. She pulls me into a booth. Her face is red and she smells like she smoked a whole carton. Luckily the café isn't crowded. Still, she takes out a cigarette and her lighter. "I think Mason's cheating on me, Kar."

"Don't light that in here, my mom will kill you," I whisper. "So what happened?"

Noelle flicks the lighter on and off, staring at the flame. "We were just sitting there in his car and I pissed him off because I always change the song on his iPod. I guess this time it was too much for the prick. All of a sudden he says 'I think we need to see other people too, I mean we can still hang out but I want to explore my options.' *Explore my options?* So I said fine, asshole, now I can go after Mr. Hoyt."

"Nice, Noelle."

She stares over my shoulder and points her lit lighter. "Mind your own business, bone lover, this is a *private* convo!"

I don't even need to turn to see she's talking to Hayden. But when I do, I smile and mouth, *Forget it.*

I feel Noelle's lighter poking my shoulder. "Whose side are you on here?"

I turn back around. "*Noelle*," I whisper, "he has nothing to do with it."

She frowns at me and sits back. "Can you stop lusting over him for two seconds to listen?"

"Fine. What happened next?"

"He just went off, saying he was only joking and he knew I had a thing for Mr. Hoyt. Mason and his friends all got stoned last weekend and one of his idiot friends brought up this crap about Mr. Hoyt. I guess Mason was sober enough to remember and trick me with all this shit about breaking up. He's such a dick."

"And what guy wouldn't love the idea of his girlfriend hoping to bang a teacher?"

"Yeah but I don't see him that way, Kar. Shit he's only a couple of years older than me. And he's not even my teacher anymore so it doesn't count. God, I need to let loose. Come on, Kar."

"It's a school night," I say. "How about tomorrow night? Maybe a sleepover?" She narrows her eyes at me. I've made a mistake. Before she can protest, I add, "It *can* be fun you know. Watching movies, pigging out on cookie dough and pizza—"

"Getting drunk."

"Okay, getting drunk, too." I was going to mention my little weed stash to seal it, but that's totally unnecessary now.

She sits up and flicks the lighter on again. "Okay. At my house, because your Harry Potter cupboard of a room sucks. Bring cookie dough. I'll take care of the rest." She stands up, cracking her knuckles. "Hey let's watch all the *Saw* movies, too. I'll call ya later." As she leaves I hear her snap, "*Forget it*, boner boy. You know she's way too good for you!"

When I whip around, Noelle's hurtling out the door. I don't even have time to yell anything to her before she gets out. My face feels hot and I want to sink down into the booth and hide.

I see now that Hayden is the only one left in the café with me, besides a couple my mom's age. The dishwasher hums in the back. I know it's not Charlie because it's his day off.

"C'mere." Hayden says, pointing to the seat next to him. He closes his laptop.

"I should go back upstairs," I say.

"You're too smart to be friends with Noelle."

So now what? I'm getting the older brother talk? "You don't know her, Hayden."

"Yeah, I know her. Girls like her. Nothing there. Nothing to see. Unlike you."

This all puts me on the defensive. I feel normal again. And it feels good. "She's pretty much my only friend these days."

Hayden chews his lip, as if wanting to say something but not sure how. "People kind of ditch you after someone close dies. Or maybe you ditch them. I haven't figured out which is which yet."

Now I don't feel so normal anymore. My pulse quickens. "What do you mean?"

He shakes his head. "Forget it."

"Did that happen to you, too?"

He nods, avoiding my eyes. "Yeah."

"What happened?"

"Look, I'm sorry, Kara," he says. "I don't really want to talk about it. But I want you to know that I understand. I know how it feels."

Thank God, because I don't want to talk about it, either. "Thanks."

Hayden stays silent for a solid minute. I could congratulate him for not filling the silence with more condolences or the need for more details.

"She drowned, right? Your sister?" he finally says. "I knew someone who drowned, too." He reaches out to pick at an old scratch in the table.

I shake my head. "Look, your friend probably didn't drown like Kellen did. Like, how many people are stupid enough to get drunk at a party and then fall into a swimming pool in October? Who does that?"

There's a *clang* in the kitchen that makes me flinch. Raul's obviously dropped something again. But Hayden doesn't seem to notice. Instead he rubs his neck with one hand and starts tapping his fingers on the laptop with the other, frowning at the screen.

I sit back and offer nothing more because I really don't want to talk about Kellen. Another *clang* from the back fills the silence and I wonder if I should go check on Raul to make sure he didn't fall or something, anything to get us off the topic of my sister.

Hayden closes the laptop. "Sorry about that. I mean . . . I hate when people are only half-there, but I do it all the time."

I nod. A rush of warmth goes through me.

"You seem pissed at her, Kara."

"Huh? Oh. Can we talk about something else please?"

"Sure."

"Where's your girlfriend?" I hear myself ask.

"Ah . . . we're on a break."

Before Charlie came back, this news probably would've put me over the moon. "Sorry."

"I'm not. Hey, remember a couple of weeks ago when we talked about my grandma, the baker? Remember I told you she was Greek? And she couldn't speak English so she showed her love by baking us treats?"

I don't remember at all. But he smiles and the fact that I notice again how incredibly good-looking he is makes me feel bad about Charlie for some reason. I don't remember us talking about his Greek grandma ever, do I? But it doesn't matter since I forget stuff all the time.

He continues. "She reminds me of you a little."

"Thanks, Hayden. I remind you of your grandma. Nice."

"No, no. Just in her dedication to what she loved doing. Baking. Like you. That's why you remind me of her. It's a compliment, trust me. Back in her village she baked for everyone. That was before she came to America. I miss her baklava."

"Really, Hayden? A *village?*"

He nods like everyone lives in a village, and I feel dumb so I quickly say, "Give me her recipe and I'll make it for you sometime."

Hayden's arm is practically around me and I feel the soft cotton of his sleeve against my neck under my ponytail. When he leans down, strands of his dirty blond hair fall over his forehead and his lips are inches from mine.

"You'd do that for me? Make me her baklava?"

"Mm-hmm. Phyllo dough is kind of tricky but I can do it."

Outside the shop a face peers in. If it weren't for the letterman jacket catching my eye, I wouldn't have noticed him staring in at us. What the hell? Maybe now that he's seen Hayden he'll leave me alone.

I'm just about to tell Hayden but all thoughts are gone because he's caught my chin in his fingers. His eyes flicker back and forth between my eyes and my mouth and then his lips are on mine.

"Thank you, Kara."

I don't have time to think about how quick the kiss is because he kisses me again, harder.

A thousand and one thoughts are going through my mind.

You're just a fuckin' baby, Kara.

It feels wrong. My arms were dangling at my side, but now I push my hands into his chest. He sits back and shakes his head, running a hand through his hair. My lips tingle. Before Charlie came back, I'd pictured this moment with Hayden a gazillion times, and in my dreams I'd been happy and floating on air. But my mind is taking me somewhere else, back to a memory, and now that it's done, all I can do is try not to be sick or cry and hope that he's not mad at me.

Again he kisses me, quick and soft on the lips before he slides out of the booth. "I need to go."

Out of the corner of my eye I catch a flash of red across the room. Kellen disappears around the corner, her black ponytail peeking out of the top of her red hoodie.

At the door, Hayden doesn't notice my sister, but turns and smiles at me, saying something I can't hear. His face looks apologetic. Or pitying. Or maybe both. Probably about how I'm just a high school baby who'd never be able to meet his college guy needs anyway.

As soon as he's out the door I want to go look for Kellen. But then I remember she's dead. I'm frozen in the booth, shaking.

FRIDAY AFTER MY SHIFT at Crockett's, I pick up cookie dough. I have Justine wrap it in a brown bag for me because a real baker should never be seen with store-bought dough. I'm looking forward to just hanging out with Noelle and forgetting the weird stuff that's been happening to me.

While I sit at the bus stop, my cell signals a new text: Chg o plans. Me & M ok. Hang @ wrk tomm?

My feet won't budge. I close the message, unaware the bus has arrived until the driver hollers at me if I'm getting on or not? I check the time of the message—an hour ago, when I was still working. Then I delete it.

I feel like I'm always standing outside those circular fences at the carnival, waiting for my turn on the Tilt-A-Whirl. I watch and wait as everyone else goes in and my turn never comes. I can't wait to get out of here and be off to college. I set the tub of cookie dough on the bench; maybe someone will want it. Then I trudge toward home.

Noelle keeps texting me: R U ok? Sorry. Hafta b w/hm. We'll do it soon. Promise.

I let her off the hook by texting her back that I have so much homework it's probably for the best.

Ok. Def good thing<3

Whatever. At the café, every table's full and parties wait. Mom blows me a kiss and mouths, *We are so blessed.* She says it so often I can read her lips.

Upstairs, I take a shower, because I don't know what else to do. With my hair wrapped in a towel, I sit in the window seat and watch the happy people strolling along the twinkly lit Ave in the frigid evening.

Down a block, El Diablo Coffee looks full and I think of Charlie.

I haven't seen him in a while and I wonder if he's there. Below me, muffled voices and laughter make the emptiness around me unbearable, so after combing out and drying my hair, I change into my favorite jeans and T-shirt.

My hand is almost on the doorknob when a loud *knock, knock, knock* scares me from the other side.

Mom wouldn't knock on the door. Noelle would knock and yell.

"Who is it?" I ask.

It happens again, only louder. Three knocks. What the hell?

I listen carefully, still hearing the muffled voices downstairs. I can't hear anything outside my door and I stand there waiting, my heartbeat picking up speed, while my cheek presses against the door to hear better.

Minutes tick away.

Then the thudding of footsteps hurrying downstairs and the amplified noise of diners as whoever was just outside my door opens the first-floor door that leads into the café. The door only Mom and I are allowed through. The door only Mom and I have a key for.

TWENTY MINUTES LATER I'VE calmed down enough to go down to the kitchen and pull out ingredients for royal icing, intending to test out a design for the contest on some sugar cookies I'd baked and stuck in the freezer.

Before I mix I creep around the corner to see if Charlie's washing dishes. Maybe Charlie came to the door? But changed his mind? This is what I'm hoping but deep down I know it wasn't Charlie at my door.

Disappointment must show on my face because Raul, the regular dishwasher, smiles at me over his shoulder.

"Hey, Kara. Charlie's off." Then he winks. "If you were wondering."

My mouth opens but nothing comes out, and I hurry back to my section of the kitchen. I try not to think of what Charlie might be doing or who he might be with.

When I turn around, Kellen's sitting on the counter.

She stares at me. There's softness in her eyes, something I never saw when she was alive.

"This is not happening," I say, maybe to her, I'm not sure. I think briefly of Mom, and of her insistence that Kellen visited her after she died. "You're dead. Go away, Kellen."

Even as I say it I'm not sure I mean it. I'm not sure about much anymore. My sister is trying to make me crazy like Mom. Even in death she has to try and get me.

Raul pops around the corner. "You okay, Kara? Who you talkin' to?"

"Sorry. It's nothing."

He nods and disappears around the corner.

My notebook sits there, opened to my last sketches. The corner of a familiar blue-gray envelope sticks out from the pages.

How did I not see this before? I think as I rip it open.

YOU'RE NOTHING LIKE THE FIRST.

JUNE: THIRTEEN-YEAR-OLD CARROT'S SUMMER ~~FUN~~ BEFORE HIGH SCHOOL

Everyone looks at us now. Kellen grabs her bag and climbs over the rope to the sidewalk. The pizza in my mouth is a chunk of wood I can't swallow. I watch my sister storm off down the Ave, leaving me there with Nick and Tad.

"Shit," Tad mutters, shaking his head. "She's a fuckin' nut job." He points at me. "You can tell her I said so!" He grabs another slice of pizza, folds it in half, and crams it into his mouth.

I'm not sure what to do, follow her or stay. I keep hoping that she'll yell for me to come with her.

"Aw, Christ," Tad mutters, his mouth full. He hops out of his chair and over the rope, walking fast in the direction that Kellen went.

I still can't believe she left me. I've been to the Ave a zillion times but never by myself. Mom only started letting me come here with friends a couple months ago. She's going to be so pissed at Kellen when she finds out.

Nick puffs his cheeks out with a long exhale. "I'll walk you home when you're ready, kid."

He wipes his mouth, sighs, and checks his watch and phone. I nod.

I've been around Nick enough, just never alone so I'm nervous about going with him. What do I say? He's seventeen. I'm thirteen and feel like more of a baby than ever. I push my plate away and shuffle my flips flops underneath the table.

"Finished?" Nick asks, looking at his watch again.

"Yeah," I wipe my hands off on a napkin and stand up. I have to pull my sundress off my butt because it's stuck there from my damp swimsuit.

Nick tosses a five on the table and walks out to the sidewalk. He waits, hands in his pockets, staring across the street and I hurry over, even though I don't want to walk with him because I see this is such a burden for him—walking the baby home.

"I can walk myself, okay? I'm old enough and I know the way home," I tell his backside as I walk past him. For some reason my eyes sting, threatening tears. I feel a hand on my shoulder and I stop and turn around. When he sticks his hands in his pockets I notice the tan and how the little hairs on his arm seem lighter than his skin.

"Look, Kara, it's getting dark and you shouldn't be walking by yourself okay?" He's in front of me and his mouth turns up with a hint of a smile. "I really don't mind. Plans are kinda shot now anyway."

I follow behind when he starts walking and when he stops, I almost walk into his back. Over his shoulder he smiles. "You don't need to walk behind me, kid."

I move up next to him and for the first time ever I notice how good he smells. Clean. Not bathed in cologne like my dad—just clean. I keep up with him and notice he's slowed down a bit. I catch a whiff of Fritos. Ugh, my swimsuit.

The peal of giggling girls comes from across the street. I recognize some of them from school but we aren't friends. Nick and I are waiting for the light to change so I move a little closer to him and smile. The noise hushes a bit and I know they're impressed and I have a feeling that if we were in school tomorrow they'd be asking me about him. Their mouths hang open, and one whispers and points at us. I don't think Nick notices them, but I flip my damp hair to one side and stand up taller. Should I grab his arm? Gaby would do it for sure.

"Kara," he starts and my stomach plunges because I think he's onto me. "Back there, what they were saying, that was . . ." He doesn't finish and we walk down toward my street. "Not right. They shouldn't be talking like that in front of you, you know?"

The light changes and the girls still whisper and stare at us as we cross the street. Suddenly I realize how silly and obnoxious they seem. I'm embarrassed for them.

"I mean, really, you're just a baby, a kid. I hope you just forget all that, everything they said. It was wrong of them, okay?"

"Yeah but I'm not really a kid anymore. I'm almost fourteen."

Nick chuckles and pats my back in a brotherly sort of way. I shrug my shoulder away from his hand, so sick of being called a baby today. I make a great effort to walk ahead of him and when I see my street, I decide I don't need him to walk me the rest of the way so I run. My flip flops are still damp and squishy and chafing the heck out of the spaces between my toes. Gnats are buzzing into my face. Nick calls out after me, but I ignore it because there's no way I'm crying in front of him and showing what a baby I really am.

10. *Beat to stiff peaks.*

. . . .

My latest ridiculous thought is that my dead sister is leaving me the notes.

It's crazy, yes. But I feel crazy right now.

I've been sitting here with Noelle, deciding if I'm going to tell her about the notes, but I see that guy with the varsity jacket. "Noelle, who is that guy over there, sitting with the jocks?"

She turns around. "Which one?"

"The guy on the end, he's looking at us now."

"Umm, I forget his name, but I'm pretty sure he had a very hot older brother. I remember him from parties, but I can't remember his name, either. Why? Are we hot for him now, too?"

I ignore this and she turns back to look at him.

"He *is* cute, but not like his brother . . ." Noelle slams her hand down on the table. "Noah! His name's Noah."

Her cell distracts her, which is good because I've changed my mind and don't want to get into the whole stalker thing with her right now.

When she gets off her cell, I avoid any more comments about Noah by telling her I saw Kellen again.

"What did she do this time?" Noelle asks, picking at the pizza on her cafeteria tray.

"Nothing, just—"

"How exciting." She takes a bite of pizza and then talks with her mouth full. "So does she say how Elvis is doing these days?"

I stare at my chicken burger, deciding if I really want lunch at all. "Can you be serious?"

Noelle finishes chewing before she speaks again. "I don't know, Kar. What do you want me to say? That I think you're crazy? Or that I think maybe you need to believe your mom when she says Kellen visited her and told her to make her Jesus soup?"

I hate that Mom's craziness could've been caused by my dead sister. But it certainly fits with Mom's current version of events: a few weeks after Kellen drowned, Mom went to the couch with her wine, and the next day she claimed to have had a near death experience where my sister waited in the light and told her to go back, sell our house, and open the café. Putting yourself to sleep with two bottles of wine could make your dreams unusually strange, right? At least that's what I thought back when it happened.

But it was weird, the way everything changed so quickly. One day she was catatonic, the next she had the first smile on her face in months, and she had a mission.

"Hey, Noah!"

When I look up, Noelle is grabbing Noah's arm, and he has no choice but to sit down next to her.

She smiles at him, takes a drink of his Coke, and gives it back. "Thanks, Noah. Hey, do you know my girl Kara here?"

Noah's eyes flick around to a few different spots before they land on my shoulder. "No, can't say that I do."

"Well, then, Noah, Kara, Kara, Noah."

He offers a weak smile with a millisecond of eye contact. I do the same. His group of friends walks by and he pops up fast.

"Well, now we know balls don't run in his family," Noelle says. "I know his brother wasn't scared of girls." She flashes a grin. "So how come we never see Charlie at school?"

"He goes to Kennedy," I tell her.

"How do *you* know?"

"He told me."

She waggles her eyebrows. "Well, well. You seem to know a lot. You kids getting a little sloppy back there between dishwasher cycles? Hmm?"

"God, can you possibly be serious for a whole minute? Some people have actual problems, you know?"

Noelle frowns. "Yes, I know. How could I not when you remind me daily? This is why our ancestors invented beer. And by the way, life is also about getting some, and getting over sad stuff and having fun, and not wasting all of your *best* years hiding in a kitchen baking cookies. You know, I put up with a lot from you and your moods, Kar." She sweeps her hand around the room in a giant circle. "Take a look. Is there anyone else here that you could call a friend besides me?"

I want to tell her to kiss my ass, but then I'd have no one else to talk to. Because she's right. But I think about how if Jen and Gaby were still my friends I'd be able to tell them things. Like how Hayden kissed me, and I've wanted him to do it forever, but then it wasn't what I thought it'd be. I could tell them that I have a stalker, and they wouldn't joke about it. But I can't tell Noelle any of this.

After another bite of burger, I drop it back on the tray. "I have other friends, Noelle."

"Mm-hmm. Where? Sometimes I worry about you."

"So stop ditching me every chance you get to spend time with Mason!"

There. I said it. My insides feel hot and twisty as I wait for the verbal annihilation that will leave me humiliated and alone in this big cafeteria.

Noelle glares at me. I've done it, somehow. Because my only friend stands up, grabs her stuff, and marches away. When I dare look up I see her leaving the cafeteria with Mason.

People watch. Or maybe they're staring at my French fry log house in the corner of the tray next to the grapes, which Noelle and I think are cat eyeballs. Maybe *he* watches, too. My hands shake when I carry my tray to the garbage. Noah's just turning to walk out the door and I see the entire back of his letterman jacket.

Bender. It's written in big script.

Noah Bender.

But I still don't know why he's so familiar.

THE REST OF THE day blurs by me and the ground is the only place that feels safe to look. In sixth period home ec I'm not in the mood to bake. I think about ditching and taking the Playtex box home, to my old house.

Later, while I robotically crack eggs into a bowl, Mr. King approaches the counter. "Kara, how are things on the contest front? Did you get permission from your mom yet?"

I can't even force a smile for him and his Captain Morgan apron. "I bought my plane ticket, earned enough money working."

He nods.

Everyone is busy, stirring and sifting and measuring. I should tell him about the notes. He's my favorite teacher. He'll help me.

But instead I say, "I've narrowed down my designs."

He stares down at me, nodding his head while his eyes do that teacher-roving-around-the- room thing.

Now, Kara! Tell him now.

He nods again and my insides twist because I know what he's asking.

"Kara, I am glad that you've raised the money, but the entry form clearly states that those under eighteen need *written* parental consent. Have you gotten it?"

I look down into my bowl of butter, eggs, and vanilla. The vanilla separates, making the egg look like it has freckles on it. "Working on it."

"Kara, you have to do this."

I have to tell him.

"Mr. King!" I hear someone yell from across the room.

Mr. King pivots and hurries toward the smell of burning pans. But I can't tell him anyway. He'd probably feel obligated to tell Mom, and she can't ever know. If she found out then she'd find out about other secrets. I go back to mixing and try to see my future in the bowl. I don't need anyone. I need to get out of this city and off to school, and maybe France, and get my own life and start over.

Dreams are all I need, anyway.

"HMM. LOOKS LIKE YOU just lost your best friend." Justine rubs hand lotion over her elbows.

"Just a crappy day," I say, restocking bags.

"I see. Sniff is at the bank, so go on."

I smile at Dickhead's new nickname. "There's just something I want more than anything in the world, and I know my mom's going to say no."

"Tell me," Justine leans over. "What? A piercing? A tattoo? Bigger tits? Not that yours aren't just precious." With that she cups both of hers, frowning and shaking her head at them. "Good Lord, what's a girl to do with these? Love to get me down a cup or two."

"It's that baking contest I told you about," I interrupt, not really wanting to talk about her boobs. "But I didn't tell you it was in San Francisco. There's no way in hell she'll let me go, but I just *have* to go."

"I *get* it. I know all about dreams. Shit, just ask her, and if she says no, find a way. You'll never get anywhere in this life if you don't try, Kara."

I nod.

"Try what?" a familiar boy's voice asks.

My head jerks up. It's Charlie Norton. He stands at Justine's register with a pack of gum and a smile for me.

Justine wags a finger at him. "Listen, we work here and we're polite to you customers, but this is a private conversation that's none of *your* dang beeswax. So let me just ring up your stuff and you can scoot on out of here."

My eyes meet Charlie's. I bite my lip to keep back a smile.

"Sorry, miss," Charlie replies. "It's just . . . I know Kara. We're friends."

Justine leans back against the cash register with a hand on her hip, clucking her tongue and looking back and forth at Charlie and me.

"You know *my* Kara?" she asks him.

"Yeah, I do." He matches her grin. "See you at your mom's later, Kara?"

My face is burning. "Okay."

She cranes her neck to watch him stroll out to the parking lot. "Mmm-hmm. Okay," she says, poking me in the shoulder. "*Who* was *that?* Huh?"

"Just Charlie."

"Hmm. 'Just Charlie.'" She makes air quotes. "Turns your face the color of my Christmas lipstick? Good Lord."

"Kara." Sniff and Jason have magically appeared with matching sodas. "Round up the carts and don't forget to grab the trash out of 'em this time. Yesterday a customer had to throw away a damn dirty diaper you left in one! Go on now."

My mouth hangs open because Jason was here yesterday; maybe it was one of his carts that had the shitty diaper. I'm so out of here after the contest.

AFTER SCHOOL THE NEXT day I sit in the café, waiting for Mom.

"Sweetheart, you're late. Was there a problem at school?" She sets a latte in front of me.

"I'm not late, Mom." I don't even bother with an excuse this time because it's true.

"Well, stay here and I'll be right back because your face tells me something prayerful is on your mind."

She's not right with me though, and every couple of minutes she whizzes by, giving me her little drive-by shoulder squeeze to make sure I haven't left her sight. Each time she passes my stomach loops into another knot because of what I'm going to ask her.

My cup is empty when Mom finally sits down. She takes my hands and I can smell the onions and garlic and lotion on them. "I feel like we need to pray first. Shall we start there?"

She can't even talk to me anymore without bringing God to the table! When she starts with "Dear Lord," I snatch my hands away.

"Mom! I don't need to pray. I need to talk to you about something important."

The bell above the door launches Mom out of her seat. But before she goes to greet yet another customer, she whispers, "You always need to pray. I'll be right back, and then we'll talk."

The dinner rush starts.

I watch Mom feed her flock. Their grumbling bellies are more important than my problems. But I already knew that.

AT 9:00 THAT NIGHT Mom walks into the apartment.

"Oh, Kara, I am worn out! Worn out and blessed!"

She lies back and rubs her foot while I stuff popcorn into my mouth.

"I'm sorry, honey, I know there's something you wanted to talk to me about. What was it?" She smiles at me.

But I can't—I know what's coming. "I . . . um, Mr. King wants me to enter a very important baking contest."

Mom sits up, clapping her hands. "Oh, Kara! That's wonderful! He thinks so highly of you! I'm so glad he appreciates your talent! When is it?"

I hand her the postcard and give her a few seconds before I say, "The contest—it's in San Francisco."

She flinches as if I hit her. "Absolutely not," she replies, dismissing me with her hand like I just asked for ten bucks, before getting up and walking into the kitchen.

The floor creaks and I hear the water being turned on and then a glass filling. Mom walks back into the living room. She stares at me and I think she might throw the water on me, which is crazy. But our life has become one big rollercoaster of crazy, so it's very possible.

I never ask for anything. Kellen wore her and Dad down, always asking for more because what they offered was never enough. This was how she got better clothes, a better car, a later curfew—which she broke anyway—and the chance to go away to college.

"Mom, I already earned enough money at Crockett's for the flight." I leave out the fact that I bought my ticket already. "You don't have to pay for anything. This means more to me than anything in the world."

"Kara." She sighs and stares up at the ceiling, or maybe heaven. "It's out of the question. You can't go by yourself, and I can't take time off from the café to run off to California so you can bake cookies."

Her whole face patronizes me, like she's trying not to smile.

I'm expected to make the right decisions. Unlike Kellen, I'm expected to get good grades, have a job, and be responsible. My dreams aren't important. Kellen didn't even know what she wanted to *do* after college, but my parents let her go off to her first choice anyway. To "find herself." Their words.

"Don't sulk, Kara. I know you want this *now*, but trust me, someday you'll thank me for saving you from your mistakes."

"What mistakes, Mom? I love baking. I want to bake."

"Kara, this isn't a church bake-off. Do you know how many people enter? Why waste all that money and time when you have so little chance of winning? I know you're talented, but really? This is not something you're likely to stick with down the road, as history has proven. Honestly, your father and I spent so much money on lessons for you—music, sports—and the *stuff* to go with those lessons only to have you quit and see our hard-earned money gone. So why waste *your* money on a plane ticket?"

"Dad already said I could go." The lie pops out of my mouth before I even fully form the thought.

Mom sits up fast. "Kara McKinley, don't you dare bring darkness into this house by lying to me. You did not ask your father. *I* am your custodial parent and you need *my* consent, not his."

I meet her gaze. "I can win a free ride to La Patisserie. And there's prize money."

"Good *Lord*, that *school*! As far as getting into *that school*, we've discussed this. The Lord's plan for your future does not involve going out of state to college! The only reason you want to go there is because it's in California! You're staying! I've already lost *one* daughter, I'm *not* going to lose another! Do you really think I need any more stress in my life?"

Disbelief dawns on me. She thinks I want to go to La Patisserie because it's out of state. But she knows that if the school was in Seattle, I'd stay in Seattle. She must. Doesn't she? How can she not know that? How can she not know what's important to me? My throat closes up and I can't speak because it will be a rush of emotion. I blink hard and swallow because I won't show it; I won't give her the satisfaction.

A minute passes with both of us staring at opposite walls. "I'm doing this," I tell her. "You can't stop me." My heart pounds because I never talk to her this way. So maybe I should tell her all of it. Tell her that I have a stalker and he might kill me and it would be nice to have this little bit of happiness in my life before I'm done.

Mom whirls, her face red. "Why should I trust you to go or do anything by yourself? When have you ever shown any responsibility in your life to make me feel like I could let you do this? I'd end up having to close the café to come down and bail you out. You're always pushing the boundary a little further, pushing me to the edge a little more! You're always screwing up, leaving things for your father and me to fix! Well not this time!"

My mouth hangs open because I don't know what she's talking about. What have I ever screwed up? I'm confused.

And then it hits me.

I don't think she's really arguing with me anymore.

She's arguing with Kellen. My mom is wishing for my dead sister.

Mom continues. "And God *damn* it I did not raise children to speak to me like this!"

Now my mom sounds more like her old self and I am almost relieved. I want to say something else, something that will piss her off even more, just to keep my old mom here. I miss her. But nothing will come out of my mouth, and there she goes, hopping off the couch and onto her knees, whispering and asking for forgiveness for taking His name in vain.

Half a minute later she walks to the kitchen window.

She looks the way she did back then, staring into the night sky, wrapped in Kellen's blue afghan. Lost in her memories. I'd put my hand on her arm, but she'd swat it off as if it were a spider. All because I'm not Kellen.

Now, the tear tracks make me wonder if she's thinking of Kellen or pissed about breaking a commandment.

MUCH LATER, BEHIND MY locked door, I'm still listening to the sounds of my mother begging Jesus to forgive me. She finally gives prayer a rest sometime around 11 P.M.

My head hurts. My mother is crazy. There's no way I'm missing the contest.

I grab the entry form and spend the next five minutes staring at it. I talk myself into something I never would've done before Kellen died. I fill it out. When I get to the parent signature, I creep to my door and crack it open. Down the short hall Mom snores in her room.

In the kitchen I find the bill box and take it back into my room.

Inside the box I find a check for the power bill Mom hasn't sent.

There's just enough light coming from the shop below and the shops across the street. It's easy for me to turn the window into the backlighting that I need. It's easy for me to place the check against the window and the entry sheet over that.

Mom's signature comes through just enough for me to trace it onto the contest sheet. Kellen taught me how to do this when I was in middle school, but I never needed a forgery until now.

After stuffing the entry in an envelope, I address and stamp it.

Ten minutes later I stand out in the cold, dropping my ticket to happiness into the mailbox.

When I get to my front porch I'm out of breath and the tears
have vanished. As soon as I reach the bottom step I feel a hand
on my back.

"Hey wait, Kara. I'm sorry back there; I didn't mean you
were a kid, kid, okay? Look I know how it is. I have older
brothers, I know how you feel," Nick says, rummaging through
his pockets. "Shit."

"What?"

"Tad has my car keys. He had to go back and stick his shirt
in the car. Damn it!" He steps away and paces around with his
hands on his hips.

I know that he lives in the U District so it's not like he can
walk home. "So, I guess you're stuck here until they come back."
I rub my flip flop over the edge of the step.

"Yeah, well, I can just go back to the Ave or something, try
to get into a bar," He grins. "Maybe you can tell them where I
went? To come get me? If it's not too much trouble?"

I stare at him, running a hand through his hair and placing
the other on his hip. My mom likes Nick. She's even hinted to
Kellen that she should go out with him instead. She'd probably
be mad at me if I didn't at least invite him to hang out here until
Kellen and Tad come back. "Why don't you just wait here? You
can watch TV."

He has his hands in his pockets, and he stares out toward the
orange sky west of Puget Sound, which is dappled with pink.
"Yeah, I guess I could. Sure."

Good thing Kellen didn't lock the door because I didn't have time to grab my key before we left. I open the door for Nick and wave him in. "You know where the TV is, right?"

"Yeah, thanks." He nods and makes his way to the door to the basement steps.

I stand and watch him disappear through the doorway, not sure if I should follow him or not.

The bolder side of me decides I should. Mom would expect me to offer a drink like we do to everyone who comes over. As I pad down the stairs, I feel the temperature drop with each step, and smell that familiar damp smell. The TV shows some action movie. Nick's back is to me and his arm is up on the back of the loveseat. I go around and stand at the opposite end of the loveseat, and my face flushes because I don't know what to say.

"Oh hey, kid. What's up?" He gives me a quick glance before looking back to the TV.

"Um, I wondered if you'd uh, like something to drink?"

"Oh sure, thanks."

I skip back up the steps and into the kitchen. When I pull the fridge door open I grab for a Coke but stop when I see beer— Bud Lights and a couple of Guinness. I grab a Guinness because that's what my dad offers to company. The cap hisses when I pop it off and hurry back down the steps.

"Here you go," I hand the beer to him.

He seems surprised and smiles as he says, "Thanks, Kara. Uh, you wanna sit down and watch with me?"

I'm not expecting him to say this. "Um, sure. But I'll be right back." I walk backwards to the stairs, my eye on Nick. I walk fast up the stairs and then run up the main stairs to my room.

STEP 2:

Watch cookies carefully so they don't burn!

11. *Flatten and repeat.*

. . . .

Over the next few days Mom acknowledges our fight by making it worse. "Kara McKinley, you'll win no favor with God by sulking over things you can't have. The Most High has a plan for you; you just don't know it yet."

I ignore her, and Hayden, who asks me to sit with him, or asks about my baking every time I walk through the café, with that same apologetic and pitying look on his face. I've taken to rushing past, preoccupied with whatever since I'm not really sure how I feel about him now. Awkward tops the list.

At lunch, I've been sitting alone. But I'm getting used to it. I can get used to anything. Today Noelle texted me for the first time since she ditched me in the cafeteria. I know we're okay.

Got cramps? Let's find us some chocolate.

She smiled and gave me the finger from across the cafeteria. I gave it right back.

I try to focus my energy on my cookie designs. But my enthusiasm tastes bland without Mom's approval, even though I'm still mad at her. And I'm mad that I care about what she thinks or feels. But I'm going. Sneaking off to San Francisco was something my sister would have done. Kellen wouldn't have cared what our parents said, and she wouldn't have felt guilty about it.

THE FOLLOWING MONDAY AFTER school, Mom thinks I'm still pissed. She doesn't have a clue. And she's too busy to say anything. Hayden's hunched over his laptop, not paying any attention to me. Behind the espresso machine, I fix myself a latte and peek again at Hayden. He smiles at me and I give him a pathetic smile because he is beautiful.

Back in my corner of the kitchen I line up my jars of food color gel, along with bowls so I can make four shades of royal icing. I stand on the old chair to gather sprinkles in my apron; eight lovely jars of sparkly sugar in shades of blue, pink, purple, and green.

I sift out confectioners' sugar, meringue powder, and water into each bowl. After adding food color, it takes me a half hour to get the perfect tint in each bowl: Grass green, lime green, plum, and pink.

It's not until I'm filling the piping bags that I hear the familiar pinging of the sprayer. Charlie's back. He's working, shooting water against a crusty pan to the rhythm of whatever plays in his ear. I pick up the grass green icing bag to outline the leaves of the flowers. I'm easing my way into the Valentine theme. While I pipe leaves, I think about walking around the corner. But I've got a good piping flow going. After I finish each cookie, I use the plum icing to outline the petals, making a dam around the whole of each one. Carefully I pipe the pink icing to make a smaller dam inside each petal.

When these are done I need time to let them dry and set before I flood them with the rest of the icing.

"Hey."

At the sound of his voice, a blob of lime green escapes the piping bag and jumps over the line of dry plum icing. I hate when that happens. I turn with a frown, but it melts.

"Crap. Look what you did." I gesture to my ruined cookie.

Charlie draws his lips together in a line and shakes his head. "Hey, I didn't touch that."

"*You* made me goof it up." I turn to wipe the blob off with a knife.

"*I* didn't do anything, Sprinkles," he says, backing up against my little storage cabinet. He folds his arms and leans against the door, smiling at me. "What'cha working on?"

"Cookies."

"Obviously. What are they *for*?"

"Um, nothing, just to sell."

"So what are your plans later? Or are you going to be here painting cookies all night?"

"Um, I have plans," I lie, and I even nod so maybe he'll believe it.

"Hayden Westcott?"

I flinch. His eyes ask more than his words do.

"Don't you think he's kind of old for you?"

I never knew Hayden's last name. "What business is it of yours?" I regret my tone, and before I can tell him I don't have plans, he's backing away, his smile gone.

"Okay then. Have a good night." He disappears around the corner.

I close my eyes and exhale. Probably he'll see Hayden out with some girl on the Ave and know that I am a pathetic liar with no plans at all. But the more I think about it, the more I wonder if Charlie is keeping tabs on me. Or more. Behind me I hear a creak and something crashes to the floor.

When I turn, there's nothing. I check around my counter and the shelves. Down the hall to the bathroom, there's nothing. Hairs stand up on my arm anyway. I peek out into the dining room, now busier. Hayden's gone. Mom's smiling and twirling around to customers all over the room. When I get back to my corner, Kellen sits on the counter, kicking her dirty pink Uggs back and forth. Her eyes are glassy and she smiles, but it's not the bitchy smile she always gave me when she was alive.

She looks in Charlie's direction and back at me, and I know Kellen's smiling over my failures. Even in death she's still smug.

"Why don't you go haunt Dad? You'd probably make his day,"
I snap at her.

I wonder if she can even hear me. What does she want? Why
won't she leave me alone?

"If you're planning on turning me into a Holy Roller like
Mom, forget it. I don't *believe* in you."

Nothing on her face changes, but she lifts her arms slightly,
almost reaching them out to me.

"No." I say this even as emotion catches at the back of my
throat, tasting the same as when it was all shocking and fresh.
When that tiny part of me still loved my sister, no matter how
she betrayed me. When I wanted her to sit up in her coffin and
tell us she was okay.

But one memory is all it takes. "You know what you did. Leave
me alone."

Kellen's gone.

Secrets buried.

In her place, a blue-gray envelope with droplets of purple
and bloody red fibers sits on top of my counter.

FIVE-YEAR-OLD CARROT

Kellen stares at me from her window. She's nine and I'm five, and I'm sitting on the tree branch Dad cleared away for us so we could play tree fairies. Kellen and me discovered last month that we could see real good into her room from the tree. I listened to her when she didn't know I heard her—she told her friend there's a boy down the street that she likes and she told him to climb the tree and she can talk to him from her window but they have to whisper.

Kellen looks mad at me. She's grounded again, this time for the whole gum incident, even though I think it's kinda my fault. My sister hides her stuff from me in her backpack so I won't get them, and she thinks I don't know, but I know. I'm smart and I watch and I know she keeps her whole gum collection in there.

I put on some of her lip gloss that she bought with her allowance. And then I took some of her gum. She bought that too, with her own money. And she wouldn't buy me any or share it so now I'm chewing it and I hope she won't find out. The gum is *sooo* good, it's my favorite kind—grape. I know I shouldn't have but I chewed another piece too because gum always loses its flavor after lots of chewing. Kellen showed me how to do a bubble once, and so I tried but my teeth were tired and sore from chewing and I accidentally spit the whole gum wad into my hair.

"Carrot, don't move, I have to rub the peanut butter in so the gum can come out, okay?"

I nod, but it's hard to sit still. Everything smells like peanut butter and grape gum.

"Stop it, Carrot! Hold still! Do you want Mom to see this? She'll be really mad at you for this so you better hold still! I don't want you to get a spankin'!"

Kellen starts combing the hair with peanut butter in it and it hurts! It's so hard to be still.

"Hey, Carrot I think I'm getting it!"

We both hear the *beep-beep* Mom's car makes when she locks it.

"Oh shit!"

"Kellen! That's a cuss word! I'm gonna tell and you'll get the soap again!"

"Oh be quiet, Carrot! Mom's home! Okay, well, I gotta cut it."

"Kellen, no!" I grab my hair and my hand gets peanut butter on it. "I don't want my hair cut!"

But she grabs scissors from the drawer anyway. "Don't worry, it'll be okay. No one will notice anything, okay? It's really just a little bit of hair."

I nod.

She cuts and doesn't show me the hair but I see it when she flushes the whole purply, peanut butter, gummy hair mess down the toilet.

"Don't tell her, Carrot. She'll be so mad if she knows about this. And stay out of my backpack and my room, okay?"

But Mom found out. Now Kellen's in her room grounded for cutting my hair.

Now I watch her window from the tree, and she holds up a sign in the window and I'm just learning to read. It says "I." I know that word for sure, and I also know "you." It's the one in the middle I'm having a hard time with: "hate."

12. *Dissolve the sugar.*

. . . .

With the lights inside the dining room on, I can see two kids setting the table for dinner. These are my favorite views because at
night, when they leave the curtains open, I see everything.

The mom works in the kitchen while the kids go back and
forth, poking and chasing each other, just the way Kellen and I
used to.

The night is pitch-black except for the icy clouds that hang
in front of my face when I breathe out. I hold the smoke in my
mouth, trying as hard as I can not to cough. By the time I get
the hang of it, my supply will be gone, I'm sure. My mind is
still clear enough to realize the irony that I sit here in the dark,
pretty much stalking this family in my old house, while I try to
forget about my stalker. The latest note baffles me.

> YOU DON'T DESERVE IT LIKE THE LAST, BUT
> STILL . . .

The mom points her paring knife at the kids, and looks like
she's yelling.

A beat-up Civic barrels into the driveway and out pops a boy
from my school, carrying pizza up to the front steps. I can smell
it; warm and crusty, the tomato and spices and cheese and pepperoni. The pepperoni smells good, but I'd still pick it off and
give it to Kellen like I used to.

When the pizza is delivered and the guy walks back to his car, I slink down a little further into my hiding place because he stops and looks up and sniffs. He looks all around but doesn't see me. Once he pulls out of the driveway, I settle back and watch the new family eat dinner.

Leaning back against the tree, my butt sits on the fattest root. It's numb from the cold. My sister and I spent a lot of time around this tree in our front yard.

I'm taking another hit from my sister's weed just as dead things crunch and move beside me.

And feet come to a stop in front of me.

Once upstairs, I grab my makeup bag and head into the bathroom, where I try to put on mascara and lip gloss. Then I decide I should brush my teeth as I'm sure my breath stinks from eating pizza. So I wipe the lip gloss off, brush my teeth, and put gloss back on. Strawberry. When I drop the bag back in my room I decide to change, too.

I slip into a clean sweatshirt because the basement gets cold. I have no clean shorts left so I run into Kellen's room and take a pair of cotton ones from the top of her pile. They're a little big but have a cinch at the waist so I'm good. While I'm at it I rub fresh deodorant under my pits. My hair has dried into waves so it doesn't look too bad. I don't brush it because I don't want to be obvious about fixing myself up.

I run downstairs, grab myself a Coke, and then back down to the basement. Nick still sits in the same spot, but I notice another beer in his hand and an empty bottle on the coffee table. I didn't even hear him come upstairs.

"Hey," Nick says as I come back into the room. "What took you so long?" He wears a smile and my insides lurch a bit. He pats the cushion next to him. "Come and sit down, it's a good movie. We can change it if you don't like it."

I'm almost too warm, and the basement is cool. I sit down on the loveseat next to him, sipping my Coke and watching the movie, but my mind is far away from the story line. I want to call Gaby and tell her I'm alone in my house with a high school boy, watching TV with him. What would she tell me to do?

Last month, Gaby French-kissed a sixteen-year-old boy and

she's still bragging about it. What would they think of me if I did the same thing? Nick is seventeen. I'd one-up Gaby. Maybe she'd stop teasing me about my virginity all the time.

Most girls my age could lie about something like that, but not me. My friends know me too well. I've spent the past few years watching Kellen and the way she acts around every boy I've ever seen her with. Kellen has never been without a boyfriend.

I turn toward Nick. His arm still rests on the back of the love-seat, behind me. I suck in a breath and bring my knees up so my feet are tucked almost under my thighs. I manage to do this without kicking Nick or toppling myself over. He looks at me for a second and smiles before his eyes go back to the movie.

My heart flutters but I lean in toward him and place my hand on his knee. My other elbow goes up on the back of the sofa, my hand under my chin. I've seen Kellen do this a gazillion times with boys. "So, Nick, how's your beer?"

His eyes go straight to my hand. I'm suddenly afraid he'll take it off him but when he looks back to me, he smiles. "It's great, Kara."

I stare at his mouth and the top of the bottle. "Oh, good," I say, keeping my hand on his knee and it feels like it's on fire.

"Have you ever tried it?" he asks.

"Um, nope," I lie, twirling a strand of hair in my other hand.

"Do you want to?" he asks.

"Um, okay," I say. "That would be a first for me."

He offers the bottle. The smooth, cool glass feels nice on my lower lip and I don't even have the urge to wipe off the rim like I do when other people offer me sips of whatever they're drinking. I tilt the bottle back and let the liquid fill my mouth. I'm thankful it's still cold because if it wasn't I wouldn't be able to swallow it.

"Mmm," I say, handing it back to him. "It's good!" I lie. It tastes horrible. The bitterness hangs on to my tongue like a canker sore.

He laughs and takes a swig. "Mmm," he says after he swallows. "Tastes like strawberry."

"Huh?" It tastes nothing like strawberry.

Nick sits back into the corner, turning toward me. He smiles and makes a sweeping motion across his mouth with his finger and thumb.

Oh. Lip gloss. "Sorry."

"So Kara, that was a first for you. Any other firsts you're wanting to check off your list?"

He smiles when he says this, and I feel a pull in my stomach. Like when I'm taking a test and I'm only halfway done and the teacher gives the three-minute warning.

I turn to the TV, grabbing the Coke and taking a too-big sip. Thank God I don't cough, but Coke dribbles down from the corner of my mouth. Before I can move, Nick's wiping it off with his finger, and the corner of my lip burns under his touch. I don't know what to say or where to look and I try to think of what Gaby would do, but I blank out and stare at the TV. Then Nick's fingers are under my chin and he turns my face gently so I'm forced to look at him.

13. *Set the broken bits aside.*

. . . .

My stomach unhinges and drops to my feet. The joint falls onto my thigh. I use one hand to pick up the joint and the other to pull my hoodie farther down on my head, as if I could hide now.

The feet belong to Charlie. I'm looking into his disapproving face as he squats down, illuminated by the street lamp.

"You should become a sniper or a Navy Seal or something, sneaking up on people like that. You scared the shit out of me."

It's Charlie and he's harmless, but I still have the urge to run.

"Well," he starts, his face level to mine as he snatches the joint from me. "You were a little busy, Sprinkles."

No words come out while I watch him squish the joint into the dead, frosty leaves and pine needles and dirt. Then he stands up and uses his shoe to bury it even deeper.

I pinch my eyes shut, my feelings split between being pissed that I didn't feel the full effects and shame that he caught me. When I open them I see the family eating pizza in my house. Too quickly I try to stand and end up stumbling forward, knocking my bag over. The angel I stole from *my* yard topples over and out, her head hitting the ground. My Playtex box of weed falls out, too.

Charlie bends over and pulls out the angel and the box. He stands up, holding my angel and my pot, his eyes flicking back and forth between them. Now it's all shame, and it threatens to squash me into the earth with the dead things. I'm afraid of how the judgment on his face will come out in words. If Noelle caught me that would be one thing; she'd beg for my lighter, but Charlie Norton is something altogether different.

"What the hell are you doing? Did you steal this? You're a thief *and* a pothead now?"

"Mind your own business, Charlie," I hiss, grabbing my treasures from him. He lets go of his hold on the angel, but the box remains clamped in his fingers.

"No way, Sprinkles."

With his left eyebrow arched and the slight smile, I'm positive he's going to insist I share it. A surge of disappointment runs through me. Maybe he's not who I think he is.

I tug on the box. He tugs on it harder as the smile disappears.

"You're too good for this, Sprinkles. What the hell are you doing?"

"Smoking it, Mr. Obvious. It was my sister's. I found it in her stuff and decided to not let it go to waste, okay?"

"Nothing good can come from you smoking this shit. Take my word for it."

We're both holding the box. I feel like if he doesn't give it back I will cry, and it has nothing to do with what's in it.

"What are you doing out here anyway? Are you following me?" I pull hard on my sister's Playtex box at the same time as Charlie. It rips and I hold the ripped part while Charlie ends up with everything else. But then the pot falls on the ground amongst the dead things.

Dead, like Kellen's dead in the ground. "That was my *sister's*! It was Kellen's, okay? Besides, she didn't smoke it all the time, you know, just when she went away. Everyone in college smokes it and it doesn't make her a criminal. It doesn't make her a bad person! And now she's dead and you've no right to take it from me!" I blink hard. "Anyway I thought you had a date with that little waitress wannabe that works for my mom."

"So where's Westcott?"

I stare at the kitchen towel lying in the dirt. "I never *said* I had plans with him."

"Huh," he says, his left foot poking at the towel on the ground. "Yeah, I followed you. But I ran into an old friend and lost you. I figured you might be headed over here because I, uh, I just guessed." He bends over and starts picking up Kellen's stash while I keep quiet. "Wow. You could sell this and buy that plane ticket." He stands up, cramming the towel back into the ruined box.

"Charlie, I would never sell . . ."

He puts his other hand up. "I know. I know you're not that kind of girl. Now give me your lighter."

I stare at the ripped-up box for a few seconds before I reach back into my bag. My hand digs around; my knuckles rub against the angel as I find the lighter.

"Let's go." He grabs the lighter from me as he nods in the direction of the house next door.

Mrs. Nguyen stands in the window, arms folded, looking at us.

I doubt she can see us out here in the dark, but I don't want to stick around. She bought me and Kellen Astro Pops from the ice cream truck a few times each summer. My Astro Pop always melted and ran down my wrist, making a purplish splash onto the hot summer sidewalk. But then I forget about Mrs. Nguyen because I'm so aware of the rough heat of Charlie's hand as he leads me down the street. We walk a few blocks and he doesn't let go until we're creeping down an alley, and Charlie's lifting the lids off of recycle containers.

I don't even ask.

Finally he props up a lid and whispers, "Bingo!" and retrieves a large coffee can.

I hear the smile in his voice. "Now we look for puddles."

I follow behind as he continues down the alley. Soon he stops and squats so I catch up to him. There's enough light from a nearby garage that we can see.

Charlie uses the can to crack the thin layer of ice over the first puddle we find. The ice floats away as Charlie sticks the can in the middle of the water.

"Keep watch, Sprinkles, okay?"

I nod and whisper. "You're weird."

Charlie stands up and faces me. He squashes the whole Playtex box into about half of its size and drops it into the coffee can. I cringe when he lights it on fire. Small flames flicker and mirror off the inside of the can.

The burning sweetness of my dead sister's weed stash makes me a little sad. Plus, I half expect her to appear and give me dirty looks for wasting it. Charlie stands up and thrusts his hands into his pockets as he looks around. Then he takes a knee and waves his arms out over the burning pot.

"God of thy glorious grass, we offer you back your wares, in the coffin of a tampon box, and ask your forgiveness. Sprinkles no longer requires the fruit of your weedy goodness, as I will show her the way to get high on life itself. For this we pray, amen."

He bows.

I find myself smiling, in spite of everything. The coffee-can bonfire reflects flames in the puddle, and the ice bits drift and bob like tiny ant rafts. The sweet smoke turns acrid, making me cough. Maybe if I get closer I can suck in some fumes, but a back porch light and the squeal and bang of an old screen door set Charlie off—grabbing my hand and dragging me down the alley.

"C'mon," he whispers.

It's scary dark and suddenly I don't want to be outside anymore. "You know I was having a great time before you showed up."

"Shut up, Sprinkles! *Run!*" he hisses as a tiny beam from a flashlight comes from behind.

Now some guy is yelling and running after us. The beam

from his flashlight bobs here and there, between my feet. The guy yells that he called the cops. I can barely hear him; my heart pounds so loud in my ears. I've never been chased before, or dealt with the cops, except when Noelle tries to get out of speeding tickets.

When we round the corner we wait. My lungs border on pain, even though we haven't run far. Charlie doesn't breathe hard at all.

He turns to me as I try digging my fingers into the brick wall behind me, like I can disappear. "I can't breathe," I say, looking down to my feet.

Charlie faces me, he's so close and I can't see his face because of the light coming from behind him.

"That was fun, Sprinkles. I—"

He stops talking and leans his face down to me. My heart pounds and I'm not sure what he's going to do, but then he lets go of my hand, turns, and heads down the street.

That was weird, but still I suck in enough breath to swallow the lump in my throat as I watch him leave.

When he turns around, I see his outline, hands on his hips. "Are you coming?"

14. *Crack and crumble.*

· ·

When he leads me to the door of the Moon Bar I stop. A small group of smokers gather a few feet away, drinking and laughing and talking.

Charlie turns around. "What's wrong?"

"A *bar*? I don't have a fake ID, Charlie." Noelle made me one but I lost it, right into the nearest trash can.

He smiles, pulling on my hand. "The bartender's a friend of mine. He won't hassle us."

A little panic flashes through me as I wait for one of the smokers to stop us. I just want to go home to the safety of my bed, but Charlie pulls me through the door.

The Moon Bar is packed. And just like when we were at the coffee shop, Charlie smiles and greets everyone because he knows everyone. What it must feel like to have the room wake up and smile because you walk through the door. Clearly Charlie's used to it. The bartender hollers something to him and eyes me while he wipes out a glass.

"Hey our seats are over there." He points to a pair of wing-back chairs by the window. "Go ahead."

I watch as he heads to the bar. Great. He'll probably bring me a beer, and I hate beer. I'll have to sip and fake that I like it, just like I do at the parties Noelle drags me to.

People are drinking and laughing and playing pool or darts. In the back of the room there's a small dance floor, and a small stage for a band but no band plays tonight. The place smells like stale beer and old French fries and sweat and dead smoke.

Charlie sets drinks down in the windowsill behind me and turns his chair to face the window. Then he turns my chair around with me in it, and hands me a cup. I'm relieved because it's dark and bubbles pop on the surface. Coke. He smiles and sighs as he looks out the window and sips.

I think he says something but it's so noisy that I can't hear, and even though we were holding hands a few minutes ago, the fact that his legs are so close to mine feels oddly intimate. His jeans are torn on the right knee and little threads grow out of it.

"Look up there." He points, yelling. "Just between those two buildings, you can see the stars. Cool, huh?"

"It's just the sky," I have to yell back so he can hear me. "It's there every night."

"I like to appreciate things people take for granted."

Why do I have to like a guy who says things Mom would? I stop myself from rolling my eyes because from the corner of my eye I swear I see Charlie raising his drink to the sky.

He yells, "You shouldn't let anger and being pissed at your mom cloud up your mind and your ability to see. You shouldn't let weed fog you up either."

"Look, I told you I—"

"It's okay, Sprinkles."

The din rings in my ears. Obnoxious laughter, music, the diesel engine of the Metro outside, the whirr of a blender, the ice rattling inside a stainless steel mixer cup. "Can we go? It's so loud in here."

Charlie stares out the window. I don't think he heard me.

I give up and watch the happy people stroll outside, some even smiling in at me as I try to look away. Someday I'll be one of them. Someday, when I'm happy and in pastry school, or working in my own bakery, I'll get the kind of happy I want and I'll be the one smiling at sad-looking girls.

"You're not much of a talker, are you, Sprinkles?" Charlie yells.

I don't have the energy to yell back that he's spent enough time around me lately to avoid restating the obvious, yet he keeps pointing it out. Instead I stare at the *e* in *Safeway* because the bulb inside flickers a little.

"So why do you hate your mom?"

I take a long sip of Coke. "I don't hate my mom. My mom is a Jesus-loving lunatic. I *hate* my sister."

Charlie's back at my ear. "There's nothing wrong with loving Jesus. How can you hate a dead person?"

His breath in my ear makes me shiver. "Believe me, it's possible. You don't know anything about it." I want to say I saw him duck into that church so I know he probably has more in common with my mom than me.

"Fill me in."

"So are you going to tell me why you disappeared freshman year?" I ask, getting annoyed.

"Did you really notice?"

"Only because the whole school talked about you nonstop."

A troubled smile flickers over his face. "Nice to know you cared."

"Charlie." I lean in closer, trying to not yell. "We barely ever spoke to each other."

"Remember we used to chase each other around during recess in first grade. You were my first kiss." And he brushes his thumb across my lips, leaving my mouth feeling like he touched it with a lit match. "Tell me about your sister."

"You should've let me keep smoking. Might've had a full confession by now. Anyway, we're not talking about me. We're talking about you. Why did you leave town?"

He pulls back and crosses his arms, saying nothing.

Fine. I can play that game, too. But when he still doesn't speak, I do. "I haven't even told Noelle about it." But I'm not even sure what I mean by *it*. There are many *it*s.

"I moved to California." He sighs, maybe not having heard me. "And it wasn't to surf or become famous."

"Kinda figured that," I shout.

"Your turn."

"My sister made my life hell from the second I took my first breath."

"That's not it." Charlie shakes his head at me like he knows everything. "She's dead. You'd have to have forgiven her for some of the stuff she did. What *exactly* made you hate her? Death sometimes cancels out bad feelings like that, or so I've heard."

I say nothing.

"You know, forgiveness is really about helping yourself, not absolving the other person of what they did. Whatever she did you should forgive her."

"Wow, are you planning to become a shrink or a talk show host or something?" I look down at my feet and then back at him. "Does anyone know why you left Seattle?"

He shakes his head.

"You didn't tell any of your friends?" I'm pretty shocked by this, knowing how many friends he had back then, and seeing all the friends he has now.

"Most of the friends I've had are just good acquaintances. There's never been someone I could completely trust."

I want to ask him if this includes girlfriends but I don't. "Not one person?"

"Nope." He sips his drink.

"I can't imagine not having Noelle to talk to." I don't really mean to say it out loud, even though I can't be sure he heard me above the din.

"You just said you didn't tell her everything about why you hate your sister."

"I know." I sip my Coke. I guess I really don't tell Noelle anything, come to think of it. "You know there are rumors? Your old friends must've filled you in."

"Memories hang on people, and when you see them, it takes you back to what you're trying to forget. So you try your best to avoid them."

"Hmm."

He grins over his Coke. "It's more than you gave me, don't you think?"

I say nothing.

"Anyway," he continues. "I should get you home. Have to be up early for the breakfast crowd." He makes an exaggerated, self-mocking show of flexing his biceps. "Scraping dried eggs off plates is a real bitch. I need my beauty sleep."

I have to laugh. But then I stand up to put my coat on and I see Hayden at the back of the bar.

Charlie is still sitting, looking at his phone, and I'm thankful for the sudden distraction. I tilt my head down as I put on my coat, keeping my eyes on Hayden, who doesn't notice me at all. He wears a white button-down shirt and a tie with jeans, and he looks older. Gone is the ball cap he always wears. Dark-rimmed glasses sit on top of his head.

A girl straddles his lap, her hands on his hips, but he doesn't touch her because he's holding a beer in one hand and a cigarette in the other. Hayden squints at her while he turns his head slightly and blows smoke out of the side of his mouth. Taking another drag, he blows smoke in her face. She swats it away and he sneers. The girl leans over to whisper in his ear. *The poor girl,* I'm thinking. *Hayden is bored with her* . . .

To my shock, he pushes the girl off him, hard, and she stumbles backwards, landing on her ass.

Suddenly there's a flash of red hoodie and bobbing black ponytail. Kellen rushes past, behind Hayden and the girl. I want to go find her, but I don't want Hayden seeing me. I don't want to bolt from Charlie either.

The girl stands up, brushing off her rear. Now she's in Hayden's face pointing while he smiles at her. I can't hear what

she's yelling at him. And no one around them pays any attention and it's the first time I've ever felt bad for one of Hayden's
girls. He smashes the cigarette into the ashtray next to him and
grabs at her breasts. She's swatting his hand away with one hand
and pulling up her blouse with the other.

I swallow. I can't stop staring. This is not the Hayden I know.
This Hayden makes me sick to my stomach. This Hayden is
nothing like the sweet college guy that hangs out in Mom's
shop and shows me funny little videos on YouTube. This is a
boob-grabbing, cigarette-smoking, tie-wearing asshole that must
be drunk. Where is the Hayden that the tiniest bit of me still
crushes on?

"Ready?" Charlie asks. I don't take my eyes off the scene at
the back of the bar soon enough, because Charlie turns around
to look for himself.

My heart pounds and I'm not sure why since I haven't done
anything. Charlie scans the room and turns back to me, smiling.
"Okay, let's go."

We walk in silence, and I'm disappointed that he wants to end
the night so soon. I'm relieved he didn't see Hayden. Maybe I
can pretend I didn't see him either. But I know I can't.

We get to Mom's café and as I start to enter, Charlie grabs my
elbow.

"Kara?"

It's weird hearing him use my name. When I look up into
his eyes, the light from the street reflects and they look watery
almost. He flicks his eyes between the ground and mine, then
releases a sort of half-chuckle, half-sigh, and shakes his head.

"Never mind. See ya." He turns and hurries across the street.
From inside Mom's shop I watch him disappear around the
corner.

WHEN I LIE IN bed later I still can't get Hayden out of my
head, or Charlie. A January storm blows in and the wind and hail

sound like fire crackling and popping outside, trying to break through the glass. Outside my window the vine maple sways out of the sidewalk planter below. Small branches scrape along the glass like fingers, clawing to get in. I get up to peek outside.

The weather's terrible, but there he is, and I shiver. He's leaning against the post box on the corner, looking up at my window. I don't think he can see me because it's dark inside my room.

Charlie.

JUNE: THIRTEEN-YEAR-OLD CARROT'S
SUMMER ~~FUN~~ BEFORE HIGH SCHOOL

Nick's fingers press into my chin a little. "Kara?" His eyes are bright as he looks between my eyes and my mouth. "Have you ever been kissed?"

I swallow hard. My heart flutters a hundred miles an hour, bouncing off every corner of my chest. I shake my head.

He tips my chin up and dips his head down slowly. I watch his eyes close as he presses his lips onto mine. His lips are soft and warm and wonderful.

"Kara," he whispers against my lips. "Mmm, strawberry. Close your eyes."

I snap them shut, feeling stupid. Nick's lips are on mine again and this time he holds my lower lip in between his. His hands are holding either side of my face. He pulls away again but only to come in from different angles. When he pulls away again I can barely breathe. I'm afraid I'm doing it wrong even though Gaby and Jen and I practiced on our hands all the time. Gaby was sort of the expert and said we did it the right way.

The way Nick smiles and the fact that his breath comes faster makes me think I'm okay.

And just as I'm feeling disappointment that it's over, he comes back at me. This time his lips press into mine harder than before and after a moment he nudges his lower lip between mine.

"Open your mouth," he whispers against my lips.

When I do I feel his tongue running inside my lower lip, and then deeper. I wrap my arms around his neck because it feels like the right thing to do. His hands move around to the small of my back. His weight is forcing me backwards into the armrest but it doesn't hurt. In the back of my mind I know this is all wrong, and I can almost hear Mom standing at the top of the stairs scolding me. So many thoughts run through me, but the only one that matters is I can't wait to tell Gaby I got French-kissed by a high school boy!

I'm not sure how much time passes before Nick pulls away, sitting back and stretching his arms over his head. "Cross that off your list, too," he says, smiling.

My face flushes and my mouth feels swollen. "Thanks." Thanks? I am a dork! I couldn't think of something else to say?

He laughs and scratches his head. "Well, you're welcome." He leans forward and catches my chin again, giving me a short kiss before he stands up. "Happy to oblige. I'll be right back."

I wish he'd kiss me again and I wonder what it all means now? He's Tad's best friend and always over here. What happens now? Does he kiss me now whenever he gets me alone? Do we forget it? Do I tell Kellen? No way. She'd tell Mom.

The weight of all of it pushes me further into the loveseat. I look at where Nick sat and reach out, feeling the warmth he left there. I pick up one of the pillows and sniff and smell Nick's clean smell. Then I throw it down and stand up, feeling like the biggest dork ever.

15. *Be careful not to burn your butter.*

· ·

Working on my final cookie design at the café, I'm careful to not let Mom see. I am a nervous wreck. I can barely sleep. The contest is next week. Entering and winning is not what I'm panicked about—it's logistics. How do I get there without Mom noticing?

Sticking my pen into the foam of my latte, I draw loopy swirls of cream and brown and wonder if Charlie is working. Dishes need washing today because the place is packed.

Most people eat Mom's holy pea soup. They smile and look at the ceiling. Some hold hands in prayer. What the hell? Mom's turned everyone crazy. People slurp it down because she says it's liquid salvation, the answer to their prayers. They actually believe this, or pretend to. I suck the latte foam off my pen and go back to my cookie design.

"Hey, Sprinkles."

I jump.

Charlie's on his knees, leaning over the back of the other booth and resting his chin on his folded arms. "What are you doing?"

Before I can answer, he scoots out of his booth and comes to sit across from me. I think of him the other night, spying and staring up at my window.

Mom comes out of the kitchen so I slap my notebook shut. When she looks at me, and then Charlie, her face stretches into a huge grin and she claps her hands together, like she approves of seeing us together. Whatever. Maybe she approves of him because he's a little bit of a Holy Roller himself. I fidget in my seat when she whirls over to the table and plants a kiss on both of our cheeks.

"Well aren't I the lucky one! The Lord sees fit to bless me with you two!" She turns to Charlie. "I still have that chocolate cream in back, shall I get it for you?"

"Sure, thanks, Meg."

Mom glows before she winks at him and twirls off to the kitchen. It's weird to hear him use Mom's name, like he knows her so well.

"Your mom is the best, Sprinkles. You're lucky to have her."

I sigh very loudly and glare out the window.

"It wasn't her fault that your sister died. She had so much grief, Kara—"

"Stop it," I interrupt. I feel the anger rising in me. "You don't even know what you're talking about."

Mom sets the plate down. "Enjoy!"

He smiles at her and she puts a hand on each of our shoulders, squeezing before she disappears.

"Kara, listen. I'm saying this because . . . my mom died." He stops for a moment and stares at the pie. "My dad couldn't take it; we didn't even have a funeral. We left, just like that—two days later. I had no chance to say good-bye to anyone. That's why I disappeared so quick . . ." His eyes are glued to the plate. His voice is thick, strained. "Man, I've been begging your mom to save me a piece of this—it's amazing."

His eyes are glassy when he looks up at me.

I feel tears prickling my own eyes. I wasn't expecting this. "I'm sorry."

"She used to make this pie for me. It's my favorite."

"What happened?"

Charlie cuts off a bite with his fork and offers it to me. I shake my head.

"No way, you did not just turn down the best pie in town. Take it."

He pushes a fork of the moist chocolate against my lips and his expression makes me smile, so I take a bite.

"I wanted you to know that I understand," he manages while I chew. He sniffs, his voice still shaky. "But right now that's all I can . . ." He exhales, pushing the plate away. "I'm sorry. Guess I'm not ready."

I stare at him, and the shock of it hits me. Charlie's mom chaperoned every field trip and made it to every school function. I can't think of a time my parents showed up for any school events, but I remember Charlie's mom brought in cupcakes for our class on his birthday.

One time my cupcake fell, frosting side down, onto the dirty linoleum floor. When I picked it up pencil shavings and grit were stuck in it. The teacher hollered at me to clean it up but Charlie's mom knelt down with wet paper towels to help me. "It's okay, sweetheart," she'd said.

Right there, my ten-year-old self wanted to tell her that I loved Charlie and that Tracy Snider was a horrible girl and that Charlie shouldn't have a crush on her. He should like me because I'm nicer and I already love him.

Now Charlie is scooting out of the booth. "Can I pull you away from your cookie baking long enough to go take a walk with me?"

"It's freezing outside. They're forecasting snow."

"All the more reason for a walk. C'mon, please?" He offers his hand.

"Okay. Give me a second to get my coat, 'kay?" I slide out of the booth and walk toward our apartment door.

"Need help? I can come up there with you." He grins.

No way. Where I live is embarrassing. "I'll be back in a sec." With that I rush to the door and upstairs.

Charlie waits by the front door for me, smiling, wearing one of those funny baseball-type caps lined with fake sheep fur. It's goofy but sort of cute. He also wears a flannel work coat that makes me think of maple syrup and pancakes. All in all, not a picture of hotness, but as we step outside into the biting cold, I'm thinking of him without his mom. My nose stings and I wipe my eyes at the same time I hear someone whistling.

The frigid air smells of baking bread, coffee, wood smoke, and diesel from the buses. Noelle and Mason are across the street, watching us. Mason gives a slight wave with his fingerless glove, while Noelle points at us, grabs Mason and thrusts her hips back and forth into his butt. Thank God Charlie doesn't seem to see my psychotic friend, who is now blowing us kisses. He's hurrying down the street.

"I just want to show you something, Sprinkles."

I nod, following, and every few seconds a question about Charlie's mom nearly rolls out of my mouth but I stop it, because I know how he feels. Charlie leads me past Crockett's and around the corner to the lot of St. Francis's Catholic Church.

I knew it. He *is* like Mom. He probably wants me to go to Bible study or something. Disappointment floods through me. I do not need any more Jesus in my face. I stop and watch as he skirts the front of the church and disappears around the corner. Seconds later he reappears, throwing his arms up.

"Hey, are you coming or what?"

I shake my head, trudging over to him.

"Over there."

I look to see an old, flat brown Ford Ranger. Tiny dents dapple the side, along with a few scrapes of different colors. There are spots here and there of the old shine but not much.

"What do you think?" he asks, smiling at the truck.

A FOR SALE sign is taped crooked in the window.

"Are you serious?"

Charlie shoves his hands into the pockets of his jacket and shrugs. "I'm buying it."

I move closer to the driver's side and see a Strawberry Short-cake ice cream bar sticker. Not very appetizing because the color has faded to blue and letters are peeling away.

"Why would you want to buy this? It's a piece of junk. An old ice cream truck?"

He sighs. "Can't you see the potential? A little paint?"

I think it sucks but I don't say it out loud. It's not like I have a car or anything.

"It beats my bike and the Metro. It has wheels, a motor; it's covered, and it's the right price," he adds.

"Which I hope isn't much."

"To get it I have to do yard work for the church for a year. Cut grass, rake leaves, prune stuff, pull weeds."

"Um, do you go to this church?" I see my breath form icy crystals on the window.

Charlie's right behind me, pretty much trapping me against the truck. All of a sudden I'm focused on the contrast of frozen air and the heat from his body so close to me. I want to turn and wrap myself into him and his flannel jacket, but instead I stare into the truck and wonder why he can't have a better car when his parents have money. I mean, surely his dad still has money, right?

It's so admirable, though. He wants to work for it, and do it on his own. Not typical of most of the boys I know on the Hill. For an instant, I feel that same feeling I had when I was ten, when I wanted to confess everything to his mother, that I loved him.

"I can't afford to pay for a car right now so it's a pretty good deal I think."

"Sure." I can barely breathe because he's almost pinned against me. Part of me enjoys being so close but the other part feels cautious. Eventually I'm going to have to turn around and there he'll be. "Plus you'll be all ready if you want to sell ice cream."

"Ha-ha. Too bad it's not mine yet, I could drive you to California, to the contest."

I say nothing. I feel his gloved fingers touching my hair. It sends a tingle over my scalp.

"So," he continues. "You're still planning on sneaking off by yourself, huh? Maybe I should go with you—"

"Listen," I interrupt, whirling around to face him. "I don't need anyone to watch out for me. I'll be fine, so don't get any ideas about coming with me, okay? Besides I already have my ticket, and don't you *dare* tell my mom."

He raises his hands in surrender but doesn't back up. His face is very close, and his scent is soapy and clean and warm, like he just came out of the shower. "Okay, okay. So will you ride in my truck with me when it's finished?"

Maybe when I get into La Patisserie, Charlie can go with me. We could pack up all our stuff into his truck and move to California. We could take the Pacific Coast Highway all the way, through Oregon and into California. Make a fun trip of it before we have to get busy and work. I'm not sure where he'd go to school but I know there is a university close by. Of course I don't tell him all of my thoughts. Not yet.

"If you dare say a word to my mom about San Francisco you won't have the chance to finish it."

He pulls me closer, smiling down at me and I stop breathing. He just stares with his big brown eyes and I think it's the first time I've really noticed how much taller he is than me—I remember when I could look at him eye to eye. But that was when we were kids.

He's not a Holy Roller like my mom. He's just the same Charlie, the same sweet boy he's always been except now he has a history he wants to escape like I do.

Charlie asks me if I'm cold and tightens his arms around me before I answer and I don't care about anything else. My mom, baking contests, creepy note writers, nothing.

I suddenly feel like I could tell Charlie everything.

But I won't.

The few strands of hair sticking out of his dorky cap are tossed around by the wind. A tiny frozen flake lands on my cheek. "Charlie, it's snowing!" I look up and another flake lands in my eye.

"C'mon, let's go," he orders, grabbing my hand.

We sneak past Crockett's on the other side of the street. A mere dusting of white would have the store filled because pantries on the Hill might go bare during the two hours we have snow. If Dickhead saw me he'd call me in on my day off like the asshole that he is.

"Sprinkles." Charlie turns and grabs my other hand, pulling me to him, just a little closer. "I'm sorry, but I have to go. If we have a snow day tomorrow we'll spend it together."

"Okay."

"No excuses, no hiding in the kitchen baking cookies."

"*Okay.*"

He grabs my hand and pulls me around the corner where it's just the snow and us. Thankfully, the chill masks the odor of rotting vegetables coming from Crockett's dumpsters.

"If your school is canceled tomorrow and mine isn't then I'll skip," he says.

Snow falls heavier as Charlie pulls me to him. Icy snowflakes flutter onto my lashes and cheeks as Charlie's lips touch mine.

I shiver when his arms slide under my jacket and around me. My hands wrap around him and go up his back, under his jacket where he is so warm. Snowflakes fall onto our faces, so cold, and his lips are so soft and sweet. When he goes deeper I can't believe after all this time that I'm finally kissing Charlie Norton.

You're just a fuckin' baby, Kara.

Bliss changes to fear. His arms tighten around me and his lips are an unbreakable seal and I suddenly can't breathe. My palms go into his chest and I'm sick to my stomach. "Charlie, I can't, I'm sorry, I . . ." I'm gasping for air.

He releases me and rubs his chin. "What's wrong?"

"I can't."

"We're just kissing."

I'm going to throw up. The memory won't budge no matter how much I push it away. "I'm so sorry, I just can't, okay?"

He looks up into the sky and lets out a short laugh. When he looks back at me he's red-faced and I know it's not the frozen air. "Did you say that to Westcott, too? Because I didn't see you push *him* away." His eyes narrow, accusing and judgmental, and I have to look away.

"I don't even know what you're talking about." My heart pounds and I watch the snowflakes trying to cover up the wilted lettuce and lumps of dead paper scattered around the foot of the dumpster. I can't believe he saw Hayden kiss me. No one was around. I suck in air so I won't puke.

"I always go through the back door to pick up my paycheck. But that's beside the point. If this is going to happen then I need the truth, Kara. Are you and Westcott over?"

His intrusiveness eclipses every warm feeling I had for him only moments ago. "Fine! Then we won't *happen!*" I jerk away from him and run through the snow.

He calls out, but I keep running. The warm café smells of smoked ham and coffee, as I run up the stairs to our apartment. When I reach the top step I can hear Charlie's voice and Mom's at the bottom, but not what they're saying.

For a minute, I sit down on the top step before I open the apartment door. I can't keep my heart from racing. Once I'm inside I put the kettle on to make tea and peek outside. The snow is falling hard, and the cars crawl along the Ave, even though it barely sticks to the pavement.

Charlie stands across the street, staring up at my window.

THE NEXT DAY I'M pulling go-backs from each checkout stand when Justine pokes me in the shoulder. "Precious girl, you're not really so absorbed in your work that you didn't hear me call your name five times?"

"Sorry." I shove a jar of kalamata olives in the basket.

"What's wrong?"

"Nothing."

"Is it Charlie?" She grabs the edge of my basket, stopping me.

"No," I pull the basket away from her hot pink nails. "There's nothing going on with Charlie. And you need to forget it."

"You know," she says, hands on her hips, "Guys like Charlie don't grow on fuckin' trees, baby girl."

"You don't know what you're talking about, Justine." I slam a can of ravioli into the basket. "You don't even know him."

She shakes her head. "I got eyes, and I know enough to see you've got your head stuck in a cloud of frosting. Don't let that one slip away because you're too busy planning what color to paint your damn cakes."

"Cookies, by the way. And, yes, I'm stressed about the contest, okay? And I'm not interested in Charlie."

"Kara." She slaps her hand down on the counter just as the intercom drowns out her words. Sniff's voice booms over us, calling Justine to the office. Her face drops. We exchange a quick look as she tightens her apron and walks toward the dark little cage where our boss spends most of his time.

Justine's only gone about thirty seconds, but when she returns she's red and biting her lip and looks ready to laugh any second.

"What happened?" I whisper.

"That fucker," she whispers. "Told me if I drop another f-bomb at the checkout stand I'm a goner."

I bite my lip to keep from laughing.

Sniff pops out from nowhere and I hope he didn't hear Justine. I can't work here without her.

"Kara, did you get on those go-backs yet?" He asks me, eyeing my basket.

"I'm just doing it now. I—"

"Well get on with it then. I don't pay you to stand here and gossip with Justine. That yogurt in the basket can be saved if it gets to the dairy case now, so get a move on." He folds his arms and sniffs three times.

I swear under my breath and grab the basket, which I then drop by mistake. I hear the clink of broken glass, but ignore it despite the trail of juice leaking from the jar of olives. Maybe someone will slip on it and sue Crockett's. Better yet, maybe Sniff or Jason will bite it.

I'm relieved I don't have to talk to Justine anymore because it's over with Charlie before it even started. I try to think of how his eyes looked before he kissed me, and how it felt to have his lips on mine but I can't. I'm wrecked and destined to be alone because I can't stop remembering.

Time has moved on. Kellen died, unforgiven, but I'm still thirteen, stuck in that memory. I've forgotten so much about that period of my life, but not that day. Not that night. It's still razor sharp. Every detail, like it happened yesterday. So I can't even tell Justine why Charlie and I are done.

I decide my workday is over, and I leave my go-backs in a basket on the floor in front of a shelf of condoms and pregnancy tests. Fuck Sniff and my job.

When I grab my time card, something falls to the floor and I stare at it, like it is shattered glass and I don't know where to start cleaning up.

I pick up and rip into the blue-gray envelope with droplets of purple and bloody-red fibers.

> I'M THINKING OF THE THINGS I'LL DO WHEN I
> FINALLY GET YOU ALONE.

I don't punch out; instead I sneak out the back door through the stench of celery and sour milk, and past the dumpsters where Charlie kissed me.

When I get to the bottom of the basement stairs, I almost crash into Nick. He's holding another beer. "Hey there! Where are you going?" He wraps his free arm around my back, rubbing up and down.

"Um, I'm really sleepy, from the pool, and babysitting last night. I think I better get to bed. Goodnight." I yawn.

"Okay then." He smiles down at me while he sets the beer down on the shelf next to him.

Nick wraps both arms around me and pulls me close. He squeezes me, lifting me so my feet aren't even touching the ground and all I notice is how he smells a little more like beer than he did before. He kisses me again and it's not as sweet as the first time. His mouth feels colder and he tastes like beer.

He pulls away and sticks his face under my chin, into my neck. I have to bite my lip not to giggle. "I'm going to stay until Kellen and Tad come back with my keys. Probably not a good idea to tell anyone about this, about what we've been doing okay?"

I nod. And he sets me down. Grabbing his beer, he goes and flops down on the loveseat.

I run up to my room, practically flying upstairs on these new feelings. I try to focus on the first kiss, not the last one. In my head I practice what I'm going to say to Gaby as I pick up the phone. Jen hasn't even been kissed like that! Unless she's holding out on us. When I scroll through the phone for Gaby's number, I remember that I'm still pissed at them for how they treated me at the pool. I need to wait until tomorrow. For more impact. It's not like I'll ever forget.

16. *Do not overmix.*

. . . .

Six days pass before I see Charlie again. He washes dishes without his usual humming, singing, or dancing. This time I don't go over and say hi. I haven't been in the mood to bake or decorate and if I'm not ready for the contest by now then I'll never be. I haven't gone anywhere except school and I try harder than ever not to walk anywhere alone, especially at school, which is hard when Noelle isn't with me.

Today I delivered a forged note to the attendance office.

Please excuse Kara McKinley through next Tuesday, as she'll be attending a funeral with her father in Wisconsin.

God bless,
Meg McKinley

Now I'm in the café kitchen, listening to the ping of the sprayer on dishes as I grab some things I need for the contest. Mom is out on errands. All week I've had to sneak around, grabbing things here or there so as not to raise her suspicions. I hope Charlie isn't so pissed at me that he would tell her before I sneak off to California.

After stowing what I need away in the apartment, I head back down to the café.

Hayden sits at his usual table.

I haven't seen him since the night at the bar. He's bent over

his laptop; I'm hoping I'll be able to sneak past without him
noticing. My palms are damp and it's feeling harder to breathe.
I take a quick glance around to see that no one looks my way,
and try to time it so that when I pass by his table I'm preoccupied fighting with the zipper on my hoodie.

"Is that how it is now?"

My face heats up because I know he's talking to me, but I pretend not to hear him as I let the door shut behind me. Maybe
he's regretting kissing me. Forget the kiss. I'm remembering
him at the Moon Bar. My shift starts in twenty minutes. For once
I'm thankful I have to work.

I head over to Hill Kitchens and go right for the baking aisle.
I sift through pans, Silpats, and rolling pins and of course, their
to-die-for collection of sprinkles. They're ridiculously overpriced, but it doesn't matter. I can't resist them.

My breath catches when I see the poster advertising the
Snowflake Sugar Cookie Bake-Off. I feel a flush of both excitement and terrible fear. I can't wait to go. Can't wait to get away
from Seattle and Charlie and Mom and Kellen and Hayden
and my stalker. But I'm scared of traveling to California alone.
I was so confident and sure of myself, buying my plane ticket
and forging Mom's signature, but now I'm scared of everything
falling apart. Now I know just how much of a dream it really is.

JUSTINE'S SLATHERING ON LIPSTICK when I get to Crockett's. She doesn't look like herself at all—no other makeup or
fancy hair or anything.

"Why are you here, Justine? It's your day off."

She smiles sweetly at me and still looks beautiful even without
all the makeup. "Hey, sweetie, nice to see you. Got called in.
Two checkers out sick." She sighs and caps her lipstick before
tucking it back into her apron. "I could use the extra money
anyway."

Out of the corner of my eye I see Sniff and Jason walking

toward us. They are laughing over something and then Sniff pats Jason on the back. I hear him say, "No problem, I'll take care of it."

I turn so I can go lock up my bag, but Dickhead trots over, like he can't wait to tell me something.

"Kara," he says. "You're filling in for Jason tomorrow. Be here at seven thirty."

With that he pivots and walks away but I follow him into the produce section. "I can't. I have plans," I announce to his back.

He turns and sniffs. "Kara, I'm sorry but I need you here."

"But I asked for these days off when you hired me, remember?"

"Things have changed and now I need you to cover for Jason. He's going out of town. Last minute."

I feel my insides boil. "I have a *plane* ticket."

"Kara," he replies. His hands are on his hips and he's looking up at the ceiling now, sniffing of course. "Be here tomorrow at seven thirty or I will fire you."

My whole body shakes with anger. I inhale fast and let it out even faster, and louder. My face heats up and I think I might be sick. "You asshole," I whisper.

Sniff glowers at me and doesn't seem to care that every eye in the produce section watches us. "*What* did you say?"

I look at his shoes and my heart pounds. Don't cry! God, I want to cry.

My total dickhead of a boss stands with his legs apart, arms folded and stares at me. So I suck in another breath before I yell, "I have a *plane ticket* and you're giving Jason the day off? Are you kidding? *You* are a fucking *asshole!*"

I turn around, swinging my bag over my shoulder as I run, my heart pounding like I sprinted a mile. When I'm finally back in my own head, I realize that I ran straight back to the stockroom, rather than out the front door. My face reddens again because how stupid am I?

Then I hear some laughing way down the hall, and a "Holy

shit!" I slide out the backdoor and find myself at the spot by the dumpsters where Charlie kissed me. I keep moving. I pick up my pace. When I run around the corner, I almost knock into Jason, who's leaning against the wall smoking. I force an exaggerated sigh and move on, not wanting to give him one second of my time. But then I change my mind and whirl around.

"You're a dick, Jason, you know that?"

Sniff's protégé gives me a half-lidded stare and blows smoke at me. Gone are the smile and that sickeningly friendly way he has about him when we're in Crockett's.

I want to say more but won't waste my breath on a loser, so I go sit on the bench at the far corner of the lot where Justine usually takes her smoke breaks, hoping she'll come out.

I feel like crap. I planned on quitting after the contest, but I kind of like earning money that doesn't come from Mom's hand. I never wanted to quit before because then she'd be suspicious about it, or worse—she'd make me work in her Jesus café.

I'm not a quitter. But maybe I am.

SEVEN-YEAR-OLD CARROT

Dad and Kellen are in the garage where he's teaching her to paint. I am sort of hiding from them behind the workbench. I want to learn, too.

"Okay, you're getting the hang of it, Kell Bells."

The support beam is in front of me. On our birthdays Dad makes us stand against it and he sticks his flat carpenter pencil on top of our heads so he can mark the beam with how much we've grown. I touch the spots where Dad has written our names.

"*Kell Bells, age eleven.*" That was her birthday last month. All the way down the beam are places Dad wrote: *Kell Bells, ghost phase,* or *princess phase,* or *Elmo phase.*

Kellen has numbers for every birthday. My last number was when I turned five. Now I'm seven. Maybe I should remind him to measure me.

For Dad my sister is always Kell Bells, and I'm always Kara. Just Kara.

I peek out around the beam and Dad sees me.

"Hey baby girl, why don't you run along and see what your Mom is up to?"

"She's at the store."

He smiles and nods and goes back to Kellen. I want to paint so bad. My teacher always tells me I'm a good painter.

Dad always shows Kellen how to do everything.

I shuffle over to watch a little closer. They are painting new lattice for the porch. Kellen takes her time and goes back and forth with the brush while Dad smiles. "Good girl. Keep it right with the grain, you're doing great!"

Kellen dips again and drips paint all over the floor this time, and on Dad's shoe. She looks up quickly at him.

"It's okay," Dad says. "We'll clean it up later."

"Can I try?" I whisper. "I wanna paint."

"Baby girl, this is Kellen's job right now. Maybe when you're older, okay?"

The paint is so thick and glossy and pretty and I want to stick my finger in it. It looks like melted ice cream, even though it smells stinky.

"Kara, go check on your mom."

"I told you, she's gone!"

Kellen ignores us. She dips the paintbrush again and brushes the extra on the edge of the can before smoothing the luscious paint over the wood he taught her to sand last week.

"Dad, please?"

He eyes me and nods before he lets out an irritated sigh. "Sure. Kell Bells?"

Kellen starts telling me what to do but I already know and I'm not listening to her. I've watched them paint and I know how to do it. I don't need anyone to tell me.

I take the brush and dip it, making sure to leave a half-inch of brush showing, like Dad told Kellen.

My hand is shaky but I set the brush down on the wood like I've seen my sister do. I smile because its fun and I look up at my Dad. His arms are folded and he watches my hand like I could stab someone with the paintbrush.

"Same direction your sister went, Kara. Nice and easy."

I nod and it looks good to me, but when I go to dip the brush again, it slips and bounces off the edge of the can, splattering paint everywhere and sinking into the bottom of the can. Only the top of the handle pokes out of the paint.

"Dammit, Kara, that's enough—you're done! Go get yourself cleaned up."

17. *Break it all into pieces.*

. . . .

"Hey!"

When I look up, there's Justine, already sitting down beside me, already lighting up a smoke. She sucks down a big drag. "Well, that was fun! He *is* a prick and he deserves that, even though I've worked for *much* worse." Ash falls from her cigarette as she exhales. With her other hand she wipes under her eyes.

"Were you crying? Did you hear what I said to Sniff?"

She's smiling, but wiping her eyes again. Movement catches my eye. Jason walks from around the corner of the store and stands there, watching us, probably waiting to tell Dickhead, so Justine will wind up fired.

"I heard you—all of us did. I laughed so much the tears just poured out. Good Lord, you only told him what we all want to say. Course now you're on my shit list because I won't be seeing you anymore."

"I'll visit, Justine."

Jason turns and looks at us again before he heads inside. Crap, I better get out of here.

"We both know you'll never come in again. Sniff will meet you at the door and tell you to scoot the fuck on out, just like he does for the people who bounce checks." She takes another drag. "So, tomorrow's the day of your big trip?"

"Yup."

"Your mama still doesn't know?"

"Nope."

"Listen, take my number and call me if you need anything. I'm giving you my pepper spray." She pulls a small bottle from her purse and gives me a quick demo on how to use it. "Oh shit, I almost forgot." She fishes for something else in her pocket and hands it to me. "Here you go!"

"Where did you get this?" I whisper. I find myself staring at a blue-gray envelope. I don't want her to suspect anything so I take a breath to calm myself down. "Justine?"

She stubs out her cigarette before answering. "Found it at my checkout stand about an hour ago. Open it! Maybe it's a love letter from that Charlie who gives you the twinkle in your eye."

An hour ago I wasn't even there. Someone knows my schedule. Knows where and when I work.

"It showed up when I ran back to pee. When I came back, *voilà.*" She waves her perfectly manicured nails over the envelope. "There it was. Woulda given it to you when you came in but I forgot."

"Was Charlie in? Before I came to work?"

"No idea. All I know is it just showed up."

I stuff the note in my pocket. I sit there with her, unsure of what to do, where to go. I have to tell her about the stalker, about the notes I'm getting. She'll know what I should do.

"Justine, I . . ."

She gives me one last squeeze before she heads inside. I watch, mad at myself for not telling her and also for feeling a weird sadness that I no longer belong to Crockett's and all its gourmet pretentiousness.

Justine turns to wave and blow a kiss, and I wish my own mother would listen to me the way she does. Just once.

TEN MINUTES LATER I creep into the backdoor of the café. The note sits, red-hot, in my pocket and I want to run upstairs. But as difficult as it is, I decide to hang out and be extra cheerful to Mom so she won't ground me for life when I get back from the contest. Maybe then one day she'll finally remember me as a good girl, not the one who ran off to another state without permission.

When I look out into the café, I'm surprised because Noelle's sitting out there—not with Mason, but with Noah Bender, the guy in the letterman jacket. I quickly sit down at the counter, back turned, because neither of them has noticed me yet.

Mom slides a coffee across the counter to me. "Why aren't you working?"

"I don't work today."

"Hmm." She stares at me, nodding, and it's hard to keep the eye contact. "Your schedule says that you do. So where were you then?"

"Um, they had too many clerks so I got sent home because I, uh, told Justine I had cramps."

Seconds tick away and her silence makes me think she found out that Dickhead almost fired me.

"Well then. What a blessed gift of an afternoon you've been given. So are you baking? Charlie's in back." She smiles when I reflexively look toward the kitchen door. "Why don't you go say hi? He's been asking about you. Have you changed your mind about him?"

"Changed my mind about what, Mom?" I act like I have no clue what she means, but I'm not sure how to answer this even to myself.

"Kara, he likes you and you like him, right?"

"Mom!" I whisper.

"What, sweetie? He's a doll. I see a lot of young men come in here with their girlfriends and they don't look at them the way he looks at you. Now that doesn't mean you can do whatever you want with him. You know I'll not condone sins of the flesh. If—"

"Mom!" I hiss again, cutting her off. "Stop trying to play matchmaker. Isn't that God's job anyway?"

Bonus points. The smile that spreads across her face confirms it.

She pulls a fake zipper over her lips as she bends over to whisper in my ear. "You're right, sweetheart. Everything *is* in His hands. I won't say anymore!" With that, she twirls away.

A FEW MINUTES LATER Noah gets up and leaves, so I go sit with Noelle.

"Hey." Her voice is tired, unenthusiastic.

"Why was Noah sitting with you?" I ask.

"No reason. I saw him walk by, so I banged on the window and told him to come in." Noelle squints at me. "Hey, you look different. What's up?"

"Nothing."

She stares at my face. "No, *not* nothing. Something's different." Now she's interested. The sparkle is back.

I roll my eyes and sip my latte.

She slaps her hand down on the table and whispers, "You've done it? With Charlie?"

"Wow, no, and can you lower your voice, please?" I take a peek at my cell even though I know there aren't any messages. "And for your information, I just kissed him."

"Oh hell." She takes out her nail file and gets busy on her thumbnail. "Okay, well, it's a start."

"We had a fight."

She scowls. "*Why?* God, Kar, why would you fight with him? He's a great guy. And he's *hot* now. Not all scrawny and skinny and—"

"It was about Hayden. I think Charlie saw me kissing him."

Noelle's eyes bulge. "You did what?" she asks, the scowl now wrestling with a smile.

"Hayden kissed me and Charlie saw, and he wasn't happy."

"Well, no shit. What the hell are you kissing Hayden for, Kar?"

"Hayden is . . ." I still feel like I have to defend him to her and

I don't know why that hasn't changed. "You know I've always had a crush on him. It just happened. I—"

"And I've always had a serious hard-on for the bartender at the Moon, but I'd never actually *let* him stick his tongue in my mouth because he's disturbed. Just like Hayden." She grabs her head and massages her temples. "I need aspirin. Did he—and I mean *Charlie*—do anything else? Touch your boobs or try to get into your pants or anything?"

I sigh. "Of course not. We were outside."

When I look up, there's Kellen—standing right behind Noelle, almost leaning on her shoulder. Her mouth is open a bit, her lower lip extended slightly, just like how my dad used to look when he was concentrating on something. She stares past me. It's as if Kellen's just another customer in the café, but no one sees her, not even Mom. Then she's gone.

"Subject change, please," I tell Noelle.

"Fine. Will you help me cook tomorrow? Maybe bake some cookies, too? Mason's parents are out of town and we're having a little get together. I'm actually in the mood to make some food instead of ordering pizza."

"I leave tomorrow. For the contest."

"What contest?"

My jaw drops. I stare at her in disbelief. She has no clue what I'm talking about.

She shrugs dramatically, emphasizing her cluelessness. "Kara? What? Oh."

"Are you so self-absorbed you've forgotten the biggest event of my whole life? I can't believe it."

Noelle closes her eyes and massages her temples and I think maybe an apology is coming. But I can tell by how she exhales that it won't happen. More than likely she's wondering how she'll manage anything in the kitchen for her party if I'm not there.

I feel myself clenching up. "Maybe you could be a real friend and stop ignoring the stuff that matters to me, because there isn't much of it."

"You know, Kar," she replies while she grabs her purse and stands. "You're the one ignoring *me* these days, for Charlie and that psycho." She takes two steps toward the door before turning back to me. "Good luck with your contest."

Then she's out the door and I'm not even mad. I just don't care anymore. Looking around the café, I have a weird feeling. Maybe one of these people is writing the notes. But I don't know any of them, and they don't know me. The only people who do know me have been around forever. And even they only know pieces of me.

UPSTAIRS IN THE APARTMENT. I feel restless, wishing it were time to leave for the airport. I strip and climb into the shower, letting the steamy water relax muscles that have been tense since I received the envelope and even tenser since Noelle stomped off, but it doesn't really help.

Fresh and clean, pajama pants and a T-shirt on, I shove in my earbuds, set the iPod to shuffle, and start packing. Thankfully I don't have to take much: clothes, personal stuff, and my favorite decorator tools—plus, of course, my designs and recipes. Snowflake Sugar will provide everything else, all of the things I can't afford to buy at Hill Kitchen.

Mom left a note: *lasagna in the freezer*. I pop it in the microwave and watch TV while it cooks. I grab a quilt from the ottoman and when I turn around, there's a shimmery mass that turns into Kellen. She's not even there long enough for me to tell her to get lost, and tonight I just can't be bothered with her.

I move to the window and think about the note in my pocket. I think about what Mom said about Charlie and how he isn't like other guys. Really, he's too good for me.

Noelle has never asked me why I hate Kellen so much. She's

never asked. But Charlie has asked, over and over. He's the only one who has.

I peek out the window to see if Charlie's bike is still there, tied to the vine maple like it is when he works. When I see it, I pick up my cell and text him.

If u want 2 no, come 2 my door now.

I creep downstairs, hoping to hear him knock, but scared I will.

Knock, knock.

"Hey." He nods once when I open the door. "Your mom says I can take my break right now."

I remember his face when he was so angry with me and when he stared up at my window. "Um, I'm ready to tell you. About Kellen. About what happened."

JUNE: THIRTEEN-YEAR-OLD ~~CARROTS~~ KARA'S
SUMMER ~~FUN~~ BEFORE HIGH SCHOOL

I read a little before bed, but I must have fallen asleep pretty fast because I wake up sometime later with the book on my pillow. With the Fourth of July a couple of days away, people are shooting off fireworks down the street, even though it's illegal. A red flash lights up my room at the same time I hear a creak out in the hall. Kellen must be home. I turn over to watch out the window while I try to fall back asleep.

I hear the creak again, the familiar warning that someone is about to enter my room. It's not like Kellen to come in and tell me she's home. She only tells me when she's sneaking out that I better cover for her or she'll kick my ass.

The old wood floor groans at the end of my bed.

Someone is in my room.

My heart starts to flutter and then it's beating in my ears. It must be Kellen, of course. I feel like the small tremors running through my body are now transferring to the bed, making it shake as I try to lie there and pretend to sleep. There's no sound but the popping of fireworks and the wild thudding in my chest. The floor right next to my bed groans. The bed creaks and someone sits down and I hope it's Mom, coming back early. But I know it's not Mom. Or Kellen.

I smell his soap smell. And stale beer. My back is still to him and I hope he thinks I'm asleep because I honestly don't know what to do. The bed creaks again and I can feel him lying behind me.

"Sweet Kara," Nick whispers so soft I almost don't hear it. I feel his cheek against my arm, and the stubble on his chin that I didn't notice when he kissed me earlier. He kisses up my arm that's prickled with gooseflesh. The stubble scrapes my sunburned shoulder when he kisses his way to my neck, and I struggle to keep my eyes tightly shut.

I can't breathe. God, where is Kellen? Please come, now, please Kellen!

He pulls back the covers and I feel his knees against my calves. I only have on a cami and the cotton shorts I borrowed from Kellen because my room was so hot. It's all I can do not to shiver. My heart pounds out of control and he must feel it and know I'm awake. He runs his hand over my side, and then my hip, and down my thigh and back up again inside my thigh, as far inside as his fingers can get.

I don't understand what he's doing and I still don't know if I should let him know I'm awake. But what if he hurts me?

His hand moves up to my hip again, and then I feel his fingertips creep down to my stomach and they feel so much rougher than when they were on my face when he kissed me earlier. I fake sleep even though I'm shaking. His hand slips down lower. My cheeks sting with the tears that are coming. I bite my lip enough to try to stop my shaking but I taste blood. I try and focus on the fireworks outside. Anything to take my mind away from what's happening.

A minute later, I feel him shaking and he breathes heavy. The bed creaks when he leans over my arm, maybe to check that he hasn't woken me up. I pray that he can't tell I'm awake when he rubs my arm and kisses my cheek.

He stays there, for how long I'm not sure but it seems like a while. Tears slip over the bridge of my nose and slide down my cheeks and over my lips and drop onto my pillow. My nose runs and I can't sniff or wipe anything because then he'll know that I'm awake.

Every few seconds he's kissing my shoulder or running his

hand along my arm. I'm calmer because he doesn't do anything but lay there. After a while I hear him sniffing.

"I'm sorry," he whispers, his voice cracked, and his breath catches when he speaks. "God. You're just a fuckin' baby, Kara. I'm so sorry."

THE NEXT MORNING. KELLEN'S asleep in her room and I have to wait half the day for her to wake up. I almost lose my nerve. I can't tell Mom, and besides, she's not going to be home for another day.

When Kellen comes downstairs she says nothing to me but grabs the coffee carafe and takes it to the sink. She has to walk past me to get the coffee grounds out of the cupboard and I notice her eyes—puffy and red, like mine.

She's scooping coffee grounds into the filter when she says, "Tad dumped me."

I swallow, unsure of what to say. Usually Kellen is the dumper.

She spins around, holding the empty coffee scoop in her hand. "Nick was asleep on the couch when I got back. He was drunk. I had to drive his drunk ass home, and fucking Tad had his car keys. I can't believe I ever let that asshole into my life. Did Nick stay here the whole night?"

My lower lip quivers and I can't stop it.

"Carrot, what?" She slams her hands onto her hips, the coffee scoop dangling from her fingers.

My sister is a blur.

"What's wrong, Carrot?" Her voice is softer now and I hear the clank of the coffee scoop as it hits the counter.

The Mr. Coffee hisses, bubbling and popping as the first drips of coffee fall into the carafe and I try to stop crying.

When I do, I tell her everything.

SHE WAS FURIOUS AT first and immediately she called Nick. When he didn't answer she called Tad. When he didn't answer, she threw a coffee mug against the wall, shattering it. After she calmed down she hugged me—the first hug I could remember in a long time.

"I'm so sorry, Carrot. I will handle it, I promise you, Carrot, I'll kill that bastard, I promise." She reassured me. "I'll deal with him."

She promised to take care of me. The whole day she tried to make me feel better with junk food I couldn't manage to eat. She tried to play my favorite DVDs but all I saw was a screen with things moving all over it. Kellen braided my hair and painted my nails and did everything she could to get my mind off what happened. For a few days after, she kept asking me if I was okay, always hugging me and reminding me she'd handle it. It felt like I had the kind of sister that Gaby had.

It didn't last long.

"HE SAID HE DIDN'T do anything, Kara!" Kellen yells at me, a week later. She had figured out when Nick got off work and planned to confront him in the parking lot. Before she left she kissed my cheek and told me she might even go to the cops after she talked to him.

"I can't believe you! How could you take his side? I'm your sister!"

We are sitting on my bed. Mom and Dad aren't home from work yet.

"He said it was you! You had a list of first times, or first . . . things you wanted to do and kissing was one of them. He said you enjoyed it, Carrot! He said you tried to seduce him, that you practically had your hand on his crotch!"

"Seduce? How would I know how to do that? I kissed him, that's it. He did that other stuff later, Kellen! The kissing was one thing, but everything else? I didn't want any of that! I was in bed, asleep and you know it! You believed me when I told you, I can't believe you're doing this to me!"

"Nick denies doing anything but kissing you, down on the basement couch. As if that's not enough for me to deal with, and try not to remember every time we're together down there!"

What is she talking about? She doesn't have to deal with anything—she wasn't messed with, and she's used to boys. "That night was my first kiss, Kellen. I wouldn't have let him if I thought he would do that other stuff!"

"You're just a baby; you don't know what you're talking about. When you told me, you didn't even make any sense. I knew you made it up. I was mad because of Tad breaking up with me. You shouldn't lie about this kind of stuff, Carrot. You could get Nick into serious trouble if you keep this up!"

18. *Cool completely.*

. . . .

Charlie paces, his face the color of flour as he runs his hands through his hair.

I shouldn't have told him.

He exhales, puffing his lips out, before disappearing into the kitchen.

I stare at the floor, counting the panels of oak. Dust bunnies converge around the base of the floor lamp. He turns on the water in the kitchen and I hear a glass filling up.

He thinks it's my fault.

When he walks back into the room, he sets the glass in front of me and sits down.

"So, you didn't even tell your mom or anyone else?"

I'm starting to get mad. Charlie can't even say anything to make me feel better about this terrible thing I've never shared. "My own sister didn't believe me, Charlie! How could I expect anyone else to? Kellen told me she'd handle it and then she didn't. The night that she died, before we knew, Mom and I went for dinner and a movie. She'd just won a big case. She was giving me a little more attention. I almost felt like I could tell her, but I didn't. Then of course she got the call from campus police the next morning and everything changed."

From the corner of my eye I see him nodding. The silence coming off him feels heavy and judgmental, and I know what he's thinking—that I'm totally messed up. I hate myself for trusting him. Maybe I'll just stay in San Francisco.

The old furnace hums and then rumbles to life, sending heat into the room. We both look toward the grate on the wall by the kitchen. I bolt for the apartment door, swinging it open. "Obviously telling you was a huge mistake, so you can go now. Besides, you have to get back to work anyway and I'm not feeling so great."

He stays. When he makes eye contact I whisper, "Please, go. I need to finish packing."

I look away, down the steps. But when he passes me I know his eyes are on me.

THE NEXT AFTERNOON I take the Metro to the light rail station at Westlake. On the train I clutch my carry-on and suitcase close. I watch everyone: a grandmother, a toddler, it doesn't matter. The pepper spray tucked into my bag gives me a little comfort, but it's sweet relief when the train gets to the airport. There's no way Mom can stop me now. She wouldn't be able to find me. But I hope the note I left her will suffice.

Mom, please don't worry, I'm fine. I'll be back in a few days.
                                                              Kara

ONCE I'M SITTING AT my gate I breathe easier, but my mind wanders to the pepper spray again. I had to stick it back into my suitcase, so now I feel less safe, like everyone's watching me, wondering why I'm traveling by myself.

All the seats facing the window are taken so I'm forced to sit and watch the main drag that runs through the terminal. My heart beats too loudly, someone will hear it, I know. Even my breathing seems unusually loud. It's like my body is trying to call out, telling the whole airport I don't have permission to travel anywhere, and that my mom thinks I'm at school.

It's not until the plane's wheels lift from the runway that I feel safe. And free.

I'm on my way to the only thing I need: my future.

For the two-hour flight I go over my contest plans, making notes for each step so that I maximize my allotted time. My heart pounds when the pilot announces our descent into San Francisco International Airport.

THE CONTESTANTS WHO CAN afford to stay at the fancy hotel where the contest takes place get a free shuttle from the airport. The rest of us poor bakers have to catch a bus or taxi to San Francisco State University's campus, where we get to stay for free in their dorms.

Thankfully, there are only five of us financially challenged contestants, so when I check in I'm told that I get an empty room to myself, but have to share the bathroom down the hall.

The small room feels big in a weird way, with two of everything: wall-mounted bookshelves, desks, and dressers, all in light wood. Is this what college is like? I can't imagine spending four years in a place like this. Thank God it has a microwave because I don't have money to eat out. My suitcase full of Cup Noodles and Pop-Tarts will be breakfast, lunch, and dinner.

A HALF HOUR LATER I hear a knock at the door.

"Miss McKinley?" a voice asks.

I walk quickly to open it because I recognize the voice of the woman who checked me in. Her face doesn't show the kindness it had earlier.

"Hi. Is everything okay?" I ask her.

I hope she doesn't want me to switch to another room. Her eyes are narrowed. Oh God, she knows I'm here illegally.

"Miss McKinley, I'm sorry to bother you but I just wanted to let you know that a boy your age stopped by downstairs a few minutes ago. He claimed to know you?" She tilts and shakes her head a little. "He said he came here with you, but I'm sure I remember you told me you came alone, from out of state, right?"

I swallow hard. I think of pepper spray. I think of blue-gray envelopes. The fear that I'd managed to chalk up to paranoia on the plane is back. "Yes, I did."

She nods, her eyes locked with mine, reading my expression. "That's what I thought. I told him you hadn't checked in yet, and when I asked if he wanted me to leave you a message, he left."

I can't respond. I'm not even sure what I'd want to say.

"Do you need me to call someone?" she asks gently. "Do you have any idea who he is?"

My nose stings. I bite my lip and shake my head.

Her forehead creases and she reaches out to touch my arm. "If you need anything, call me. The number for campus security is on a sticker on your phone by the bed. They are very fast, so no need to worry." She gives a half-smile and turns to leave.

I close the door and lock it. My body feels shaky and weak. Could my stalker know I'm here? It sounds crazy. After I get my things ready for the morning, I fix myself some noodles and crawl into bed. I've never been on my own like this. I'm far from home, far from a soul who knows me. But I've longed for this, wished for it for so long. I dig in my carry-on for the last note I got, the one left at Justine's check stand. I put off reading it because I've learned to lie to myself—that if I don't read the notes then my stalker isn't real.

The paper feels so familiar now, and I pull it out and tear it open.

DON'T THINK YOU'LL EVER FIND A PLACE I CAN'T REACH YOU.

I cram it back into my bag and crawl into bed. Then I get up to make sure the door is locked. I try to sleep but of course I can't. Does that mean he followed me? But how? Justine only gave me the note yesterday. How can he know about the contest? I've hardly told anyone.

There's noise outside in the hall so I sit up. College girls giggle and chat with each other as they walk by my door, the sounds fading as they move on down the hall. The space between the floor and the bottom of the door is illuminated by the light in the hallway. A third of the gap is dark, right in the middle.

Someone is standing outside my door.

I flip on the lamp and grab the pepper spray from my suitcase. Maybe I should call campus security. I pull the phone closer to me and check for the sticker the woman mentioned. Light rolls in from under the door because the feet, or whatever blocked it is gone.

When I lay back down, I'm shaking and I can't get warm enough. My breath rolls in and out, so loud I'm almost grateful I can't hear anything else. The clinical room feels like a hospital or jail. My brain won't turn off and I worry that sleepiness will strike me in the middle of the contest tomorrow.

I HAVE NIGHTMARES.

I pipe out white royal icing and it crawls, slithering and curling into a thousand maggots. A shadow hovers above my work area. I'm handling a fat hunk of slippery, moldy cookie dough. My rolling pin slips along the slimy surface so I press down harder, trying to flatten it, but I press too hard on the pin and blood explodes from inside the dough, splattering my face and arms. I hear a *tsk-tsk* and the scratching of a pen against paper as the shadow moves away.

I win the contest. My faceless stalker hands me my prize and then reaches out to slice my throat.

♥   ♥   ♥

SNOWFLAKE SUGAR HOSTS A breakfast for all contestants before our official 10:00 A.M. check in. When I arrive at the hotel it's beautiful and pompous and fussy. The contestants are given IDs on lanyards to wear around our necks, and I see lots of people my age, going into one of the auditoriums where breakfast is served. Everyone but me seems to have a supportive mom or dad with them, even the other poor kids who slept in the dorm. I grab a bagel and a yogurt and head to the bathroom. I don't want to call attention to myself by sitting unaccompanied at a table. Besides, the buzz of excitement and chatter just makes me feel emptier.

An eternity later, it's my turn to check in. I give my name and the registration official smiles sweetly and gives me a map of the stations, highlighting where I'm to work.

I walk around carefully, hunting for my station. The judges' tables line the wall and I can't look directly at them. They are royalty, unapproachable, ticket holders to my future.

Everyone's dressed in the white chef coats that match the ones us contestants wear, right down to the tiny Snowflake Sugar logo embroidered on the chest. It's almost comical how we all look the same. But at least now I'm not alone. I'm part of the pack. Still, my coat feels big and bulky and I don't know how I'll function in it. Why couldn't they just give us aprons? Usually when I bake I wear a T-shirt.

Not hard to find my station. My name is printed in big red letters on a sign underneath the Snowflake Sugar logo. Seeing my galley-style workspace makes my mouth drop open—so tiny. Down the line are at least a dozen identical stations. My neighbor—a girl my age with a messy bun piled on top of her head—nods and smiles because I think she understands. I smile and nod back, but say nothing. Mr. King told me not to talk to my competition. Stay focused.

As I set out my decorating tools my hands shake. Please God make it stop by the time I have to pipe out icing or I'll be in trouble. The KitchenAid mixer of my dreams towers over my station like a queen.

When I look around the giant auditorium, I notice I was mistaken: I am alone. Every baker has an adult hovering over them. Bun-head next to me nods frantically at a woman with a giant purse slung over her shoulder. When I look back a few moments later, the two are actually bent over the counter, head-to-head, hands clasped together and I know they are praying.

I feel a pang, albeit a small one, of missing Mom. If she was here now, and I had her blessing, she'd close her eyes and raise her hands to heaven before she'd wave them over my station. I can almost hear her, asking for the Holy Spirit to come down and bless my butter.

Over the loudspeaker, contestants are directed to report to their stations; spectators must please find a seat and silence their cell phones. We have a few minutes to orient ourselves before the clock starts, so I organize all my tools and ingredients in the order I'll use them. The room buzzes from the cheering section.

Doubts tiptoe through me as I scan the room. Everyone looks like they belong there, even though they're all close to my age. They can't have more knowledge than I do. Or can they? Mr. King would never have recommended me if he didn't think I could cut it, right?

I glance at the judges' tables again and a wave of nausea folds around me. I feel hot and my forehead is sweaty. As if reading my mind, a man with a cart of water bottles in ice rolls up and offers me one. I thank him quickly and drink, but not too much because I don't want to waste one second running off to pee.

The clock reverberates in my ears, ticking down the last few minutes until our four-hour time allotment starts. I run my hand over the glossy top of the KitchenAid mixer. I wish I could fold it up and sneak it home in my carry-on.

The girl next to me clenches hers fists and goes up and down on her toes.

All at once, I feel better. I'm *not* alone. These are my people, and suddenly I'm awed to be in their midst. Pride bubbles up in me. So many people with the same dream as me. I know I need to see them all as my competition—to be hated—but I can't. How can I fear or loathe people who love what I love? Are they like me, counting on this contest to make things better? To get away from a crappy life? Or do they just do it for the trip, the excuse to get out of school?

The CEO of Snowflake Sugar looks as if he eats a little too much of it. But his smiling face is full of kindness as he wishes us luck before he counts backwards from twenty to signal our begin time. "Twenty . . . nineteen . . . eighteen . . ."

TIME HAS FROZEN. BUT at the word "Go," I bolt around my station. Since the contest organizers didn't make sure the butter came to room temperature, I stick mine in the microwave. Every ten seconds I check because it has to be perfect. I pour in sugar and vanilla. My mind starts tormenting me like it did all night, and I'm thinking of the last note I got. Who asked for me at the dorm? Where is he now? In the audience? Watching and waiting until I'm alone?

I stir sugar and butter and vanilla.

But there's something that doesn't belong. I hear a rattle and clink on the bottom of the bowl. When I turn the dough with my spatula, I see them: teeth. The dough clings to the roots of the teeth like torn, ragged flesh.

When I crack the egg into the bowl, blood spills out of it.

The bottom of the bowl is Kellen's dead, gray face. Blood splashes up the sides of the bowl, coating it, and onto Kellen's eyes and nose and mouth.

EIGHT-YEAR-OLD CARROT

I'm eight and Kellen is twelve. I'm sitting in the tree again because I'm upset. Kellen is in her room.

They didn't know I was home; they thought I was still with Jen but her mom dropped me off early. They didn't hear me listening because it sounded like Kellen was in trouble so I stayed on the stairs. I didn't want to be in trouble, too.

"I hate it! Why do you make me do it? I wanted to try out for cheerleading."

"You're so talented, Kell Bells, we don't want you to throw away your future. Stick with piano a few more years and if you want to go out for cheerleading in high school then we'll support you."

"Dad's right. You've been at it too long to give up now."

"I already told them all I was quitting."

"What?"

Silence.

"Yeah, I did. Why do you make me keep doing it when you let Kara quit everything. You let her quit ballet and piano!"

"Oh stop. Your sister is, well, she's not a natural like you are. Things don't come to her as easily."

"Mom's right. She's . . ." Dad stops and chuckles. "Listen, kiddo, she's not like you. She gives up on everything. That's just her nature. It's something we've gotten used to. But you, you're so naturally talented. We won't let you give up on yourself."

"You baby her, and she gets away with everything."

"Hey, we're talking about you here not your sister," Dad says.

"We expect great things from you Kell Bells, we can't let you quit and give up on yourself," Mom agrees.

"So you're making me do it even though I hate it?"

"Kellen you also need something to keep you out of trouble."

"Why, Mom? What have I ever done?"

"You always have to push it, you always have to fight us on everything! Why is that? Your sister doesn't do that. Now get downstairs! One hour on that damn piano, right now!"

"No."

"What did you say?"

"You heard me, Mom."

Silence.

Silence.

Silence.

"Meg—"

"No, I'm done reasoning with her. Done!"

"You heard your mom, Kellen. We'll talk about this when you're not upset."

"But for now, go, get to your room! You're grounded."

"Meg, really?"

I hear the squeak of the floor as they approach Kellen's door so I bolt, out the front door and up into the tree.

I wait and watch for Kellen. It's starting to get dark. Mom's not expecting me until after dinner and I'm not going in the house until I have to, even though it's so cold out.

Kellen's blinds go up after a while and she opens her window. She sticks one leg out and looks back inside before tiptoeing across the roof and around the side of the house. A few seconds later she's making her way to the front walk where a boy stands even though I never saw him appear. I can't hear what they talk about, but she shrugs and rocks back on her heels.

He does something with his hands and I see a cigarette glowing as he offers it to her. My sister takes it and doesn't even cough. Then he puts his hand out and she takes it, and they disappear down the street, into the dark.

19. *Watch carefully so you don't burn the nuts.*

....

I stand back and close my eyes. I tell myself the horrible vision isn't real. My mind races so fast I think I'm forgetting to breathe. When I look back into the bowl I see a bright yellow egg yolk, sliding into the crevices left by beaten butter, sugar, and vanilla. I decide to switch my brain off. I blend the mixture to the right consistency, listening to the hum of mixers from all the other contestants. Only the music of baking. No talking, nothing else. I start sifting my flour mixture into the bowl and set the mixer to the lowest speed, while a judge with short gray hair, huge earrings, and a ton of makeup walks up to my station.

My gut plunges. I'm caught.

Mom must have called. Or maybe she's here! Oh God, I'm in trouble. It's a cruel joke: I'm finally praying like Mom wanted. *Please, God, no, if you ever cared about me please let me stay here and finish this—my life depends on it.*

But the judge only jots a note on her clipboard before she moves on to the next station.

I shove everything else from my mind. I'm back into action, finishing off my mixture by hand and turning the dough out onto my floured board. Five minutes later it's covered and chilling in the tiny fridge and I start on the royal icing. I need four shades.

Very carefully I dab food color gels into four bowls of icing. I have to go slow with my tinting to get it just right. The red tint is the most difficult. I add gel, but it's not perfect. It looks like an orangey-tomato red and I realize it might be the bright fluorescent lighting overhead, which I'm not used to. A rush of panic courses through me because I'm not sure how to fix it. I work on the other colors while trying not to freak out.

We are to be judged based on design, presentation, and of course, taste. I speed through the last bowl of icing, and I take a second to peek around, relieved when I see others still in the final stages of dough-making.

I'm ahead, just a little.

My confidence lasts only for a few seconds because now I'm back to dealing with crappy red icing. We have access to the pantries and refrigerators lining the wall on the far side. I walk quickly over there to figure what I can do to solve my problem. I feel my heartbeat, ticking away precious minutes while I stare at the various supplies laid out for our use.

I pass every fridge and shelf twice. On my third scan I see a basket of raspberries and remember last year when Mr. King taught us to make sauce for cheesecake out of the berries. I grab them, a saucepan, some cheesecloth, and a squeeze bottle and run back to my station.

As fast as I can, I get raspberries, water, and sugar boiling into a puree. I pour it through cheesecloth to strain out the seeds and stick it into the tiny fridge for later.

Will it solve the problem? When I start rolling out a disk of sugar cookie dough, I have the feeling that I'm being watched again. Of course the spectators are watching me; they're watching all of us. Ready to cut out dough, I look up because the feeling is so strong.

Maybe it's Mom. If she somehow made it here, I hope she'd at least let me finish before she kills me. I scan the crowd—Mom isn't there.

But Kellen is; she stands out in her red hoodie. It's like she's dancing through the crowd, not even aware of me. Until she turns and stares. At least I think she's staring. I can't make out her face too clearly.

Then I catch a flash of another face.

Familiar, but I can't place it because of the rows of people in the way.

Kellen's gone. I scan the crowd again and there's no sign of her. The other face is gone, too. Or maybe it was never there in the first place.

The auditorium smells of sugar and butter. Some of the contestants already have cookies in the oven, so I focus on my cookie dough again. I wonder if I'll hallucinate and see Noelle or Charlie, too. Maybe it's the fact that I'm here alone, and my subconscious wishes for anyone familiar.

BY THE TIME MY first batch of cookies is baking in the oven, I have two hours left—halfway through our time. I start rolling another batch to make sure I have plenty of stock to decorate, in case I screw up. The gray-haired judge comes by twice more, crinkling up her nose at God knows what when she sees me rolling dough. What is her problem anyway? None of the judges look very happy, and I've noticed some of them shaking their heads when they jot down notes. I'm praying the icing incident is my only snafu.

The timer beeps for my first batch in the oven, and then timers go off all over the room.

One and a half hours remain on the clock when I start decorating the first batch, working in layers as I always do. I set down one color first on each cookie before I gather the next piping bag. I lose one cookie to an air bubble in the bag, three to my nerves, and one to the floor when I look back up for that familiar face I thought I saw in the crowd.

We have to turn in a tray of designed cookies to the judges. Each cookie has to look the same. Out of my first batch I'm happy with half of them. With the next batch, even more.

With three minutes left, I quickly arrange my cookies on the tray with my contestant number and carry it over to the judges' tables.

Other contestants bring their trays, too.

A picture-perfect girl made cookies that look like little wedding cakes, dripping and sugary with tiers and fondant and sugared flowers. She bows to the judges after she deposits her stupid little entry.

She should be disqualified. It's not a cake contest.

I'm suddenly afraid my cookies might look and taste like shit. For a second I consider dumping the tray into the garbage.

Despite my feelings I set the tray down at the table. The gray-haired judge almost cracks a smile as she looks at my entry, and I hope it's not because she thinks mine's a joke. I turn fast to walk back to my station.

THERE IS AN AUDIBLE gasp from the judges' tables, and when I turn around many of them have converged on my tray. I hear whispers and see a lot of frantic note-writing. They don't ask the contestants to explain their designs. I'm thankful. I've never been excited about the required Valentine theme. Maybe if Charlie and I were together I might've been inspired by sick and drippy love and happiness. Instead, I took inspiration from what Kellen did to me, and then to my family.

By their smiles I know the judges see what I intended them to see: pretty sugar cookies with pink icing and raspberry puree, and glossy black accents piped in careful precision over the top, highlighted with glittery sugar sprinkles. They think I've stuck to the Valentine theme, and they've spotted the X on the bottom with the smaller O on top.

They see a kiss and a hug instead of the skull and crossbones silhouette. They don't realize the pink cookie piped with glittery black lines is the cage of my chest, twisted inside out. They don't know that the raspberry-filled heart shape is just an empty cavity, a bloody, pulpy hole.

When I look back I see one of the judges smiling and chewing as she jots something on her clipboard. Then she dips part of my broken cookie bone into the bloody hole.

Biting my lip, I walk back to my station. I don't want to look too confident. I clean up quickly, washing my tools and stuffing them into my bag, wishing I could walk around and look at the other entries, but we aren't allowed to do that until tomorrow when the winners are announced.

I'm unscrewing a decorating tip when the feeling of being watched comes back.

Now I have time so I stop and scan the audience again.

And that's when I notice him, staring at me.

Charlie.

20.   *Roll flat and dust.*

. . . .

I turn and peek again to be sure I'm not hallucinating. His face is so unexpected; like waking up on a Monday-morning school day and looking out the window to see everything buried in snow.

Most of the other contestants have left the auditorium when I finally carry my things out. There's a velvet rope about ten feet away that blocks non-contestants from entering, and Charlie waits on the other side of it. His eyes start smiling before the rest of his face does, and he nods once as I walk toward him, parallel to the rope. Neither of us can seem to remove our eyes from the other as we make our way on either side of the rope. I have to look around every few steps to make sure I don't run into a wall or people in front of me. It's all I can do to not jump the rope.

We don't say anything. My stomach feels empty and jittery.

"Dear?"

"Uh, huh?" I only realize the checkout lady is talking to me when she gently taps my hand.

"Name, dear?" She smiles sweetly. "You are checking out, correct?"

I look back to Charlie, smiling with his hands in his pockets. "Uh, Kara McKinley, and yeah, I'm done."

"Did you enjoy yourself, dear?" She hands me a pen.

Charlie stands there, and I'm fiercely proud that he's here for me, even though no one else gives a crap. I stare at the pen, having no clue what to do with it.

"Dear, you have to sign out here. Right here." She points. "Go ahead."

I take my eyes off Charlie long enough to sign and hand the pen back to the kind lady.

"Good luck, dear. I sure hope you win." Again, she smiles so sweetly I actually believe she wants me to win.

I walk toward him. His hands are tucked into his jean pockets and he rests a shoulder against the wall, one leg crossed over the other. His smile is tentative. He acted like a jerk the last time I saw him, and maybe he's remembering that. But now I don't care, because he's here, and when he reaches out an arm for me, I drop my stuff and walk right into him, letting his other arm find me, too.

"Sprinkles." His breath is warm when he whispers into my ear. "I'm sorry, I didn't know what to say."

He presses my head against him, and my forehead rests below his chin. With his other hand he reaches down to weave his fingers into mine, lifting them to his lips. After a minute I speak.

"Why are you here?"

"Nice to see you, too."

I pull away and pick up my bag.

"Your mom, Kara."

"What! Is she here?"

Charlie puts a finger to my lips. "She got your note. I told her what I knew, just to calm her down a bit. I mean, she went nuts."

My hands go to my head as I walk around the corner to find somewhere to sit down. Other contestants walk past, happily chatting and accepting congratulatory pats on the back from the parents who traveled with them. I find a little alcove with a bench on one wall and a mirror on the other.

Charlie sits next to me and opens his mouth, but I don't let him get a word out.

"I planned on calling when I was done! And wait a minute—you only came down here because of my mom?" I turn to find the answer on his face and feel crushing disappointment.

"Kara—"

"I'm so stupid." My face is hot and tears threaten. For two seconds I actually thought he came because he cared about me, because he wanted to be with me.

"I bought my ticket the day after you bought yours," he says in a rush. "I always planned on coming down here. I talked your mom out of coming, and I told her I'd take the quickest flight. She just didn't know I already had the ticket."

"You shouldn't have come."

"I didn't want you to be alone."

I catch myself in the mirror on the opposite wall, in my white chef's getup. Even though it's bulky and obnoxious to wear, I felt so proud to put it on this morning. Now, my hair is dusty with flour and it sticks up in all the wrong places. Black and pink icing smears decorate my boobs, and raspberry puree has bloodied my cheek. "Why?"

Mirror Charlie turns to face me but I keep watch on his reflection as he speaks. "Because, Kara McKinley, I've loved you since I was five. Besides, who else here would tell you that you have frosting in your hair?"

21. *Ice and sugar them.*

. . . .

Before I told Charlie my secret, I started casting him in my bakery daydreams. In my dream he works with me and puts peach pies in pink boxes. He slides baguettes, crusty and warm from the oven, into paper sleeves. He rings up a baker's dozen of pastries and hollers to me that we're out of cinnamon twists and raspberry scones again. He carefully places snicker doodles into small, sticky, and eager hands.

I've loved you since I was five.

Charlie rides a bike everywhere.

Charlie is trading yard work for that tired old truck because he doesn't have money.

But he still bought a plane ticket so I wouldn't be alone.

I lean over and take his face in both of my hands, kissing him full on the lips.

"Where are you staying?"

"I hadn't really planned that part. I'll check and see if—"

"Stay with me. I have two beds," I reply, noticing the giant Snowflake Sugar contest poster hanging in the hotel lobby. "We're having Cup O' Noodles for dinner."

"The valet told me the best cheeseburgers in town are a block away."

A black icing smear keeps pulling my attention to my chest. "I don't have cheeseburger money."

He reaches out and cups my chin. "It's on me."

♥   ♥   ♥

WE EAT OUR DINNER at the back of the bus on our way to
the dorms. When I'm done I send a text to Mom, telling her I'm
fine, and that I did awesome. I add that I'm happier than I've
ever been, so please don't spoil it. I don't say I'm sorry, because
I'm not. As soon as I get home, I'll be grounded for life, but I
don't care.

If I win first place, my problems are over.

I turn the phone off before she can call me back. That makes
me feel bad, but she's put me through a lot, too. I'm sucking
down the last of my milkshake when it occurs to me. "Charlie?"

"Mmm?" He answers with a mouth full of burger.

"When did you get here?"

He finishes chewing but I notice he won't look at me. "Late
last night. Really late."

I'm thinking about the guy who was asking after me. Maybe I
should tell Charlie, but I push the thought away.

We don't talk much for the rest of the bus ride. I'm exhausted
and Charlie hasn't stopped eating since we sat down. "Where's
your stuff by the way?"

He grins. "Only brought what I could stick into the pockets of
my jacket. Toothbrush and clean skivvies."

THERE ISN'T ANYONE AT the front desk when we get back
and I'm relieved because how else could I sneak Charlie into
my room?

Once we're inside he disappears with my soap and shampoo,
and I barely have time to think about our sleeping arrangements before he's back, wearing only his jeans. The pit of my
stomach warms and so does my face. I smell my soap on his skin
as he leans into the mirror and runs his hand through his wet
hair. I can't take my eyes off of him. The warmth inside of me
spreads and I want him close to me.

"Do you want to go do something?" he asks.

"Uh, I'm kind of tired and I don't think we should risk it since they don't know you're here. Probably safer to stay in." I know eventually I'm going to have to shower and change. Thankfully when I picked out pajamas I knew I'd probably be sharing a room, but I'm still not sure I want Charlie Norton seeing me in them.

"Yeah, you're probably right."

My eyes follow as he sits on the edge of the other bed, flipping through a magazine. He turns quickly, catching my stare and I pick at the blankets.

"What time do you find out tomorrow?"

"Eleven. We have to be back at eleven." The thought of it twists my stomach. I have to win.

"Crap," he replies. "My flight leaves at ten. I'll miss it."

"It's okay, it was sweet of you to come anyway, even though you didn't need to. I can—"

"Take care of yourself, yeah, I know, you told me." He sets the magazine down. I'm not sure how much longer I'll be able to stand him so close to me, all clean and still without a shirt on. But the fact that it makes me want to kiss him is probably a good thing. Maybe I won't be screwed up forever.

"I'm going to go, uh, change and stuff." I stand up slowly because my lower back hurts and I didn't bring any pain relief with me. I gather up my toiletry bag and clothes and head to the door.

Charlie stands up and grabs his shirt, pulling it over his head. It flattens his damp hair but he sort of shakes it out. "I'll go to that rec room down the hall and find something for us to do."

When he passes me in the doorway, he leans down to kiss my cheek. I watch him walk down the hall, whistling.

Since it's Saturday and a lot of students have gone home for the weekend, the hallway is blessedly empty, and the bathroom even smells clean, like no one has set foot inside in days. The shower is wonderfully hot over my body and massages my achy back. I didn't realize how cold I was before. My skin turns red but I stay in a long time.

Now that Charlie isn't distracting me, I can't help but think back to the contest. I could've done better. Maybe I should've done something more traditional and Valentine-y. But the only cookies that made me second-guess myself were the ones that looked like mini wedding cakes—and this wasn't a cake contest. The other entries looked like a gazillion other cookies I've seen in my life, packaged up in pretty little bakery windows in boxes with ribbons.

I hear the bathroom door open and cold air from the hallway rushes in, creeping up my legs. Slow footsteps from hard-soled shoes click their way in until I hear the creak of a stall door. I stay in the shower, listening above the trickles and splashes of the water.

No more sounds from outside.

The water heats me where it touches, but where it doesn't I'm frozen and I shift under the shower, telling myself it's only the chilly bathroom making my skin crawl with gooseflesh. I turn off the water and listen carefully while I dry off and put on pajamas.

Still nothing.

Either the person left or they're still in here. My skin glows red hot under my flannel pajamas, but my exposed skin feels frozen. Except my fingertips. My pulse throbs down into each one, and a droplet from a soaked strand of hair slides down the back of my neck, finding its way down my pajamas, making me shiver.

The stall door creaks. Shoes tap out a slow pattern as they move out of the bathroom. No toilet flushing. No hand washing. No nothing.

I grab my stuff and creep out to the hall. When I'm sure it's empty, I run back to the room.

Charlie is waiting for me. He's turned on all the lamps and the room feels cozier for it. I'm relieved he's here, but still I can't help but glance down at his shoes, kicked off and left carelessly at the end of the bed. Sneakers would squeak, wouldn't they?

"Why are you breathing so hard, Sprinkles?"

"Nothing. I was cold." I stare at his face, waiting to see if he'll ask more, waiting to see if it's the right time to tell him about my stalker.

But I don't because he nods and takes a bite from the Cup O' Noodles in his hand. I can't believe he has any room for noodles after the cheeseburgers he ate. He's adorable and I can't help but smile when he waves his hand over the Monopoly game he's set up on the bed.

I start to pull the curtains closed for the night. Outside, thick fog crouches over the quad. Only the fuzzy lights that illuminate the paths and walkways are visible. No one's outside that I can see.

Every few minutes when Charlie's laughing about some victory over me, I almost tell him about the notes I've been getting and how scared I am.

But I don't, because I'm also thinking about other things while Charlie acquires Boardwalk and I end up in jail more times than in my whole Monopoly-playing history. I can't stop thinking about our sleeping arrangements. There are two beds but only one has sheets and blankets. I could strip the bed and give him half but then neither of us will have enough covers to keep warm.

He looks at me and smiles before folding up the game, sending his hotels plummeting onto the bed. "I'm tired, how about you?"

I should tell him about the notes right now. We're here alone and there's no one else to hear—like Mom. Or would he call her anyway? I don't know what they talk about when he's there

working. Mom says he asks about me, so what else do they dis-
cuss? He seems pretty comfortable with her, so maybe he'd feel
like he had to tell her. I don't want her to know. Ever. Right now
I'm alone in another state with Charlie and that's all I want to
think about.

"Kara, what's up?"

My heart starts pounding. "Um, what do you mean?"

"You have this look about you sometimes—like you're on the
verge of saying something, and then you don't. I've noticed it a
few times. Are you worried about the contest?"

"Yeah. Um, I'll be right back." My face feels like fire and I hop
off the bed and run to the bathroom with my toothbrush and
paste. After the slowest tooth scrub ever, I walk back to the room
and let Charlie have the toothpaste.

IN BED, I CLOSE my eyes and try to take deep, long breaths.
The mattress Charlie sits on creaks, and I wait for him to cross
the space between us. The other bed has nothing on it but some
of my stuff and a thin blanket folded up. When I open my eyes,
Charlie's lying down with the flimsy blanket covering him.

I sit up and look over at him. I definitely want him with me,
but I'm afraid. Still, I try anyway. "Charlie, you're going to freeze
with just that little blanket."

He rolls over and smiles at me. "I'll be okay."

I can't make the words come out, but when I fold back
the covers and pat the spot next to me, he quickly stands
up, abandoning the blanket, then sits down next to me and
swings his legs onto the bed. I've never, willingly, been with
a boy in bed and I am self-conscious like I've never experi-
enced in my life.

Charlie props himself up on an elbow and smiles down at me.
Instinctively, I pull the blankets up around my neck so he can't
see me shaking. This must be funny to him, and he chuckles
before bending down to kiss my cheek. His brown hair hangs

over his forehead, tickling my face, and he smells of toothpaste and shampoo.

Lying back on the pillow, he clasps his hands behind his head and smiles up at the ceiling. I wonder if he's going to turn off the lamp. I'm not tired but head-to-toe aware of his body next to me and the heat coming off his naked chest. I can't help but notice the smooth panes of his muscles and the line of hair that starts right below his navel and disappears under the blankets. I scoot nearer to the wall so I don't accidentally touch him.

"Do you remember when we saw each other at Red Lobster the night of the freshman dance?" He props himself back on his elbow and looks down at me. "You were with Brian what's-his-face?"

I nod, and Charlie shakes his head and smiles. "I faked food poisoning on the way to the dance. I totally ditched—uh, I forget her name—my date, so I wouldn't have to see you with Brian."

"You should've told me."

Charlie never gave me any clue that he was interested back then, except for being nice at school. I remember Katy Morgan bragging in the locker room about him. I could've gouged her eyes out.

"I think it was girls-ask-guys only."

"Katy told the whole locker room that you'd asked her."

Charlie shakes his head. "Nope. Anyway, I'd never been jealous before, like that. You were so pretty in that shiny pink dress. I couldn't take my eyes off you."

That dress. I took it from Kellen's closet but couldn't fill it out like she did. Too long and loose on me. I didn't really care anyway, because I didn't want to go in the first place. And Mom didn't even look at me when I came downstairs wearing it.

I stared at Charlie the whole evening. "I couldn't even eat my dinner."

"I know, I watched you the whole time," he says, smiling.

This embarrasses me even though it happened two years ago, and I pull the blankets up right under my eyes.

Charlie laughs and brushes hair from my forehead. "I dumped Katy off at the dance with Grady, and still had a half hour left on the limo. So I had the driver pick up my buddy Cal, and his brother's stash of PBR, and he dropped us off in Ballard."

Charlie continues. "Cal and I got drunk down at the Locks. Not sure how many I had before I started calling you. I hung up the phone every time your mom answered."

But I wasn't home yet. That night while Noelle and her boyfriend made out in the backseat, Brian shoved his hand under my dress. Noelle had him in a headlock after he called me a bitch for puking on him. I stare up at Charlie. "What would you have done if I answered?"

He grins and lies back down, hands behind his head. "Cal kept asking me that, too." His eyes are on me now. "I probably would've said something lame and you would've hung up."

Charlie sits up and turns toward me. "You were so different, Kara. I realize now, when I think back, that you pulled away from everyone when school started that year. I remember how you were before she died. It's like you were closed off and didn't want anyone around. I wanted so badly to talk to you, but I was a chicken shit. I was afraid you'd turn me down."

My words are a whisper and I can only look at his chest. "There was only you, Charlie. And then you left."

"I'm sorry." He leans down to kiss my forehead.

When he lies back I want badly to touch his bare skin. He keeps his hands clasped behind his head on the pillow, watching me. Under my skin my heart drums my pulse down into every corner of me.

I touch him, tentatively. His chest is warm and both soft and hard at the same time. My hand travels over the muscles there and up toward his shoulder, tracing the lines of his bicep. I run my palm over his shoulder and up his neck to his ear and into his hair. I do this a few times, staring at his body. Suddenly I feel stupid. But when I look at Charlie's face, I can tell by the way he holds my gaze that it's not stupid at all.

Charlie is safe. Charlie would never hurt me, so I keep my hands on him.

He reaches for me, but then he stops.

I think he understands.

I kiss him.

Sometime before dawn, I fall asleep on his chest and it's the happiest night of my life.

JUNE: THIRTEEN-YEAR-OLD ~~CARROTS~~ KARA'S SUMMER ~~FUN~~ BEFORE HIGH SCHOOL

"Kara, your attitude lately sucks," Mom said. "I don't know what's wrong with you. You're not talking to us, and now your friend Jen tells me she's come over every day for the past two weeks and you won't answer the door? Or the phone when she calls? Whatever it is with you, I hope this time away will help." Mom hands me my last bag before getting back into the car to go home.

Now I'm curled up on my cot in the corner of the cabin, facing the wall. Mom thinks summer camp will cure me of "my sudden onset of bitchiness, hormones, end of middle school, or whatever it is." But it's not just me. Everyone in the house seems different. It's summer and why does my Mom have more work than ever? And why does Dad? And why does no one talk about the fact that Kellen is leaving for college at the end of summer? Everything at home is changing, but everyone is fixated on me and my "sudden" problems. I don't think Kellen told Mom what happened with Nick.

So I'm here and that's one less thing my parents have to deal with. Now they can completely bury themselves in their work so they can forget about their favorite girl leaving.

I hate it here. I want to go home, yet I don't want to go home either.

Every one of my cabin-mates came here matched up with a friend from home.

"What's with you, anyway?"

"We have to bunk with her? She's got like permanent cramps or something."

"Yeah, look at her."

"Hey you guys, she doesn't talk. Maybe she's one of those mute people?"

"Does anyone know sign language?"

Laughter.

"Sorry, it's the only sign language I know."

"But she's so pale. Maybe she's a vampire."

"Uh-oh, better roll up in your sleeping bags tonight, she might bite ya."

Shrieks and laughter.

"Hey, vampire deaf girl, why don't you do us a favor and go sleep in another cabin?"

"Yeah. I'm not gonna be able to sleep with her in here."

"You guys, if she went tanning she'd be pretty, you know. She just needs a little sun."

"Maybe, but vampires can't tan or be in the sun. She'll fry herself."

"Good, then we won't have to bunk with her."

Giggles.

Outside, a bell rings, signaling dinner. I wait until I hear their feet move and the screen door squeal and slam before I get up. But when I do, a few are still there and one of them is in my face.

"Vampires don't eat food. I bet you wanna suck my neck, don'tcha?"

I recognize her voice as the one who hurled most of the insults at me. She smiles, her braces shine and her face is so close to mine I can't help it.

I punch her in the mouth and it hurts so badly because her braces scrape across my knuckles.

She looks at me in shock, holding her hand over her mouth as she does, her eyes rimmed with tears.

"You bitch!" She blinks hard. "Oh, its so on!!"

And she pushes me.

I don't know how much time passed but I woke up in another

cabin with a doctor or nurse or someone staring at me, along with one of the camp counselors.

"How are you feeling? You hit your head pretty hard on the edge of the cot." The nurse/doctor says.

The counselor steps in front and cuts her off. "We'd normally ship your little butt home for starting a fight, but we can't get a hold of your parents. So I think I'll make your stay with us just a little on the crappy side and then maybe you'll learn."

I try to open my mouth to say it wasn't my fault, but I'm groggy and can't speak.

When I get better, I have KP duty for the rest of camp. Three hours a day.

It sucks: physical labor in the kitchen with the cook. His name is Big Mitch and he's been working here forever. He's tall and skinny and looks underfed, probably because he doesn't eat any of the camp food and I don't blame him, even though he cooks it. Big Mitch doesn't say a lot—mostly he frowns and mumbles and points to tell me to sweep or mop or wipe down tables or rinse out trays, or take out the garbage.

The work is tiring and sweaty and hot. The kitchen feels like a furnace in the summer heat, and I'm so tired by the time I crawl into my cot at night that I only hear the Legally Blondes making fun of how I smell for just the minute before I fall asleep.

On my fifth day of KP punishment, Big Mitch actually lets me off early. He seems like he's in a good mood. I only think that because he's not frowning as usual. I'm about to walk out the door to my diving lesson when I see him frosting a cake.

It sits in the middle of the giant wooden island in the center of the kitchen, which I just cleaned. As I watch, Big Mitch doesn't just frost the cake, he has different bags of colorful frosting and they have these pointy things on the end of them and I'm completely mesmerized, watching the frosting come out all ribbons and loops and twists.

He doesn't know I'm watching. With a few quick twirls of his hand he's made the most perfect rose out of pink icing.

I walk over to stand right behind him because I'm fascinated.

"Hey, I said you could go." He doesn't take his eyes off his work.

I swallow. "Um, that's pretty. What are you doing?"

Quickly he glances over his shoulder before looking back to the new rose he makes. "It's my girlfriend's birthday tomorrow."

"You're really good at that." I can't think of Big Mitch with a girlfriend or a life outside of this place.

He swivels around and I'm sure he's going to drag me by the neck and toss me out. But instead he looks at me and sighs. "Would you like to try piping?"

I grab a bag and squeeze it like toothpaste and icing blobs out and my face goes red. "Oops."

"Okay. Let's try on something you can't wreck, like a piece of bread."

So we spend the next two hours together before he has to start dinner, with him finishing his girlfriend's cake and me going through a loaf of stale bread practicing my piping. I pipe all kinds of lines and even little hearts and flowers. They all look like crap, but I'm having so much fun that I don't care.

"Listen," Big Mitch says, "I'm only letting you do this stuff because you're the first kid who's had KP that actually does a good job, doesn't bitch, and doesn't ask when they can leave. Since you're already here, may as well stay because we gotta get dinner going."

I swap the piping bags for a potato peeler, and I'm feeling better for the first time since I got here. After dinner clean-up, Big Mitch tells me to stick around again tomorrow and we'll make a pie. And when I quietly ask if we can make a cake to decorate, he says the day after we'll bake sugar cookies and that way I'll have lots to practice on for when I screw up.

And just like that, I love camp.

Every day when I'm supposed to be at diving or archery or horseback riding, I sneak off to the kitchen and bake with Big Mitch.

He shows me how to make donuts and cookies and cakes, and more pies and bread and cinnamon rolls. I learn everything. And I love all of it, and Big Mitch doesn't talk much but it's okay because I'm not really into people or talking these days either.

I've never been so happy learning something, and it's the first time I've ever learned anything that Mom and Dad didn't pick for me.

When it's time for me to leave camp, I hug Big Mitch, because if I say good-bye with words then I know I'll cry, and as it is my eyes water anyway when I leave the kitchen.

But I'm a little excited to go home and tell Mom and Dad I've finally found something I'm good at.

22. *Flatten each one.*

. . . .

Call me. Ur the best baker I know <3

Charlie's gone, flying over Oregon by now.

Meanwhile I try not to float away on memories of last night.

We all stand, waiting silently and barely breathing, while the judges thank all of us for our hard work and commend us on our creativity.

My hands won't keep still and neither will anyone else's waiting in the room with me. I have to imagine everyone else is like me, listening to our pounding hearts as the judges blather on about how we're the future of the industry. In a roundabout way they even praise us for choosing a creative outlet such as this rather then getting wasted or high or pregnant.

The judges announce the ten honorable mentions, which get nothing but a certificate your mom can stick on the refrigerator and a voucher for free Snowflake Sugar. I keep my smile on because I don't expect my name to be called for an honorable mention, and I'm not surprised when it isn't. Maybe it's Charlie, I don't know, but I feel an odd sense of confidence.

I'm one step closer to my future now. I wish Charlie could've stayed; I wish I had someone to be happy with. I keep one ear on the head judge while I let the rest of me figure out how I should react when I win. Just casual and thankful? Or over the top excited? No, I could never pull that off.

They announce third place.

It's a boy, one of the poor five who had to stay in the dorm. He squeals because he's won the mixer I've wanted my whole life. I am happy, even though I am also jealous. I clap for him like everyone else does.

The applause dies down while the judges prepare to announce second and first place. With every moment that passes, my grin wanes along with my confidence. The head judge's microphone screeches feedback. The audience laughs because nothing could be funnier. Any second now I'm going to need the bathroom so I can puke and I'm thankful I didn't eat this morning. My whole body burns like a furnace, and I punish my lips by sucking them in and biting them.

I never thought this would be so hard, the waiting. I close my eyes so I can calm my insides down. My bakery daydreams play behind my eyelids, brighter and clearer than before. I imagine my shop always smelling of butter and yeast and cinnamon and sugar. Flour sacks sit on shelves, waiting to be turned into love, and I smile when I hear people complain to Charlie how they're all getting fat on my pastries. I picture Charlie changing the light bulbs that are too high to reach, and I swat his hand when he steals doughnuts because he thinks I didn't see him. Always in my dreams he runs out and makes deliveries for me, and he never leaves without kissing me good-bye.

Static crackles over the microphone as the head judge bellows out the name of the second place winner.

"Kara McKinley!"

I CAN'T MUSTER EVEN half a smile when the judges shake my hand and give me the second place prize in an envelope. And I still can't register any emotion when the gray-haired judge with the giant earrings tells me, "Congratulations, Kara!"

My ears ring, making her words thin out and die.

I don't hear the winner's name, but the auditorium erupts

and spins around me, a deafening, shrieking mass of colors and applause.

I am second place.

Second is nothing.

Second place means no scholarship to La Patisserie.

Second place chains me to the life I hate, stuck with my crazy mother.

I watch the first place winner: Wedding-Cake-Cookies. She hugs twenty people on her way up to accept her prize and when she offers her arms to the judges, I'm sick.

I wait for them to say something else—that they missed something. How can they pick her? How can everyone in the room be so happy for someone who didn't even follow the rules? For someone who decorated little fancy cakes when they should've been cookies? For someone who doesn't even want it like I do? I wait for the judges to announce "Oops, we meant to call you, Kara, we made a mistake. *You* win."

I've worked toward this forever, letting my hopes soar only to see them now, punctured, destroyed, and dead at my feet.

La Patisserie is so expensive, so difficult to get into. They only take on a handful of new students every year, and most of them are over twenty years old.

Mom refuses to let me go.

This was my only chance.

I'm breathless, twisted and pulled from the inside out when I see my dream clutched in Wedding-Cake-Cookie's hands. She stole it and now she parades it around for the entire auditorium to applaud her. Behind my eyelids, I burn red and hot. I can't swallow the rock in my throat.

I hate her. Everyone in this building cheers for the wrong person. I want her gone, knocked off the podium into the crowd of screaming hands where they can rip her into pieces and she can die like I am dying now.

JULY: THIRTEEN-YEAR-OLD ~~CARROTS~~ KARA'S ~~SUMMER FUN~~ HELL BEFORE HIGH SCHOOL

I've been home from camp an hour and I'm sitting in the kitchen, watching Mom. She's been weird since I got home, fussing around the kitchen, wearing an apron.

My excitement over telling her and Dad about what I learned from Big Mitch has dwindled for two reasons: first, how do I explain why I had KP duty, and second, Mom hasn't asked me one single thing about camp, except if I have a better attitude now.

I'm grabbing a Coke out of the fridge when she says, "We have a guest for dinner, Kara, so why don't you go shower and change out of your camp clothes."

She rushes out the back door where Dad is at the grill.

I shower, dry my hair and change into a sundress before I go downstairs. We don't usually have sit-down dinners together, especially with guests.

I step out of the sliding door—and freeze.

Kellen sits at the table.

And so does Nick.

"Kara, you know Nick, right?" Dad asks, offering me a corncob as I sit down. "He's been joining us for dinner almost every night this week, and we're sure glad your sister finally came to her senses about Tad."

Mom comes to the table, kissing Dad's cheek. It's weird for her to do that, but that's not really what I'm focused on right now.

I stare at Mom's hand resting on Nick's shoulder.

Kellen sits very close to Nick and neither of them looks at me.

"So, Carrot, what did you learn at camp?" Dad offers me a piece of chicken. "Did you finally learn to dive, or are you sticking with the belly-flop?"

He and Mom think this is hilarious and both laugh and cover their mouths with napkins, looking at each other and the others. The whole thing is ridiculous because we never have dinner together like this, so why are my parents putting on this whole act for him? I want to know what they've talked about every night that I haven't been here.

Mom puts salad on her plate. "Did you learn archery? Horse-back riding?"

Kellen uses her fork to roll her corncob back and forth, back and forth.

Nick cuts his chicken very slow and careful, like it's the first time he's ever used a knife and fork.

I can barely whisper. "I learned to bake."

Dad looks around the table and laughs, covering his mouth because he's chewing at the same time. When he finishes he says, "What?"

Mom looks at Dad. "She said she learned to bake." Then she turns to me, sipping her wine. "Oh, Kara, really? Is that all? Did you learn anything else?"

I glare at Mom because she could've asked me in the car.

But I don't want to say another word, and I don't want Nick to know what I did at camp. I don't even want my family to know because it's something that's mine and has absolutely nothing to do with them.

I shake my head, staring into my plate.

"You mean you spent the whole three weeks there and never learned how to dive?" I can hear Dad's shoved another mouthful of food into his mouth. "You know, diving is a skill you'll have for life. But you learned how to make cakes? I could've saved us some money, Meg, and bought a few cake mixes—she could've learned from reading the back of the box!"

Mom and Dad both laugh at this. I don't know what's up with them. They're both so weird, putting on this act.

I hear forks hitting plates and glasses clinking. In the distance kids holler, lawnmowers buzz, and dogs bark. Kellen and Nick's plates are barely touched and I wonder how they can sit there together, knowing what he did.

Dad laughs again. "Well, Kara, if you think I'll be forking out more money for another hobby that you'll quit next week, forget it, kid, not happening this time. Maybe when you show a little stick-to-itness with something, then we'll talk."

"I didn't," I start, biting my lip because I'm not sure how much longer I can stand this. "I didn't ask for money, Dad. I'll be doing a lot of babysitting."

The Clarks down the street asked me before I went to camp if I'd babysit. If I'm busy for the rest of the summer then I don't have time to see Jen and Gaby, and I don't have to tell them about what happened. I can also stay away from my family as much as possible.

Mom raises her glass and her eyebrows and starts giggling at my dad for some reason. Kellen and Nick don't even look up from their plates.

Mom drinks her wine and Dad uses his corncob to point toward my sister and Nick. "Well you two sure are quiet tonight. Not hungry?"

After a few moments Dad puts down his corn and wipes his mouth. "Kell Bells, don't you think that's funny? Your sister spent three weeks at camp and learned to frost a cake." He leans over to Kellen and whispers something, nudging her and laughing.

Kellen doesn't laugh.

Dad looks at me. Some of the humor slowly drains from his face and he stuffs another bite into his mouth, looking around at all of us.

We are all picking at our food, and my sister and her new boyfriend have not made eye contact with anyone since I sat down.

Nick lifts his glass to drink.

I am going to throw up.

"Kara?" Mom says.

I stare into my plate, which becomes blurrier by the second.

"Well," Mom says, "obviously camp did nothing for you and your attitude."

Suddenly Kellen bolts out of her chair and runs down the deck stairs. Nick mumbles something like "Sorry" to Mom and follows my sister.

My parents stare in surprise after them for a moment and then they both look at me, because I'm to blame.

I KEPT AWAY FROM Kellen all summer—easy enough because she was always out with Nick. She broke it off with him at the end of August before she went off to college. I only know because I heard her tell her friend over the phone that she wanted a fresh start. I never saw Nick again.

The last time I saw Kellen was when she climbed into her car and left for college. That Halloween she drank so much at a party that she fell into a pool, bumped her head, and drowned.

I always thought it was an odd way for her to go.

STEP 3:

Serve warm! Your cookie monster awaits!

23. *Half lengthwise and scrape.*

. . . .

I land in Seattle with the rain pelting the little plane window. It's saying, *fuck you, Kara, you're stuck here forever.*

Mom and Charlie sent too many texts to count while I flew home. I turn my phone back off and shove it in my coat pocket when the red light above the baggage carousel starts whirling, warning that my suitcase is coming.

I leave without it.

When I get to the bottom of the escalator, someone is standing there.

"Hey, Kar," Noelle says.

I say nothing. But I notice she's wearing a ponytail, which she never does, and she's wearing the blue pearl earrings I got her for her birthday last year. Earrings she said she'd never wear because she said they looked like "a snake's balls."

"Um, Charlie's working. He told me what time your flight got in. I'm sorry, Kar. Really. I feel like such a bitch for what I said and I'm sorry. Mason's out in the car."

I nod.

When we get to the car, Mason hops out to hug me. He takes my luggage. For the whole ride home we listen to music, and neither Mason nor Noelle asks me about the contest. Thank God. Noelle only turns around once—to ask if I want Taco Bell or McDonald's or anything.

♡   ♡   ♡

AT 10:30 P.M. I unlock the café door and trudge through the semi-dark, wondering when Mom will pop out to kill me, or ground me for life, or just ask me to pray with her and tell me "I told you so." Probably some combination. I don't care because I can't feel worse than I already do. When I reach the door at the top of the stairs, I hear the TV.

Mom lets out a soft sob and rushes over, pulling me to her before I can even shut the door. Her hand is in my hair and she whispers, "Thank you for bringing my baby girl home safe."

I say nothing. I feel nothing.

She gives me a last squeeze and then pushes me back to look at me. Her brow crinkles into a frown and I see how puffy and red her eyes are. "I did not raise my daughters to be so deceptive. How could you do that to me? Do you know what I've been through?" Her voice shakes.

"Kara, if it weren't for Charlie I would've called the police. You could've been a little more sensitive to what I'd go through considering what happened with your sister." She smoothes her palm over my forehead. "Are you okay?"

She becomes a blur.

"Oh, honey, you lost, didn't you?"

I swallow and wipe my eyes fast. "I lost. Got second place. Happy?"

Mom smiles and tucks hair behind my ear. "Well, second place is nothing to get upset about, with so many contestants! You should be proud of yourself." It's the worst thing she could possibly say.

I rush off to my room, slamming the door and locking it. She knocks as I crawl into bed in my clothes.

"Kara, you're grounded for a month."

Here we go, I think.

"You will be in church with me every Sunday morning so you can pray and ask forgiveness for your deception. I hope you will soften your heart the next time you speak to me."

And that's it. I was right about what she'd do, but of course I was. I turn over and pull the quilt over my head. I have nothing left. There is nothing to think about, nothing to look forward to, and nothing to dream about. And my mom, who is *supposed* to be on my side, doesn't even care about the only thing that is important to me.

MOM DOESN'T HASSLE ME when I stay in my room for the whole next day. I skip school because the note I forged said that I'd still be absent anyway. Monday night I come out of my room to pee and run into my suitcase. The airport must have delivered it.

I forgot about charging my phone. When I turn it on the next morning there aren't any new messages from Charlie, and I'm sure by now he knows I lost, and I should talk to him, but I can't bring myself to face him.

INSTEAD OF GOING TO school, I take the bus downtown, where I blend in with the shoppers and workers and runaways. Every shop that has anything to do with cooking or baking stands as a brick and steel reminder of what I lost. I head to a corner in the bookstore and stare at a pile of magazines.

Too many people around me are happy and I can't stand it. When I'm ready to leave, buzzing on the cheap drip coffee I drank all day, a red hoodie catches my eye.

Kellen peeks from behind a shelf and then she's gone.

I don't even care enough anymore to want to find her.

ON THE WAY HOME, I stop at my old house. Winter has stripped away the layers of my hiding place, but I climb into my old tree, not giving a shit if anyone catches me today. I sit there, letting my legs dangle from the tree and staring at Kellen's window.

SEVEN-YEAR-OLD CARROT

"Carrot, let's go, he's coming!" Kellen runs out to the street with me close behind. She is eleven and I'm seven.

"Kellen, I don't have any money." I squint up at my sister and watch the irritated look come across her face. We can't tell which street the ice cream man is on but know he's close.

"Oh! Carrot, I don't have enough for you, but I guess I'll share. Wait!"

I watch her run back into the house and emerge thirty seconds later with Mom's swear jar, half full of quarters. Kellen sits down on the porch steps with the jar between her knees and fishes out coins.

She runs to catch the ice cream truck just as it stops in front of our house. "I'll pay Mom back with my next allowance, so *shhh*, don't tell her okay?"

I nod.

Five minutes later we're sitting on the shady tree branch so our ice cream bars won't melt.

"Oh crap." Kellen slinks down a little.

I look up and see Mom, who has walked around from the back of the house, her swear jar clutched in her grubby gardening gloves. She eyes us in the tree and my stomach does a little dive as she starts to march toward us. Uh-oh.

"Kellen McKinley!" Mom stops a few feet from the tree and looks up at us. Her eyes mean trouble, but she doesn't even look at me. "Why in the hell is my money jar on the porch? Are you stealing from it?"

Kellen looks at me and I look at her, deciding what we should say. I'm just about to open my mouth when Kellen blurts out, "Mom, Kara didn't have money, and I didn't have enough to buy an ice cream bar for her. I promise I'll pay it back."

Mom has her gloved hand over her eye as she squints up at us, even though we are in the shade. "Get. Down. Right. Now."

"Mom, I'm—"

"Down!"

Kellen looks at me and sucks her lips in as she makes her way down the branch. Mom looks at me quickly and I look away. Now my ice cream bar tastes like wet paper. I look back down at Mom and try to speak, to tell her it's my fault. "Mom, Kellen didn't—"

"Just eat your ice cream bar, Kara," Mom hollers up to me. "Are you going to need help getting down from there?"

Kellen's on the ground now, her eyebrows arched high and she blinks widely, which is what she always does to keep from crying. As she shuffles over to Mom, melted rivulets of ice cream run down her hand. "Mom," my sister's voice is shaky. "Kara didn't have money, I told you I—"

Mom grabs the half-eaten ice cream bar and throws it into the bushes before she points in my sister's face. "You don't steal from us! I did not raise you to be a thief! Get your butt to your room, now!"

My sister looks down and walks toward the house, her butterfly coin purse peeking out of the back pocket of her shorts.

Mom follows my sister up the porch and my ice cream drips all down my arm and into the crook of my elbow. I throw it into the bushes where Mom threw Kellen's.

I stay in the tree for awhile and watch for my sister to open her window and talk to me. I keep readjusting my position so I can see and make sure she's okay. The blinds in her window suddenly drop, and where my sister stood a little while ago, there are tiny pools of ice cream, drying on the hot sidewalk.

24. *Coarsely chop.*

· ·

When I get back to the café, Mom doesn't ask me about my day. Instead, she insists that I sit down at a booth. Her shoulders are hunched and her face droops. There are rings under her eyes and she massages the back of her neck. "Listen, you need to help me out here. The school computer called so I know you skipped everything after first period. Grounding you is not a huge punishment, Kara, because you never go anywhere."

My eyes wander out the window and across the street.

"I know you're upset about the contest, but it's not the end of the world. You got second place. It's not like I'd let you go away to that school anyway. It's out of state. You need to get that out of your head right now. Just *forget* it."

I turn toward her, my eyes now on the cross around her neck. "Any chance that you'll *ever* give a shit about what I want?"

"Satan must be pretty comfortable, dancing on your tongue, when you can speak to your own mother that way. After your sister, your dad—"

"Oh my God, Mom! You're unbelievable, you know that? And you're not the only one who lost them!"

I've crossed the line and there's no going back. I'm aware of all the eyes in the café on us. But she doesn't seem to notice. Her eyes seethe with anger, something I haven't seen in a long time.

"I'm finished talking about this," she says. "You broke my

grounding rule of going nowhere but home, school, and work. So now, since I hear from Crockett's that you no longer work there, you will help out here, every day."

She disappears into the kitchen.

I try to scoot out of the booth, but someone slides in next to me. I smell Charlie's soap, and out of the corner of my eye I can see he's staring straight ahead, rather than at me. He stretches his arms out on the table, clasping his fingers together. I focus my gaze on his hands. He grabs a Snowflake Sugar packet out of the holder. His knuckles are rough and dry. He folds all the corners inward, spins it around, and then flicks it off the table.

The café is virtually silent. After a minute, people start to talk again.

I bury my clenched fingers under my chin.

"So," Charlie finally says. "Did you lose your phone?"

The booth seat creaks as he shifts.

"It's one thing when someone tells you that they love you, to not say it back. I get it. But was it too much trouble to let me know that you made it back to Seattle?"

I can't say anything.

"Look at me." He reaches over and clasps my chin in his hand. "Is this because you lost? Really? You got second place and you should be damn proud of that. Or is this about something else?"

My eyes are wet so I close them. He kisses me on one cheek, then the other, and then his lips are on mine. He lets go of my face.

"Is this about us?" he breathes.

There's something about the word *us*. I'm pinned in between Charlie and the wall, and my thirteen-year old self shrinks down into the vinyl seat, hoping she can hide or disappear. But there's no escape from that ugly queasiness. The shame of everything, always lurking, always waiting, threatening to swallow me up.

I shove Charlie so he'll move over, but he doesn't budge.

Instead my fingers claw at the vinyl as I climb up onto the seat. I throw my body over the back of the booth.

Charlie's grabbing for me. "Kara!"

I bolt out the door. At the corner I'm stuck because of the bus blocking the street I feel his hand grab my arm.

I swipe the back of my sleeve over my eyes and face him.

"It's a big deal, Charlie," I whisper, staring at the cold gray sidewalk. "It was my only shot. I'm screwed up, okay? You don't seem to understand that. No one does. You shouldn't be with me. Go find a happy girl."

His hand still holds my arm. "Kara, please? I want to help, okay? Why won't you let me help you through this?"

"Let *go* of me!"

Something's different in his eyes. A flicker of hostility? Something I've never seen before. "Don't, Kara, please!"

"Get the fuck away from me, Charlie!" I pry his hand off my arm and run across the street. Once I'm on the other side, I turn back to look.

He still stands there, watching me.

25. *Remove when puffed around the edges.*

. . . .

Weeks pass without a note.

They also pass without a single spoken word between Charlie and me.

I work at Mom's, bussing tables, taking orders, bringing out food when it's slow. I've scrubbed every inch of the place when it isn't busy. Splatters of sticky old sauce and soup used to freckle the entire café, but now there's not a corner of the floor or wall or underside of a table that hasn't seen my hand. It looks pretty nice in here.

When it's busy I stay behind the cash register and help train the new girl, Jessica. She has thin, over-processed hair, high on her head in a ponytail fastened with a bow. Just like a five year old. And she grasps absolutely nothing the first, or even the second, or even the third time around. Mom doesn't pay me for training her, or for anything else. She's harder on me than Dickhead ever was. As part of my punishment, even my tips go to church.

Every night I go to bed with a sore body. The collapse is my only relief. But I would never ever tell Mom I'm thankful for the exhaustion that steals away my ability to think about baking, my future plans, or Charlie.

I haven't baked a thing since the contest. My heart won't let me. Mom won't let me either—as punishment. But the joke's on her.

Charlie and I have developed a pattern when we see each other at the café:

I take tubs of dirty dishes back to him and say nothing, but my whole body still reacts because it's Charlie.

Charlie says nothing,

I rush out quickly. Each time I swallow a bigger lump because each time I miss him a little more.

Rinse. Repeat.

TWENTY DAYS AFTER THE contest, I'm over the absolute shock of it all, but still numb. I carry back a tub of crusty bowls, setting them on the end of the triple sink for Charlie. His apron sits low on his hips, reaching all the way down to his ankles. It's tied sloppily in back and I can't help but think about him in the dorm room with the towel, half naked and beautiful.

"Need something?" he asks. He grabs a soup bowl while he keeps his eyes on the sink.

Before I can say anything, he squeezes the trigger on the rinse hose, blasting pea crust off the bowl.

These are the first words he's spoken to me since our fight.

But I don't know what to say anyway, so I just watch his bicep flex under his white T-shirt sleeve while he shoots another dirty bowl. He keeps his back to me, grabbing dishes while I try to think of anything I could say to him.

Charlie's head turns slowly until he's pretty much glaring at me over his shoulder. I know I owe him an apology. The rational side of me realizes that, but the rest doesn't care.

"Kara!" I hear Mom yelling from the front.

I head out there.

Mom smiles, her teeth pressed together. I know she needs to tell me something, and I infer from her look that it's about Jessica, the new girl. I know what it is, too: Jessica screws up the register every single shift. But Mom will never fire her. Mom needs to *save* her. Now Jessica has table-bussing duty, so I don't have any reason to go into the kitchen.

"Kara," Mom whispers. "Jessica just charged someone five hundred and sixty-five dollars for their soup. I need you to stay on the register."

Jessica carries a dish tub past us, and given the blissful look on her face I imagine she'd skip back to the dishwashing area if she could.

I watch her over the next hour, noticing how she carries half-full tubs back, which puts her in the kitchen a lot.

When I catch her carrying a tub that holds a single fork, I decide to call her on it. "Jessica, you need to wait until a tub is full before you take it back to the dishwasher."

She tilts her head, like maybe she's confused. "Charlie likes me to bring him every single dirty dish, right away. I think he *needs me* to bring him the dishes as they get dirty, don't you?"

I stand in front of her, trying to figure out if she's as stupid as she pretends to be, which seems impossible. "It's a waste of effort for you take back *one single fork* when we have a lot going on out here!"

"Whatever." She sighs, scurrying around me, her straw-like ponytail whipping side to side under that bow, back to Charlie.

I wipe the counter. I hear Jessica's squealing laughter. Charlie's laughing, too, and I know they're talking, but I can't hear what they're saying. My hands shake. I almost knock a glass to the floor. If they don't stop it back there I'm going to knock Jessica on the floor, too.

When I look up, I see Noah staring in the window. He has both hands framing his eyes, like he's trying to get a better view.

I set the rag down and walk around the counter, flushing a bit because now he's looking at me. He smiles weakly and gives me a little wave before he turns and walks quickly down the street. Must've been looking for Noelle, I guess.

I pick up the cleaning rag again as Mason and Noelle walk in.

Mason plops down at the counter. "Hey, McKinley, 'sup?" he asks while he sticks his earbuds in.

I wipe down the espresso machine and I nod in the direction of the kitchen. "I have to train a dumbass and I don't even get paid. That's what's up."

Noelle sits on Mason's knee with her elbows on the counter.

"Where should we do lunch tomorrow? Should we try the Indian place? Or do you want to come back here for Jesus soup? You pick."

Noelle's changed since I came back and told her everything that happened at the contest and with Charlie. She's nicer. Whenever possible, she sneaks me out in her Mini and buys me lunch. She's worried about me. Which I guess is good. At least someone is.

Jessica's obnoxious giggling erupts from the back.

"See what I mean?" I mutter.

Noelle perks up. "Uh-oh, she's falling for Mr. Sudsy back there. Hey, it's not her fault you gave him up."

I wipe the end of the steamer nozzles. "Whose side are you on here?"

Noelle takes a quick peek at Mason, who's bobbing his head to what's playing on his iPod. "The truth hurts, Kar. If Mr. Hoyt ever dumps his fiancée, I'll be on him before self-gratification even crosses his mind."

"Nice. You're sitting on your boyfriend's lap."

"He can't hear me. And we're not married." She readjusts so she's straddling Mason in a particularly grotesque way at the exact moment Mom passes by.

"*Ohhh* no you don't!" Mom scolds. "You've heard me before, Noelle Butler. You save your grinding for elsewhere. Now either hop down from there, or scoot!"

Noelle climbs down and takes the stool next to Mason. I notice the pink in her cheeks when she sips her Coke. She'll never back-talk my Mom—ever.

Jessica emerges from the kitchen, red-faced as usual and fanning herself. She steps in next to me behind the counter and elbows me like we're BFFs.

"Do you think Charlie has a girlfriend?" she asks.

Noelle leans across the counter. "Hey, Jess?"

Jessica pulls back, frowning. "Nobody calls me Jess. Who are you?"

Noelle cracks her knuckles and leans forward. "It doesn't really fucking matter who I am. But here's the thing, Jess, and I want you to know this because I'm worried about you. If you hook up with a dishwasher, he *will* expect you to suck on his bubbles the first date."

Noelle is clearly too much for Jessica to process. The poor girl blinks several times. Finally she gasps, "You're disgusting."

"I just speak truth. Ask Kara. Now, if you want a Prince Charming, then you need look no further." Noelle turns around and makes a gun with her hand, pointing at Hayden.

"WHAT IS GOING ON with you and Charlie?" Mom asks later, when Jessica takes her break, and Noelle and Mason are gone.

I rearrange the bills in the drawer. "Nothing."

She follows me to the supply closet. "Kara, I think you need to talk to him. He's been so miserable, distant, and short-tempered with everyone lately."

"Doesn't seem miserable."

"Kara, what's wrong? I sent him down to California to bring you back. I know I should've gone myself. I was so swamped here and I couldn't go, and you two are just kids and you were down there in San Francisco together, unsupervised by *anyone* but God himself. I can only pray that you didn't partake in sins of the flesh because that—"

"Jesus Christ, Mom!"

"That only separates you from God, Kara. He *commands* you

to wait until marriage. And *damn it anyway!*" She whacks the supply closet door. "Stop using our Savior's name in vain!"

I ignore Mom and walk back to the counter at the same time that Jessica bounces in and hands me a blue-gray envelope. "Sorry, Karen, I forgot to give this to you. Has your name on it. Someone left it on the counter."

My heart pounds, but I still correct her. "Ka-*ra,* the end rhymes with Jes-si-*ca.*"

Mom turns, frowning at me, but then her face relaxes a bit and her eyes are questioning.

No, Mom, please don't ask me anything. Please.

A group of customers walks through the door. When Mom rushes over to greet them, I turn my back, shoving the note in my pocket.

"I'm taking my fifteen," I say to Jessica, grabbing my coat and lukewarm latte, and heading out the door. February blew its way into Seattle with a lot of snow. The Ave, dusted with white, is also barfing up Valentine's Day. Everywhere it's red and pink, reminding me of the loser that I am.

The door jingles and Mom zips out into the cold, all bundled up. At first I think she's chasing after me to continue our argument, but then I see that she's holding the paper take-out bag she thinks hides the bank bag so well. Anyone keeping track would notice how Mom leaves at the exact same time every day. Robbing her would be a cinch.

I sit down at a table outside and watch until she's vanished. Then I take the envelope out of my pocket, tear into it, and read it.

IN THE DARK DO YOU THINK OF ME?

Cramming it back into my coat pocket, I walk back inside. Jessica's rushing into the kitchen through the swinging door, leaving no one to look after the cash register.

I don't even take my coat off as I bolt through the door after her.

Already she's talking and laughing with Charlie.

"You can't leave the counter when no one is there, Jessica!" I yell at her. "You are so stupid!"

She's holding the dish tub when she turns to me, her mouth open in surprise.

"Whoa, Kara?" Charlie stands in front of her, blocking her from me. His hands are up and I see tiny bubbles of soap on his palms. "Do you really need to talk to her like that? She's new. She doesn't know everything yet."

"She doesn't know *anything*, Charlie! The fucking cash register could get robbed if no one's out there watching it! A *normal* person would get that, obviously, after working here two fucking minutes!"

Of course Jessica starts crying now.

"She made a mistake, it happens," Charlie says. "Back off."

Charlie puts his arm protectively around her shoulder while he tells her I didn't mean it and that everything will be okay.

I bite hard on my lip so I don't say anything else. What a dumb cow. And he can't see that? I turn and bolt back into the café.

The front door swings open with a gust of wind, blowing Mom through it, along with Raul, the other dishwasher, to relieve Charlie.

Mom smiles. "Kara, you can be off now if you'd like."

I don't respond. I grab my coat and head outside because I don't want to go upstairs yet. The sky is dark blue and black, a clear night, and I'm standing against the wall when Charlie rushes out the door, not seeing me. He still wears his apron, and it flaps against his legs as he walks.

I want to talk to him, *need* to talk to him.

So I follow him toward the bus stop that would take him home to the most expensive side of the Hill.

♡   ♡   ♡

I KNOW CHARLIE'S NEIGHBORHOOD well. Gaby and Jen and I always used Halloween as an excuse to stalk the homes of boys we had crushes on. For us it meant going to a bunch of houses because Gaby loved lots of boys at the same time. We always lied to Jen's mom about our reasons for being dropped off in the most expensive neighborhood.

There's just a dusting of snow, now frozen. Most of the sidewalk has been salted so I don't have to worry about the sound of crunching snow under my feet.

Charlie's walking briskly and I stay about twenty feet behind him, in the shadows.

But he passes his bus stop, walking straight down the Ave and past Crockett's. I can hear Justine's loud voice as a customer enters through the automatic doors.

"That'll be one fifty-nine, young sir."

I wish I could go in and talk to her and tell her what a mess I've made of everything.

Charlie stops and turns around. I freeze. Shoving his hands in his pockets, he steps toward the store. Then he stops, maybe thinking for a moment before walking in.

"Well hey there, you cutie of a stranger!" Justine's voice cries. "I hate to tell you but your Kara—" Her words fade out, cut off by the automatic doors.

Something in the dark catches my eye and I see the glow of a cigarette. My heart jumps a little. Jason steps out into the light.

"Hey, Kara." His voice sounds like a robot's.

Whatever. I'm not even answering. I'm too baffled to be creeped out. I peer through the glass doors, careful not to get too close so that they'll slide open and give me away. Jason vanishes back into the alley like a troll backing into his cave.

Charlie stands at the end of the checkout stand, his head strained toward Justine. She's standing a little too close to him, cleavage on display. Oh well, that's Justine. I immediately feel bad for thinking she might have intentions. Her smile is friendly and she is listening to him, nodding the entire time. I watch her lips to see if they form my name at all. Charlie nods. She blows him a kiss and he turns to leave. I dash to the safety of some snow-frosted evergreen bushes as the doors part and he exits. He continues down the Ave and I duck out into the street so the parked cars can hide me. He starts whistling. This ticks me off because maybe it means he's happy, and how could he be happy when we aren't together?

The old Catholic church where he took me to see his old truck looms ahead. I have to hustle to keep up with him. He runs up the steps and disappears inside the big wooden double doors.

Oh no.

It all hits me. I *was* right. He is totally a Holy Roller. It explains why he started working at my Mom's café in the first place. It explains why he's so tortured. Why he has such gentlemanly ways. Why it's impossible to hate him. Why he can walk into a bar, underage, and be greeted with cheers. Why he defended that idiot, Jessica. Always amen-ing and hallelujah-ing my mother's Bible babble. Charlie's becoming a priest, isn't he? Holy shit.

I hold the old iron door handle, wondering if I really want to do this—as in, talk him out of it. I'd probably go straight to Hell.

I have to plant my feet wide apart to get the doors to open, even though he threw them open with ease. It's dark and silent inside. Cavernous. Echoey. Holy. I have no business being here and no clue where Charlie disappeared to.

I hide in the corner so I can scope out the place from behind a back pew. In the front pews I see a few solitary people kneeling in prayer, but I don't see him. An old lady makes her way toward me, clutching a rosary to her chest. Small candles flicker against the wall nearby, where a woman kneels. Charlie is gone, but there's a door behind the altar, and that's all I can see as a possible escape route.

I leave and walk back out into the cold. Off to the side of the parking lot sits Charlie's truck, moved from where it was last time. I walk around the church, figuring that the door behind the altar must lead somewhere. Each step I take toward the back of the church sends my pulse higher. A bus thunders past and somewhere in the distance sirens wail.

My feet crunch into a half-inch of snow. I notice thin yellow light slanting out onto the walkway behind one of the basement windows. Tiptoeing along the edge of the rhododendrons, I crouch just outside it.

There's a cot-like bed made up neatly against the painted concrete block wall. A small bedside table holds a lamp, an alarm clock, a Bible, a stack of books, and a picture of a woman. An ugly green throw rug lies on the concrete floor. Maybe so the person who gets out of that bed can avoid the frigid shock each morning. The rug grows darker as a shadow moves over it and into my line of view.

Charlie.

His feet are bare and a towel is wrapped around his waist.

Charlie's at the church half-naked?

He disappears and returns pulling what looks like a portable heater. It must be freezing in there. When he moves toward the window I fall on my ass. I scoot back in an awkward crab-walk.

I turn away when he drops the towel. If Noelle were here, she'd be trying to snap a picture by now. When I turn back, Charlie is pulling on a T-shirt to top off some sweats. He crawls into the cot and starts texting someone.

Maybe he's texting me. I can imagine what he'd write.

Hey, peep show much?

My cell stays silent.

Charlie sets the phone down and lies back in bed.

I'm frozen and I need to get out of here before he turns off the light; before the glow from the street reveals the pervy girl outside his window.

Why is he sleeping at church? Don't priests in training sleep in a priest dorm or something? And they surely don't sleep half-naked. So maybe that's not it. He said his dad went to California. But he came back, right? Why isn't he living with his dad?

When I reach Charlie's truck my spine prickles, reminding me that I'm out in the dark alone.

And that's when I hear the noise behind the tree next to me.

26. *Poke the middle to check for doneness.*

. . . .

The night sky is black and starry, with fuzzy gray edges to the west.

I hurry around the side of the Ranger to the sidewalk. The noise could be anything. It could be a homeless person I don't want to offend by running away.

But as I step onto the sidewalk I hear ice crunching behind me. I start to run because now I don't care who I offend. The footsteps behind me are fast and deafening and my heart is thumping in my chest. Adrenaline gives me a little boost and I run faster than I've ever run in my life. The safety of light streaming from Crockett's interior lies only a block away, and I run for it because my life may depend on it.

I scream but it comes out as a breathy wail that no one could possibly hear. He's on my heels and it's a wonder I haven't been knocked over yet. I hear breathing and hard-soled toes hitting the ground behind me. Trees line the yard I'm passing so I launch myself into them, hoping to throw him off, but he's still there.

He slams me sideways against a tree. Half of my face smashes against the icy bark while he pins me there with his entire body. My pulse knocks in my eardrums. My limbs are weak and rubbery. His arms are on either side of my shoulder and he presses his chest into my shoulders. I can feel his thighs against me as he towers over my head. I can't even turn to see who he is.

Again I try to scream, but nothing comes out. My vocal chords are frozen and I can't even ask him why he's doing this. He thrusts his body against mine again, trying to flatten me against the tree. The bark scrapes my face, stinging my cheek.

Lights move down the street and I feel air around my back. Frozen leaves crunch.

Then he's gone.

I clutch the tree. Sap sticks to the burning scrapes on my palms. When I pull away from the tree my legs buckle and send me down to the frozen dirt and twigs and pine needles. I know I should run because he could come back, but I don't. I'm frozen.

The air, the sky, everything holds on to silence. And then, all at once, the noise returns: bar laughter far in the distance, barking dogs, and even the horn from a ferry boat. I stand up and brush myself off. My palms sting badly and two fingers on my right hand are stuck together with sap.

When I start walking down the sidewalk toward home, I realize I'm going in the wrong direction and stop. The suffocation of my life strangling me loosens its hold and I start crying.

"Kara?"

Hayden stands in front of me.

I collapse against him and his familiarity. His arms catch me and wrap around my back. He holds me to him and my arms go around him. My sticky fingers touch his backpack and I want him to carry me away from here. He holds me for a few minutes and I try not to cry. But there's no use. I keep quiet, because I don't want him to know what happened.

Hayden's fingers are in my hair, stroking my head and reassuring me that I'm okay. I'm safe.

When he whispers into my ear, tingles cross every inch of me. "Kara, what the hell are you doing? You shouldn't be out here by yourself!"

The streetlight overhead offers enough light for me to see him, his baseball hat a little askew as he pulls away to look at me.

All I can do is stare at his mouth and his eyes and how he's here, protecting me, really saving me. This Hayden always asks for the broken, reject cookies I make because my baking reminds him of his grandma. This Hayden laughs at Ninja Cat videos and smiles at me from under the bill of his baseball cap because he knows it makes me blush.

I've crushed on him forever and I don't care about anything, or that he's too old for me. I know it shouldn't be that way, especially after what I saw in the Moon Bar, but then maybe he was drunk? He had to be drunk. Or maybe it wasn't really him at all. And even if it were, he wasn't being his real self. We've all done things we aren't proud of, right? I grab the collar of his coat anyway and scatter all the bad thoughts as I go on tiptoe to kiss him. My whole world is off kilter right now and I only mean to thank him, but his hands press me into him and our kiss goes on, deeper, and the frozen earth at my feet spins around us.

Hayden kisses me like he's done it forever, and he pushes me against the wall, kissing all the way down my neck. His fingers undo the top buttons of my coat and he opens it so he can kiss me lower on my neck.

No. This isn't the place. Someone might see. Charlie might see. But we're done so what does it matter anymore?

Charlie.

A small cry catches in my throat and tears rush to my eyes again. What is wrong with me? I pull away from Hayden.

"I'm sorry. I shouldn't have done that." I look down and rebutton my coat so I don't have to see his face, my fingers shaking.

He leans down and kisses me again. "Of course you should have."

"No, Hayden, I'm sorry," I say to his neck.

"Don't be sorry, Kara," he whispers. "I'm not sorry."

I feel bad, and I'm looking at his face now. "I'm really a mess. I'm sorry, okay? I can't do this."

"It's okay."

It's not okay. I'm horrible. "Can you walk me home? I'm afraid to go alone."

His hand brushes across my forehead. "No problem."

Every step back to the café is difficult, and I feel like the shittiest person I know, kissing Hayden when I really just want Charlie. I'm not that kind of person. I don't go around kissing whoever is convenient. I keep telling myself the situation wasn't normal.

As in: I don't walk around at night getting *attacked* by psychos.

The silence between us is thick and awkward. I catch Hayden's face in my periphery and I know he spends the entire walk to the café watching me. My guilt feels heavy and I'm putting my key into the lock before I can speak again. "I'm really sorry, Hayden. I shouldn't have kissed you. I'm sort of getting over someone."

He leans down so we're eye to eye. I take a step backward. "Like I said, I'm not sorry. And I know you're not that kind of girl. But I think you know I've had a thing for you for a while. You know, it's the reason your friend hates me so much."

I nod and try to swallow the sudden lump in my throat. No, actually, I didn't know he had a thing for me. What the hell? Why couldn't he have told me this a couple of months ago? I would've been his. And why didn't Noelle tell me she liked him? No wonder she's so nasty to him—he must've turned her down.

His eyes are soft and I've never seen him look at me this way. I bite my lip because I couldn't feel like a bigger bitch. Kellen did this kind of thing and she bragged about it, how fun it was to play guys, tease and torture them and wind them up and then shut them down with nothing. I don't understand how she could get a thrill out of being so insensitive.

"Hey, Westcott! You coming?" Some guy across the street calls out.

He grabs my shoulders and leans close to me. "When you

change your mind, Kara, I'm yours. Now get inside and take care, okay?" He kisses me quickly and jogs across the street.

I LIE IN BED shivering because I can't get warm enough. The cold may have a little to do with it but not a minute passes without me remembering the attack. I replay it in my mind, trying to figure out who the guy was. But I get nowhere so I start thinking about Charlie.

I love him.

I know it. I love him, and I pushed him away because I can't deal with my life. I can't deal with my stalker anymore either— he's dangerous, and I can't go another day without telling someone. I'd like to believe Noelle would understand and help me, but I'm not sure.

Charlie has to be the one I tell.

But what if he doesn't listen? What if he doesn't believe me? I barely believe me. It makes no sense. Since that summer, and since Kellen died, I've kept to myself for the most part, so I can't understand why anyone would be interested in me.

Charlie will help because he always does. Tomorrow I'll tell him everything and maybe he'll take me back. And maybe then he'll tell me the truth about what he's been hiding, too.

27. *Let it rest.*

. . . .

I rush through the courtyard to the Arts building. The wind blows so hard I wouldn't be able to hear anyone following me anyway. All day I've practiced what I'm going to say to Charlie when I see him. Mr. King has cut me some slack since I came home from the contest, letting me reorganize stuff and categorize his favorite recipes for future projects.

"I think you're being too hard on yourself, Kara," he said my first day back. "Second place in a *national* baking contest is nothing to feel bad about! Not to mention your thousand-dollar scholarship from Snowflake, although I think they could've given you more than that. Anyway, the school newspaper wants to interview you about the contest."

I appreciate his kindness, but he doesn't understand that for me, he's wrong. It doesn't matter—second place means nothing. There's no second place free ride. He doesn't understand why I can't talk about it.

Now I sit at his desk, pushing aside a can of Coke, a giant 7-Eleven coffee, and an unopened Red Bull. No wonder he practically flies around the room.

"Kara," he says, placing his hand on my shoulder. "Fetch the mail from the office for me?"

I nod and head for the door, not eager to go through the courtyard again. Or the empty halls. I can't see anyone watching so I run through the courtyard, expecting any moment to feel hands clawing at my back.

I make it in, and the hallway is long and empty.

Except for my sister.

Kellen moves down the hall as if she's a student, disappearing around the corner to the office. I run the rest of the way, looking for her, but when I get to the office, she's gone.

"Mr. King's mail," I tell the substitute secretary breathlessly. The office smells like an overheated copier and chicken soup heated in the microwave. My eyes dart around for a sign of my sister. The sub hands me the mail and when I turn around, I'm facing the big window that has the best view of the parking lot and of students like Mason and Noelle, who like to sneak off campus for lunch.

Someone walks through the parking lot, away from the school. A guy. But I can't see his face.

On his head he wears a dark beanie and a big puffy vest over some kind of flannel jacket.

I whirl around. "Excuse me, was that guy in here?" I point at his back, hoping she'll see him before he disappears behind cars.

"Oh yes, dear. He was just checking to make sure his brother made it to school. Apparently they had a fight last night and he was worried and wanted to make sure he was okay."

It takes a second for her words to register but I'm not sure why. They are leading me somewhere, but the thought vanishes before I can connect it. "Oh, so is his brother here today?"

"You know, it's funny because I thought he wanted to see him. Instead he just wanted me to check attendance. I thought that was odd because if he was worried about his brother then why didn't he ask me to call him down here so they could talk? Seems like the obvious thing to do."

"What's his name?"

"Oh shoot, I'm sorry, I'm just filling in today so I don't

remember. I probably shouldn't be telling you anyway, given all the privacy laws we have nowadays. I—"

"What was his brother's name?"

"Oh, dear, I don't remember that either. I do know that he's been in before. Just last week I filled in for Suzy and that nice young man was bringing his brother's lunch. So sweet."

I watch her, hoping she'll give me something, but instead she grabs the clipboard off the counter and stares at it.

"Oh damn, and look how I forgot to have him sign in. Shoot! Well, that's just our little secret okay, hon? I could get into trouble for that."

I stare at her kind face, which is turning red now.

AN HOUR LATER I'M still thinking about it, trying to figure out who the guy was, while I wait for Charlie to arrive for his shift.

I feel a weird kind of excitement about the relief I'll feel sharing everything with someone after all these months. Telling someone has to make it better. It's not like I expect the notes to stop just because I tell someone, but I won't have to go through it alone anymore. And hopefully I can convince Charlie not to say a word about it to Mom—or anyone else.

Charlie rushes in the front door, his apron tossed over his shoulder. I try to catch his eye but he looks straight ahead without acknowledging me.

My heart squeezes in on itself for a second. This won't be easy. I'm glad Jessica's not here, but I better do it quick. I'm heading for the kitchen door when he comes back out.

"Hey," he says.

The words I intend don't come out. Nothing comes out.

"I asked your mom if we could go for a little walk before my shift starts."

"Okay," I say. Well, that was easy.

Charlie walks to the door and I follow. When we're out on the sidewalk, his arm brushes mine.

The sky, whitish and heavy, looks like snow might fall. The wind brushes damp and frigid across my face. We walk past a row of tiny boutiques—wine, organic crap, and yarn. My old closet is bigger than any of these shops. The sidewalks are crowded and two people bump me while I wait for Charlie to speak first. I can't help but remember last night. As if I'll forget it anytime soon.

"Listen, Kara, I know I haven't been straight with you. I've kept a few things from my past private." He pauses. "I know you followed me home last night."

I freeze. My whole body feels on fire with the embarrassment of being caught.

"You need to work on those ninja skills," he continues, but his voice is soft and forgiving. "When I came out of Crockett's, I saw you . . . and I saw you again outside the window. Sorry, I know that's kind of creepy, but I didn't know what else to do, since we haven't really been talking much these days."

Now I want to die. I keep quiet and let him talk.

"I'm sure you have questions?"

I nod.

Charlie jaywalks across the street and I follow him to the church. My face flushes as I follow him through the same door I entered on my spy mission. We walk down the stairs toward the source of light I saw last night. It all happens so fast, I feel as if I'm in a dream, as if time can shrink and expand like a sponge. The hallway outside is decorated with paper crosses obviously made by children.

Charlie opens a door a ways down the hall, the room where I peeped in on him.

"Are you becoming a priest?"

He chuckles. "No way."

I stand in the doorway, watching him turn on the lamp and sit on his cot. He pats the space next to him. I figure I've come this far, so I might as well. For a minute we sit in silence together.

"Father Bill keeps asking if God is speaking to me, whether

I have a vocation. I haven't told him there's this baker I know, and I like her a little too much." He bumps my knee with his.

I could cry. Maybe my plan will work after all.

"Okay, here's the thing. My mom died in an accident, hiking with my dad."

I think of her again at school, always helping, or offering me another cupcake when mine fell on the floor. "I'm sorry, Charlie," I whisper. "I didn't know."

Charlie looks down for a moment. "Yeah, no one did. I'm not sure if you remember when I left school. It was right before summer vacation. Mom and Dad went with friends to that cabin on Lake Chelan for the long weekend. I went camping with Cal's family so I wasn't there. Dad said she tripped on a root and fell down into a ravine.

"Two days later, Dad came home with a motor home and he said I had an hour to pack only what was truly important. Then we were on I-5, headed south to California. We camped in different places and eventually settled in a trailer park outside of Monterey.

"We were okay for a while and then Dad started acting weird, not himself. I figured it was because of losing Mom. Then one day he took off. Left me a little money and a note on the table, saying he had to go.

"I didn't know what to do, I don't have relatives close to me and I didn't want to end up living with some weird aunt so I took the Greyhound back here and came right to Father Bill. He arranged for me to go to Kennedy, and now I live in the church basement for as long as I want. I have no idea where my dad is. So I guess I'm kind of an orphan."

He scrunches his eyes and sort of massages his forehead. I feel stupid, not knowing how to help him, how to ease his pain and confusion.

"Now you know all my secrets," he says. He smiles and I'm relieved for it. "And, Kara, I know it's hard, but I want you to remember how we were in San Francisco. I'll be here waiting for you when you're ready."

I nod and my eyes are closed, threatening tears. I swallow it back, stuffing it in because I can't tell him about my problems right now.

He has to get back to work. It can wait till after his shift when we've got more time.

NINE-YEAR-OLD CARROT

My sister is crying.

I look up at her window before I get into the car to head off to the lake cabin with Jen's family. Kellen's grounded because she got caught kissing a boy at school. Well, she didn't exactly get caught. Gaby's sister told Gaby, who told me. I sat on the information for half a day until Kellen called me a baby for crying over my broken goggles, even though I used all my allowance for them. And now she's in big trouble because I told Mom.

She's crying and her hand is pressed to the glass.

She hugged me before I left, telling me she's worried I might drown in the lake and she won't be there to rescue me.

My sister is crying because she's worried about me.

She stops enough to fog up the window with her breath and then draws a heart.

Mom said Kellen knows that I'm the one who told on her.

28. *Put it on the rack.*

· ·

The café is empty and since I have no customers I decide to run upstairs to grab my history book to study. But when I get to the top step I freeze.

A blue-gray envelope with droplets of purple and bloody red fibers is lying there.

I manage to get downstairs when I hear the bell above the door jingle. Somehow I am able to make lattes for a group of college kids. Afterwards I sink down to the cold floor by the cash register while I open the envelope. If anyone asked, I wouldn't be able to offer a single detail of how I did it. Sort of like how I take the bus home from school some days and don't really know how I made it home because I can't remember a single detail of the trip.

My knuckles are white and I try not to shake while I read the words over and over. It's like I'm seeing them but not really and maybe if I read them again, they'll change, disappear and this won't exist. The college crowd laughs, outside the Metro thunders by, and I smell coffee grounds and bleach. My left hand presses into the dirty crumbs and bits on the floor, while the other holds the note so I can read it again.

> Do you know where I watch you?
> You're just a fuckin' baby, Kara.
> What will you cross off my list?

29. *Drizzle before it hardens.*

. . . .

Everything is slow motion when I turn toward the kitchen. My feet slog across a floor that sticks and pulls and tries to suck me into it, and I can barely get my body through the swinging door. There's only one person who could write this note.

But it can't be.

Charlie's filling the sink with water and bleach, and he turns with a towel clenched in his fists. Raising it over his head, he smiles and pulls it tight like he's doing some sort of stretch.

The smile fades and he shakes his head, looking puzzled. "Sprinkles?"

I can't speak. Charlie steps closer to me and I step backward.

"Kara, what's wrong?" he asks, grabbing my wrist, pressing his thumb into my veins and it hurts. He spins me around and grabs my waist with the other hand while he leans down into my face. "What is it?"

"Oh!" Mom appears out of nowhere, grinning and slapping her hands together. "Patched up have we? Oh thank you, Jesus!" Charlie's thumb pinches my wrist even more. Mom's face turns serious. "But very soon I *will* sit down and have a *serious* talk with the two of you about sexual boundaries. Not today, I have too damn many errands to run."

"Okay," Charlie stares at me now that Mom is gone. He blinks hard. "*What* is going on?"

It can't be him.

He can't be back.

Nick.

My mouth hangs open, my tongue touching the inside of my top teeth, but I can't say his name out loud. The words I want to say to Charlie are stuck there, and I can't speak or swallow.

Mom comes back out of her office and I don't want her to see my face, so I shake off Charlie's hands and rush for the apartment.

I'VE LAIN IN BED for an hour, staring at the ceiling. For the first twenty minutes Charlie called or texted every other minute. I shut the phone off because I don't know what to do, so how can I talk to anyone? Charlie knows my secret so I know I should tell him. But he's still working right now so I have to wait. Or maybe I should call the police?

But then I'd have to tell them what happened back then, and Mom would find out, and I'd have to tell her that Kellen did nothing about it. And she's happy now, she doesn't need that. She doesn't need to know about this. The only person I should tell is Charlie.

When I flop over on my side, there's Kellen, sitting on the edge of the windowsill.

She kicks her legs back and forth while she stares at me.

Her face usually looks the same and she rarely moves a muscle of it. But there's a difference today. A glimmer in her eye, and I hate it.

I stare hard and blink harder, like maybe I can blink her away. But she's still there.

"Do you even know how much you hurt me?" I whisper. "Do you know that *you* hurt me more than he did? By turning your back on me, abandoning me? If you were the kind of sister I needed then you'd know that your thirteen-year-old little sister had never dated or even been kissed. You'd know that she didn't even know how to kiss a boy, let alone seduce one who was four years older."

Kellen stares in the direction of my closet, like she's done before. I'm ready to break something, a window maybe.

"*Look* at me you dumb, dead bitch!"

She can't hear me. Or if she can, she chooses not to. She just eyes the closet.

"He practically raped me, Kellen, and you did nothing. And then you have to go ahead and be so stupid and die? You poison yourself with so many drinks that you end up drowning? How could you do that to Mom? You are the most selfish person I've ever known, Kellen."

She stares hard in the direction of the closet, and I wonder if she hears me at all. "Yeah, I know about your pot, I smoked it. Your stuff is mine now and I think I'll have a good-riddance bonfire with it. I'll let the ashes sink down into your grave and cover your bony, rotting face. Good-bye and good riddance to you forever."

I throw my fake Ugg boot at her, but she's already vanished.

I turn to the closet.

ELEVEN-YEAR-OLD CARROT

These mean girls from school keep walking by my house on their way home. They stop and point up at my window and laugh. I try not to peek, but it's hard not to and every time I do they somehow always see me. So embarrassing. I hate them.

Gaby and I had a fight and then she blabbed my big secret about starting my period. These girls that laugh at me found out somehow, and every day for the past week they've stopped in front of my house. I don't know what's so frickin' funny about starting your period. I'm eleven—that's not too early to get it, right? I hate them laughing at me. Last night I cried myself to sleep about it. I hate them.

I get off the bus fast so I can get into the house and pull down the blinds before they pass. But today I stop as soon as I get to our walkway.

There are signs on the windows, and I stare in confusion until I hear something above me in the tree. Kellen hisses at me from above, on the tree branch. She is sixteen and so bossy all the time. I'm really sick of her these days.

"Carrot, get in the house right now."

I stare up at her. She's holding a tampon by the string—without its shell—in one hand and a big can in the other. A big pink tampon box sits next to her on the branch. My sister's shelling tampons, and the shells are all around the tree, a couple of them rolling with the breeze. She whispers again and her face means serious business. "Carrot, go, run into the house, NOW!"

So I do. I run all the way to my room and peek out my window at my sister in the tree and not long after, I see those two horrible girls. They giggle and stop in front of my house like they have every day, laughing and pointing. But they quickly stop because they see the signs across the windows.

The smiles fall from their dumb faces as they read the posters taped there:

WHAT

IS

SO

FUNNY?

DID YOU SEE

YOUR REFLECTION

IN MY WINDOW

YOU UGLY BITCHES?

The girls look at each other, confused.

Things fall from the tree.

The girls jump, moving and batting at their shoulders and heads because things are falling on them and they are screaming. Tampons, bright red and dripping from whatever Kellen is dunking them in, are dropping from the tree branch. Falling on their heads, shoulders, feet and splattering and rolling all over the ground, and I see one, sliding down the back of the meanest girl, leaving a bloody red trail on her pretty pink coat. This makes me giggle.

The girls stand there because they are too dumb to get out of the way. They scream and look up and one gets a red, gushy tampon in the face. Then suddenly, Kellen drops from the tree and they start running and she runs after them, pelting them with bloody tampons.

Kellen runs into the house soon after and we laugh together

for an hour. But the parents of one of the girls end up threatening to call the cops on my sister. So for all this Kellen gets her car keys taken away for a month and Mom won't let her go to the junior prom.

30. *Knead and work it thoroughly.*

. . . .

After dragging the big box out of the closet, I sit down and trace the words *Kellen's stuff* with my finger.

The rest of my sister's boxes are in storage, but these were her college things, still warm with Kellen's life, waiting for her to come back. Mom refused to look at this box. Kellen's roommate literally shoved everything in there, including a half-empty package of Oreos and an unopened can of Red Bull.

What a fucking idiot. What kind of person thinks a grieving family needs stuff like that?

I pull the giant box between my legs and sift through it. The last time I did this I found her diary and the tampon box of weed. I'm hoping for more weed. I really need it right now.

I pull out Kellen's toiletry bag. I remember admiring it on the kitchen table after Kellen and Mom went dorm shopping. It contains her makeup, toothbrush, toothpaste, and her birth control pills.

I snap open a case of eye shadow. The dark colors are worn down, showing the mirrored pan underneath, and I wonder about the last thing my sister saw before she died. I wonder if this eye shadow was on her dead eyelids. The case goes back into the bag.

My hand plunges back into the box. This time I pull out a Washington State University pom-pom on a long stick. Something sharp pokes into my palm, startling me, and I feel some velvety fabric. It's a drawstring bag.

Knitting needles. Ten rows of loops are attached to one needle, leading to a big ball of lime green yarn. She took up knitting. Weird.

The official police report stated that Kellen went with friends to a Halloween party and that she started drinking as soon as she got in the car. Some concoction in a huge water bottle that a friend of a friend made up for her.

Once at the party, her friends lost track of her after she hooked up with some guy. A good guy. A trustworthy one she knew, everyone said so. Her friends left her at the party and drove back to campus because they couldn't find her.

No one could find her.

But the next morning someone did find her. In the pool. She had hit her head and drowned. And the police say if she hadn't been high, or drunk, she might not have fallen.

I know what the report said because Mom made me read it when she started talking again. She wanted it to be a warning to me so I didn't end up like Kellen.

More items come out of the box: Kellen's iPod, a small alarm clock, greeting cards from Dad telling her he loved her and missed her and to stay out of trouble. There were some boxes of Tic Tacs, some socks, some cash—not much—a few pens and chewed pencils, some flash drives, actual tampons, gum, hair scrunchies, black glittery nail polish, a calculator, and a half-burnt vanilla candle. There's a pocketknife, too. Hot pink. Weird. I put it back in the box but then change my mind and toss it onto my bed.

The bottom of the box stares up at me without any weed. Only her coffee travel cup and some more toiletries.

Her friends from home had decorated the cup for her before she went away. All of the pictures show Kellen and her skanky best girlfriends holding red Solo cups.

I unscrew the lid, betting on smelling some putrid trace of the hazelnut lattes she loved.

But when I peek into the cup I see a big wad of rolled-up paper. I sniff into them just to be sure, before I try dumping the whole lot onto the floor. They won't budge so I stick my finger into the middle of the wad to try and pry them apart. Slowly the bundle comes out, exploding onto the floor. It's a bunch of envelopes.

The thick paper feels rough in my fingers. They don't start shaking until my brain registers the familiarity of what I'm seeing.

The first thing I notice is the K on Kellen's name, written with the monstrous K that looks as if it's trying to eat the rest of her name.

The way the *K*s in my name are written.

On the notes from my stalker.

I hold an envelope out in front of me and pull the paper from it.

GIRLS WHO TEASE SHOULD NEVER WALK ALONE AT NIGHT.

A note for Kellen?

I'm on my feet too fast and the room tilts and swings as I run to the bathroom. My hip bangs into the corner of my dresser, but I make it to the toilet in time.

After I clean up I carry a glass of water back to my room. I want to close my eyes and lie down but I need to keep reading.

I race through each note, all on the same thick, buttercream paper. I read each one, and then pick them up and read them again. Every note looks just like my notes.

WHO WILL HEAR YOU WHEN YOU SCREAM?
DO YOU KNOW WHERE I HIDE?
I'M GOING TO TAKE YOU.
I DREAM OF YOUR BLOOD ON MY HANDS.
DID YOU FEEL MY FINGERS IN YOUR HAIR
WHEN I WATCHED YOU SLEEP LAST NIGHT?

I WILL MAKE YOU SUFFER.
I STILL SMELL YOUR SKIN.
SOON YOU WILL KNOW MY FACE.
SOON YOU WILL DIE.

My heart pounds in my ears and I feel like I'm underwater.

I want my sister back to tell me about the notes—and when and where she got them. Obviously they came from school. The whole box came from school.

Her diary. Where did I put the diary? I tossed it somewhere, too grossed out over her detailed sex life to read it.

I've never wanted my sister to visit me so badly, to show me the way.

I don't know what to do.

I sit with her box of stuff and stare at the pile of notes and envelopes, and I have no idea what to do about it, or what it all means.

She got notes like I'm getting.

I reach into my backpack finding my last note. I start comparing Kellen's notes to mine. I don't need to do this to know it's the same writer but what else can I do? Up on my knees, I start rummaging through my room to look for Kellen's diary.

My suitcase from California sits on the floor next to my bed, gathering dust. I slide it over and look under my bed. Nothing but masses of dust bunnies. I check the closet, and when I'm almost done there, I remember where I put the diary.

My dresser in the tiny hallway. I dig into the back of each drawer until my hand touches the smooth, hard surface of the faux alligator cover.

I never wanted Mom to see any of this. My sister chronicled her sex life with every guy she ever dated. I already read enough the first time so I scan the entries. They are long in the first half of the diary and the second half gets shorter. I search through for key words.

It doesn't take long to find what I'm looking for.

31. *Fold it all together.*

. . . .

Dear Diary—
Two this week and they are scaring the shit out of me.

I've had the whole night to read and think about Kellen's diary. Mr. King attends to a burnt pie on the opposite side of the classroom as I sit at his desk reading the diary again because he's giving me this last day to get over my contest depression and get back to work.

This entry was dated two weeks before she died.

All day, I felt like someone was following me to my classes. I still
don't know who the creep is.

The next one was written a few days later.

I called Mom today. She was supposed to call me back but forgot
I guess. I don't know what to do.

Before I read her last entry I scan back through the earlier pages, trying to catch a glimpse of what she was going through. I stop on one written at the end of September.

I can't believe I gave that D bag 3 nights I can't get back. We're
so done. He's creeping me out. I woke up this morning with him

staring at me. It really freaked me out. I know we did it but I was
high so I barely remember. Not ever again! He was so sweet before
and now he's a psycho. I think he's obsessed or something. Met a
junior on the quad today. Baseball player. Super hot. We're going
out Friday.

He's finally leaving me alone. I haven't heard from him in
two weeks, it's a miracle. We still have math together but I can
manage to stay out of his path. I really like the baseball player. I
started calling him The Cup, for many reasons. Deets later. I'm
too hungover to write more.

The Cup is really growing on me. I think I may keep him. I
may finally be in love. I got a weird secret admirer note today. My
math prof said someone left it on his desk. Weird.

The rest of the entries detailed her dates with The Cup and
listed the notes she received.

Her last entry was written the day before she died.

Today I got the worst one. He all but promised to kill me.
I've hidden all the notes and on Monday I'm going to talk to
campus police. I feel relieved just knowing I'll take care of it
soon. I called home and Kara hung up on me. I'll keep trying.
I dialed Mom's cell but then changed my mind. I don't want
her to worry. Maybe after I talk to the cops. I found something
today and I think I know who it is. His ass is so done when I
talk to the police.

Tonight is the Halloween party in Moscow. It'll be good to get
away from here, from the notes, from him. I need to get wasted and
forget everything for a while.

I close the diary. I feel bad for hanging up on her. I always hung
up on her. I wonder if she died the way the police said. I wonder
if I hadn't hung up on her if things would be different.

How could Nick have had anything to do with Kellen when

she was away on the other side of the state? He was supposed to be going to school in Arizona.

Maybe he didn't go to school in Arizona. Maybe he followed my sister and stalked her and wrote all the notes because she dumped him. But I remember hearing Kellen on the phone before she left for college: she said Nick got over her quickly because he already had a new girlfriend.

What is going on? I don't know what to think of it all.

"Kara." Mr. King smiles down at me. "Mail, please?"

I muster a half-smile while I stuff the diary into my bag. When I step out into the hallway, he's there, lingering outside my class.

Noah Bender. He's weird, no matter how much Noelle tells me he's just nice and quiet. I don't have time for weird right now.

"Look, Noah, I know we haven't talked to each other a lot before, but it seems that I always catch you hanging around. If you have something to say, spit it out. What do you want?" I feel a tad bitchy for how it comes out, especially because I've caught him with his mouth hung open.

When he shuffles his feet, I spot his right hand tucked close to his thigh. He's holding his hand in an odd way—flat—fingers together and two corners of paper stick out.

"Hey," he says before he nods at the door. "King in there?"

I keep staring at him and notice that his eyes won't meet mine now that I've seen the paper in his hand. Briefly, he glances at me, and then the floor when his right hand moves behind his back, to hide the paper from me.

When I gasp, I can hear the catch in my throat. Noah dropped it on the floor behind his feet.

It's not just any old paper.

Purple droplets and bloody red fibers.

My eyes feel dry and my breath comes out loud and shaky. "If you move I'll scream, Noah," I say, sounding calmer than I feel.

He swallows. I see the pulsing tendon in his neck.

His face turns to chalk.

"Kara, I'm sorry. He—"

"Give it to me!"

He nods fast and his breath rushes out, as shaky as mine. He bends even faster to pick it up and his hands are trembling.

"Why do you have that, Noah? It's for me, isn't it?" My legs are wobbly. I need my legs. I may need to run because I know I won't be able to scream.

He clutches the note. "Kara, I'm sorry. He *paid* me. I needed money, to pay for a speeding ticket. I couldn't tell my folks! I'm sorry!"

He paid me.

The dirty, scuffed floor in front of me draws closer, giving me the feeling of it rising and me falling backwards. I close my eyes and inhale so I don't fall down. "Who paid you? For what?"

"Look, I know it's a shitty thing, me spying on you at school and reporting to him. Leaving these for you." He waves the note. "But he paid me, I had to do it."

"*Who* paid you? Who is he? Oh my God, Noah, who?" I need him to *say* it.

"I, I don't know who he is. I only saw him once. He said no one would be hurt. He said they were just love notes for you and he was shy. I mean, if I knew who he was, I'd tell you. I didn't recognize him. He wore a hat and sunglasses that one time. He leaves me all the instructions and the notes here at school and online."

The door swings open and Mr. King pokes his head out, smiling. "Hey kids. Everything okay? Kara, did you get my mail?"

"Uh," I reply. "No, I, uh, felt sick and Noah here was looking for a garbage can for me to be sick in." I look at Noah and hope that Mr. King doesn't notice how pale and sweaty he is.

"Uh-oh, sounds like you better get to the office, maybe have them check your temperature. Let me grab your backpack just in case you end up going home."

I stare at Noah's colorless face while I wait for Mr. King to come back.

"There you go, Kara. Young man, maybe you can walk Kara to the office? Make sure she doesn't get sick?"

"Uh, sure."

We walk slowly down the hall, and I speak first. "So you don't know who he is?"

"No, I swear it, Kara! I don't even know what he looks like except that he's taller than me. I only met him the one time and I haven't seen him since. He uh, he brings me the notes here, in lunch bags, and I deliver them wherever he tells me."

"You went into my apartment, Noah, my bedroom!" I hiss.

"No! I never did that, Kara—"

"*Shh,* lower your voice okay? I don't need anyone hearing this."

He nods his head and backs up against the wall. "Kara," he starts, his voice a loud whisper, "I swear! I never went in your house! The other notes, yeah, but not in your *house.*"

I stand next to him, my back against the wall, too so I can watch out for people who might walk by. "You swear you don't know him?"

"I swear it! I'm always looking for him here, you know? It's freaked me out thinking he could turn on me, turn me in for doing this to you, for practically stalking you!"

I can't believe this.

"I'm sorry, Kara. I won't do it anymore, okay? I'm done! I'm supposed to get another delivery today, and I'll go and try to meet him and tell him I'm finished!"

We're halfway to the office when he turns and offers me the envelope. "Look, I better get to class. Do you want me to do something? Tell someone?"

I shake my head, taking the note.

"Kara, I'm so sorry. I didn't mean to scare you, really. I just figured they were love notes, like he said. But your face—obviously something else is going on. I'm, I'm so sorry." He pivots and walks fast down the hall.

I watch him, unable to speak.

Instead of going to the office I duck out the side door and down the path through a small cluster of evergreens where the smokers hide out. Since we're halfway through sixth period the place reeks already, but the smokers ignore me as I scramble down the hill. The Metro rounds the corner when I cross through a gap in the fence. I hop on the bus and get off at my old house.

Someone's home today. And it's daylight so I can't very well sneak back to the trampoline or even sit under my favorite tree, still naked with winter.

But as I turn to go I see Kellen.

My sister stares out at me from her bedroom.

She's seventeen and I'm sixteen. She's not wearing the brown and pink monkey pants, but instead wears the sundress she wore on the night she left me at the pizza place.

My sister was stalked.

Maybe my sister didn't just drown in a pool.

The envelope from Noah rests on top of dirty tufts of moss beside me. I hadn't even noticed that I'd dropped it. When I look back to the window, Kellen's gone.

The wind rustles frozen leaves as I pluck the envelope from the ground and tear it open.

YOU BELONG TO ME. I'M COMING FOR YOU.

32. *Watch carefully.*

· ·

Where do I start?

When I make it to the Ave I sit down on a bench and stare at the police station down the street. I don't know what to do. I don't want my mom to find out. Mom is over Kellen's death. Why make her remember and suffer even more?

I hear sirens. A lot of sirens, off in the distance. Taking it as a sign, I decide to walk home. Snow flurries about, landing wherever the wind drops it. Maybe I could stop by Crockett's and tell Justine, or at least tell her what I found out about Kellen. But the explanation would require a lot longer than her ten minute smoke break. Besides, Justine has her own problems— she doesn't need to worry about mine.

When I get to the café I peek in the window for Charlie. I want so badly to see him, but I can't face him right now, not with how I've treated him yet again. I'll figure things out tomorrow. Maybe I'll try to talk to Noah again, see if I can get more information because my list of questions grew the minute he left me.

Tomorrow.

I'll tell Noelle and maybe she could take me to the cops, and they could start looking for Nick.

No. I can't! If the cops are involved, Mom will find out for sure. God, Mom doesn't even know what Nick did to me. I can't let her find out *that* and now *this*, too.

I peek inside the café again. Mom has a handful of customers finishing up. She sits across the table from a woman, and I recognize her as the lady Mom introduced me to a few months ago—she used to run the bake sales at Mom's church. Her husband died last year, so she won't bake anymore because he isn't there to steal bites of cookie dough when she isn't looking, Mom said. And she comes to the café for dinner because her husband isn't there to tell her that her fried chicken is the best on earth.

Mom leaves the woman and goes to sit with a father and daughter who come in at least once a week. The man is young, mid-twenties maybe. His eyes droop and have dark circles like those of someone older and so tired and burdened. His daughter looks about four and behaves as if she's older, too.

The dad rests his forehead in his hand and now I remember— Mom told me his wife died a couple of months ago.

Mom sits next to the little girl whose hair is pulled back into the sloppy ponytail that could only be done by the hands of a little girl or a daddy—strands bulge out, making the top of her head lumpy. Loose pieces of hair hang over earlobes where too-big earrings dangle.

Too-big earrings. Grown-up-girl earrings.

A mommy's earrings.

She uses her fork to roll a meatball around on her plate before using her fingers to bury the meatball with strings of spaghetti. Her fingers get wiped off on her shirt, and her dad doesn't see but Mom offers a napkin. Then she pops up and rushes back to the kitchen, returning a minute later with a plate with one of my flower cookies from the freezer, setting the plate just out of reach. The little girl unburies that meatball and stuffs the whole thing into her mouth.

Mom moves the cookie plate closer, kisses the little girl's cheek, and squeezes her dad's shoulder.

My mom loves these people.

They are like family. And this is what she does with her

family—she feeds them dinner, and asks them about their new project at work, and if they passed their math test, and if they're speaking to their best friend anymore. She asks them about the best part of their day, and she bribes them with dessert so they'll finish dinner. She rubs their backs when they are tired and offers a tissue when their hearts can't take it anymore.

She does this because she doesn't have her own whole family—me and Dad and Kellen—all together to feed anymore.

My mom is happy and I won't ruin it for her. I won't ever tell her about the notes or Nick. I've gone this long; I can figure the rest out on my own.

When Mom disappears into the kitchen, I sneak up to the apartment. To clear my head I soak in a bubble bath until I prune and the water's tepid. I toss a frozen burrito into the microwave and get into my pajamas. After two bites of burrito I throw it away and brush my teeth. I'm tired and need the crazy thoughts out of my head so I steal my laptop from Mom's room and climb into bed with it and a DVD.

"Sweetheart?"

"Yeah, Mom?" I feel a little bad about not getting up to open the door but I'm too tired.

"Café's closed up early and I'm off to Bible study," she says. But the floor makes no noise so I know she's still standing there.

Half a minute passes.

"I love you, Kara."

"I love you too, Mom."

The floor creaks and when I can't hear her anymore I turn the movie back up.

My cell buzzes with a text and I see that Noelle's called me five times in the last half hour. She calls again.

"God, Kar! Where were you? Didn't you hear what happened?"

I sit up, fully alert. "No."

"Noah Bender, Kar. Someone beat him up in the parking lot.

That's why we had the lockdown. Can you believe it, the last five fucking minutes of school and we have a lockdown. Shit, where were you? I texted you! We were going crazy, hearing the sirens and wondering what the hell was going on."

I can't even get a word out before she speaks again.

"Noah's in the hospital and a bunch of us are going there, to see how he's doing. Mason and I will pick you up in like forty-five, 'kay?"

"Did they catch the guy who beat him up?" I ask.

"I don't know, the cops were there and people with cars couldn't leave. Listen, I gotta go. Be ready!"

"It's like the middle of the night, Noelle."

"What? It's only seven o'clock!"

She hangs up before I can say anything.

I WAIT DOWNSTAIRS. THE cafe rests, quiet and bundled up for the night. Chairs stand on tables and the floor has been swept and mopped with a chalky-smelling solution Raul always uses. The espresso machine is turned off and since it takes too long to prepare I go into the kitchen to grab a Coke from my stash inside the walk-in fridge.

Noah lies in a hospital bed and it strikes me that I might be the reason. I can't think of a single person who has ever been hurt because of me. Even though he delivered all the notes, he didn't know his actions hurt me. I think of him peeking at me at school and how at first I thought he just wanted to ask me out. I think of how he shook, and how the color disappeared from his face when I caught him.

And now he could be dying in a hospital.

The fridge drones and clicks and I'm taking my first sip when I hear something out in the dining area. My first thought is that Mom's home from Bible study, but I know it's too early. I set my Coke down on the stainless steel prep counter. For a minute I'm still, and I listen, but all I hear is the Coke bubbling and reacting inside my body. I tread lightly to the swinging door, opening it just a crack before I walk through.

Only the front counter section is lit. Inverted chairs are black shadows, all corners and edges against the radiance of street lamps outside. This makes the dining area unfamiliar, and I have to focus to orient myself. Out in the front of the shop, people stroll by laughing and talking. A couple passes by, walking their dog in the frozen night.

I'm jumpy and skittish and I know my mind is playing tricks on me. The sounds I've heard must've come from outside—there are still lots of people around.

Making my way back into the kitchen, I stop behind the counter because I hear it again. When I turn around, lights scroll along the far wall of the café, casting shadows because of the bus thundering by.

But the night silences itself enough for me to hear more sounds coming from inside. There shouldn't be anyone here but me, and this realization keeps me locked in place and I don't know what I should do. The door leading upstairs stands open just a crack.

Each step of the worn staircase up to the apartment has its own sound.

So I know by the familiar creak I'm hearing now that someone treads on the last stair before they enter my apartment.

There's silence now and I hear nothing but my pounding heart. Then, above me, I hear the slow thump of footsteps, and the groaning pop of the old oak floor. Kellen flashes across my vision and is gone before I blink. I make my way to the stairs and slowly climb them. By the time I've reached the last step, my skin crawls with goose bumps and everything inside of me loosens. Any second I might be sick. I climb over that last step so I don't make more noise and enter the apartment.

Once I'm inside I regret it. I should've called the cops, even though nothing looks out of place and I can't see anyone. The apartment stinks of the burrito I tossed into the little trash bin. I creep along the wall, past the tiny kitchen, and into the hallway. Every other step I stop and listen and hear only my breath, my heartbeat, like I'm underwater. I make my way past the dresser in the hallway and into my room. Everything appears to be the way I left it.

A *thud* comes from my mom's room next door.

Kellen's pink pocketknife and Justine's pepper spray sit on my nightstand. I hope I never get close enough to use the knife so I grab the pepper spray and tiptoe out of the room. Mom's door is open and something moves in there. With my arm outstretched and my finger on the trigger I push the door open quickly. But there's no one there; only magazine pages fluttering from the wind coming through the open window.

I drop the spray on Mom's bed and rush to the window to see if anyone climbed out. Mom leaves her window open sometimes even in the winter and I always yell at her because we live in the city. I stick my head out even though I know no one's there. They'd need the hospital if they jumped, and only an incredibly agile person could make it to the tree outside.

I close the window on the night. Safety is mere feet away, really. I think about opening the window again and yelling for help, but I'd feel dumb if it ended up being nothing. I'd have a lot of explaining to do. Most likely I'd be ignored.

Suddenly I hear the floor creak in the hallway.

I squat down and hide behind Mom's bed and my mind betrays me, making me think of the words he's written for me and Kellen.

. . . *watch you.*

. . . *your blood . . .*

. . . *make you suffer.*

. . . *ways to kill you.*

. . . *coming for you.*

My heart hammers. The creaking and popping has moved to the living room. I wait on the floor by Mom's bed trying to stop shaking so I can figure out how to get to my phone downstairs. I know I left it on the counter by my Coke.

I don't hear anything more, so I stand up. My legs are unsteady as I walk back out to the living room. It's empty. I stop at the top of the stairs and listen but only silence comes from below.

My hands clutch the banister as I make one foot and then the other move down the stairs. At the bottom I hold my breath and try to see my phone, but my view is blocked by the cash register. I wait, hearing nothing but the evening sounds outside. I rush to the counter. My Coke's still there, but not my phone.

I'm about to go check the kitchen when a movement against the wall makes me stop.

The street lamp's glow reaches that wall, so there's enough light for me to see the black form rising out of the dark booth. My pulse starts to throb in my wrists and ears.

I recognize the shape of him before the light touches his face. He moves slowly toward the counter and my shoes are frozen, stuck to the floor.

The counter separates us. I'm not sure how he even got in here since Mom should've locked the door on her way out. I let out a half-relieved sigh, even though the fact that he hid in the dark, not showing himself earlier, is not lost on me.

"What are you doing here?" I ask him. "We're closed."

"Your mom let me stay here to wait for you. I brought you that recipe for baklava. Remember? I told you I'd bring it?" Hayden pushes the recipe toward me.

Mom left hours ago. Hayden smells of sweat and wood smoke and the outdoors. His cheeks look pinched from the cold.

"Hayden, were you . . . upstairs? In my apartment just now?"

The answer to my question is in his eyes, so I don't wait for him to confirm it. "It's kind of late. You could've brought the recipe by tomorrow. Or—" I stop because now I *see* what is on the paper.

He's printed it off the computer and written my name at the top.

KARA, HERE IS . . .

"I was going to leave this on the counter for you," Hayden replies. "That's why I started leaving you a message there at the top."

Kara

Kara

"I should go. I have a lot of studying," he continues.

My hand rests on top of the paper and I see how my fingers lift and tremble before I feel anything else in my body. His hand is on the paper, too, an inch from mine.

It's the *K*.

The same monstrous K, trying to eat the rest of my name.

Like the notes for Kellen.

Like the notes for me.

I look up at Hayden's face. He's unnaturally calm, and his eyes are fixed on mine from under lowered lashes. His face answers a question I haven't yet asked.

"Hayden, what did you do to Noah Bender?"

He is still, offering nothing.

My insides shake, and I try as hard as I can to keep my fear from showing on the outside. I don't have to speak because he fills the silence.

"You look so much like her."

His eyes flicker with a glint of something I haven't seen in him before. At the same time, our eyes go to our hands, so close together. I pull mine away fast but he's faster, grabbing my wrist. I'm able to wrench it free but Hayden hops over the counter, backing me up against the wall next to the kitchen door.

His arms cage me to the wall, like when I let him kiss me the other night. He hunches over, his face in my face. My fingertips scrabble along the wall, hoping to dig up a hole or something I can escape into.

"When I saw your picture, right there in her room . . ." He takes one hand off the wall to run it down the side of my head and face. His hand is icy from the winter night. I'm frozen and I can't swallow. "I had to have you, too, Kara. That night, after I followed her to the Halloween party, I tried to talk to her, to get her away from her friends. We sat outside and I kept giving her more drinks, and more pot."

He smiles into my face, and his mouth is twisted, like when I saw him that night at the Moon Bar with that poor girl. "God, it feels good to let someone in on my little secret. Secrets are hard to keep. You know a little something about that, now don't you, *Carrot?* Your sister talked about you all the time, when we were together. She told me about how she had done that horrible thing to you. How she pretended it didn't happen. She just kept rambling about you and being sorry and wishing she had done something but that too much time had passed and it was too late. She was stoned, but I believed her."

My arms are bruising where he pins me against the wall but I cannot speak. I'm trying hard not to let it show how scared I am; if I let him keep talking and confessing maybe I'll make it out of here in one piece.

"That night at the party, I was going to give Kellen another chance. I knew she had it in her, somewhere, to be the girl I thought she was. When she wasn't putting on the act she gave everyone else. But then Kellen went right back to it—started telling me about her new boyfriend. I couldn't have that. Kellen belonged to me. Just like you do. As soon as she was gone I knew I had to find you. The way she talked about you, I knew. That night after she died—"

"After you killed her." I'm going to vomit if my sister's name crosses his lips again.

He grins like the crazy person he is. Noelle knew it.

"That night I went to her dorm room to do some, uh, research if you will, while her roommate was away." He lifts one hand to run his finger along my jaw and down my neck. "I went through her stuff, I read her diary, and I found out a little more about what happened to you, Carrot."

"You're sick, Hayden." His grip on my arms tightens.

"It's the girls like you that are the most interesting. You can't see that, can you? The girls who are hiding something. Secrets, their true selves, anything they want to keep from the world. So much fun finding out what's underneath, what they are hiding. You're so much like your sister in that way, Kara. You don't even see it. I mean sisters usually are alike in some ways. But then you two are so different . . ."

I shake my head.

"Kellen was tough, but underneath everything she was showing the rest of the world, there was so much good there. She wasn't just what she wanted the world to see. I saw her. I *saw*. She wasn't the partying loser she showed to everyone else. What she showed me was so different. Do you know the hard classes she was taking? She lied about them to her friends. She diminished them, said she was only in college to party and get away from her parents. Such a lie. Did you know what she planned on doing with herself?"

"No," I whisper.

"She tried to hide things from me, and she tried to hide her good side from me. Especially when she talked about you. But then one day I'm not sure what happened. She zipped back up into that fake self, her I-don't-give-a-fuck-about-life self. I couldn't see her anymore. I couldn't even reach her anymore. And then she met *him*."

He takes an arm off the wall to run his hands through his hair. But he catches himself and I'm caged again.

"I didn't plan on killing her. Sometimes things happen."

"Hayden—"

"*Shh*," he interrupts. "Don't you see that you were always so much more than Kellen?

"You want the world to think you're just a pot-smoking shadow, waiting for a ride out of your miserable life. You don't see that your hope, your passion comes out in everything and you couldn't hide it even if you wanted to. You can't hide all that from me. Your real self. And you knew it, you couldn't hide it from me, and here we are."

My eyes dart around the café, frantic for any kind of escape. "Please stop. You're sick."

"San Francisco was *fun*. But now it seems I need to finish this." He moves his mouth over to my ear, his breath hot on the side of my face. "But no need to rush *this*. I know you've always wanted me. You were gasping for it."

I'm going to throw up. I look away, up to the ceiling, as he presses his body into mine, his hands wrapping around my back, strangling my middle. Hayden kisses my neck and my chest and then he pulls away. When his hands slide down to my hips, I see my chance; his eyes are fixed on where he's touching me. I push my hands hard against his chest and he stumbles back into the counter.

I look at the front door but there are so many locks and I hear Hayden behind me, so I bolt for the apartment. I can call the cops when I get up there. Thank God I left the downstairs door open. I hear the thudding on the stairs behind me and don't even want to look, but I do. His eyes are wild and angry.

"You belong to *me*, Kara. You read the notes. There's nowhere for you to run where I can't get you. I can find you anywhere."

His words are muffled behind the thumping pulse in my ears as I run into my room, slamming the door and locking it. Kellen's pocketknife still sits on the nightstand and I grab it, clenching my fingers around the handle.

Hayden kicks the door and it swings open. He rushes at me

and his face is crazy. There's no hint of the Hayden I crushed on, only a psycho, crawling on top of me. The pocketknife is under my back, and Hayden's pinning my wrists together above my head with one hand while the other works at the top of my jeans.

He's straddling me, almost sitting on me. I want my mom. I've never wanted or needed my mom more than I do right now.

He's going to kill me and I feel a strange calm about all of it. He killed my sister. And how many others?

I see Kellen. She's right behind Hayden and for a second I think she might actually do something to help but she can't.

FOUR-YEAR-OLD CARROT

I'm four, standing on the edge of the pool. Mommy squints against the sun and holds her arms out to catch me because the water's way over my head. I jump and water, cold and burning, splashes my eyes but I see Mommy's smile. She cheers for me and kisses my cheek and tells me I am a good girl and she's so proud. Kellen squints at me, smiling at me from behind Mom as she clings to her shoulder. She leans over to kiss my cheek, too.

33. *Press until it springs back.*

. . . .

I can't breathe. Hayden's on top of me. His fingers rip away the last button of my jeans. The shame, the helplessness, the sickness in my middle is back, making me feel *that night* again because Hayden's lost in kissing me and I lay there like bones and meat. He's gnawing, chewing away at the carcass of my thirteen-year-old self. Because I'm disappearing. I'm gone, far away.

I'm in my bakery, rolling out dough on my big work counter all dusted in flour. Sugar cookies bake in my giant oven. The kitchen smells of warm, buttery sugar and yeast. The sun shines in through the back door I've left open. Charlie's out front ringing up customers, chatting with them, making sure they plan to come back tomorrow and buy my cookies and cakes and pies and breads.

My lower back is killing me but I don't care because I love the work. Charlie comes into the kitchen, smiling at me as he holds delivery bags. He comes around the counter to kiss me and ends up with flour all over his shirt.

"Hey there, Sprinkles. I'm off to make a delivery. Watch the front for a bit?" He kisses me again. "There's nothing I won't do for you."

34. *Add sprinkles if you wish.*

· ·

Now the pocketknife burns into my back.

"Hayden, stop, free my hands so I can touch you, too, okay?"

He stares down at me, considering the offer. "You'll make it worse if you try anything."

I nod. The pocketknife is molten under my skin. "We have time, right?"

He lets go of my arms and stares at me, testing me maybe. I reach up and pull him down to me and when we start kissing I stick one hand into his hair. The other hand moves slowly, under my thigh and up until I feel the handle of the knife.

I have a firm grip on it when I reach around to his back and massage there with my clenched fist, not letting the knife touch him. While I figure out how to open the knife without him hearing it, I'm afraid that he'll realize I'm disgusted by his tongue in my mouth.

I cry out at the same time I click open the knife. Hayden pulls up and off me and I know I'm caught. But he's smiling at me with one eyebrow raised; maybe he thinks he's given me some kind of pleasure. Bile rises in my throat but I manage to smile back. I pull him down for another kiss at the same time as I swing the knife out in front of me. He smothers me with his body while I thrust the knife toward his belly.

Kellen's twirling next to me, like we used to when we'd wear dresses or skirts. She's smiling. Smiling and twirling. Her hair is free and flowing and outlined in gold.

Hayden's blood runs warm and sticky over me.

Noelle and Mason walk in the door with Mom right behind them.

That's the last thing I remember.

35. *Make a fresh batch.*

. . . .

Two weeks ago I almost killed Hayden.

That's what Noelle told me, anyway. With some pride, I might add. But Mom says she and Noelle and Mason pulled Hayden off me before I could seriously hurt him with the pocketknife. We were both in the hospital—me hooked to monitors I didn't need because I wasn't physically hurt, and Hayden cuffed to the bed, due to wind up with a scar on his belly he'll never forget. Noelle faked being his sister and visited him. She snapped a picture with her cell.

Now he's in jail for attacking me, and Noah identified him as the person who beat him up in the school parking lot. The police are gathering evidence, including my notes, to try and charge him with murdering my sister.

I want to forget it all, but I know that won't happen. Instead, every day I go back to my old house because usually it makes me feel better.

I keep hoping to see my sister.

Sometimes when I leave the house I go to Charlie's church. I'm not sure what I believe about the life after this one but I know that sitting in the quiet, empty church, next to the candles I light, also makes me feel better. Mom found this out and has tried to get me to go to Bible study with her. No way.

But today my old house feels different. I look at the trampoline, surrounded by tall, dead winter grass because the new family doesn't have time for yard work, I guess. I can picture the pink balloons tied all around it and the bow that Mom stuck right in the middle of it for my eighth birthday. I can taste the cherry frosting from the cupcake I dropped onto it an hour later.

When I look one last time down the side of the house, I see Kellen jumping on the trampoline. Her hair is loose, free from the ponytail she usually has. She smiles. My sister's black hair bounces and flies all around her face, and the hood of her jacket flaps behind her head. With one hand she pushes black hair out of her eyes. Her other arm stretches out toward me, and her palm is up, her fingers waggling back and forth.

My sister wants me to jump with her.

I step forward and she's gone.

When I look up at her window, I see her.

My sister Kellen is forever seventeen. I'm sixteen, on my way to a lifetime of possibilities.

Birthdays, experiences, and new memories waiting to happen, and not a single one of them will ever include my sister.

The rest of my life. Forever.

Without my big sister.

I see Kellen behind a big heart drawn on her foggy window.

She peeks behind her and then at me, and presses a hand to the window.

And then she's gone.

I know that's it.

I've lost her.

I can't remember my sister's voice.

I don't belong here anymore.

"You okay?"

I turn around to see Charlie. He leans against the tree, his arms folded, and he's smiling at me.

I walk into his arms and bury my face in his chest. He's quiet, just holding my head against him.

After a while we walk back to the café. Mom twirls around with utter giddiness at seeing us, hand in hand.

"Hmm, now there's the power of pea soup," she whispers in my ear as I walk Charlie to the door of the kitchen.

I only smile because she's crazy. But I'd rather have her happy and crazy than no mom at all. And her new family, her café family, loves her, too, no matter what.

"Why don't you bake me cookies?" Charlie suggests as he ties on his apron. As he walks toward me, I step backward to the wall. He pulls me to him. "That would give you an excuse to hang out back here with me." He kisses me. "What do you think?"

"That you might be fired if that happened. But call me later when you're off?" I give him a last peck before I duck under his arms.

I'm yanked back by his hand. "Hey!" Charlie hugs me tightly before he kisses the top of my head and turns to the sink.

I walk back out to the dining area and sit down with Noelle.

Noah Bender is there. His face tells me he didn't plan on Noelle being here.

Noelle's eyes flit from me to Noah and back again. Noah scratches under the cast on his left arm, and I can see Noelle revving up to start something. I see a lot of my sister in her, so I'm happy that she's my friend. Even after Hayden attacked me, I only got one week off from her snark.

I'm actually meeting my old friend Jen Creighton for coffee tomorrow. She came by the shop and left a note for me when I missed the week of school after what happened with Hayden.

Kara—

That last summer, after 8th grade. Did Gaby and I do something to hurt you? You left the pool that day and never talked to us again. Whatever we did, whatever I did, I'm sorry and I miss you. I hope it's not too late. I don't know why you're not at school

*now and I hope it's not something bad. Please call me. If you
want to. I miss you.*

—Jen

No one at school knows what happened with Hayden except
Noelle and Mason. Noah didn't offer any info because I guess
he's embarrassed. He's been to the café a lot lately, just to stop
by and say hi, working off his guilt. He has to testify against
Hayden when he goes on trial for my sister's murder.

Jessica pops over to our table and ignores everyone except
Noah. There are other customers in the place who were here
before us and I see the annoyance on their faces. But then all of
them are older: no one Jessica can drool over.

"What can I get you?" Jessica leans over, smiling at Noah.

"Oh, *Jess*-ica?" Noelle sings.

I squirm in my seat, waiting for it.

"Yeah, what?" Jessica scribbles on her notepad.

Noelle cracks her knuckles and elbows me. "Noah, there.
He's *single, and* he's applying for the dishwasher job. Remember
what I told you about dishwashers?"

Jessica grunts and huffs off to another table.

"You're such a pig, Noelle," I tell her.

"I'm aware, and yet you stick with me."

Mom twirls by and drops an envelope in front of me. Reflexively I don't even want to touch it but when I turn it over I see
the postmark and the return address: It's La Patisserie.

Mom leans over to whisper in my ear. "Whatever that is, I
promise that we'll talk about it, okay?"

I nod as I pull a piece of paper from the envelope. Clipped to
it is a business card with a picture of the gray-haired judge from
the baking contest. In the picture her arms are folded and she
smiles at me, wearing her double-buttoned chef's uniform.

I set the card down and my heart skips a little when I read the
handwritten note.

Dear Kara—

You are quite a talented pastry artist. I hope you will pursue a career in this field because you have a remarkable future. Please consider applying for a scholarship, and since you need a reference to apply for entrance into our school, I'd be honored to write a letter for you. Please see my contact information on the enclosed business card. I wish you the best of luck!

Sincerely,
Kate Connors
Dean of Students
La Patisserie Pastry School

I read it three more times, until Noelle pulls it away from me to read it herself.

"Wow, Kar. Very awesome." She smiles and tosses the paper back to me.

It is very awesome. I stand up and tell everyone I'll see them later. Then I walk back into my corner of the kitchen. Charlie notices and blows me a soap bubbly kiss. I move the crap that other people have loaded onto *my* work counter and I'm not even pissed about it.

How can I be pissed when I'm in the mood to bake?

INGREDIENTS:

1	cup (2 sticks) of unsalted butter, at room temperature
2	cups sugar
2	eggs
2	teaspoons real vanilla extract
4	cups flour
1	teaspoon baking powder
1/2	teaspoon salt

KARA'S PRIZE-WINNING SUGAR COOKIE RECIPE

PREPARATION:

Mix butter and sugar with electric mixer until fluffy. PS: If you didn't have time to bring your butter to room temperature, then put in the microwave and heat on half-power and check it every 30 seconds so you don't end up with melted butter. FYI: melted butter doesn't work, trust me.

Mix in eggs and vanilla.

Mix together flour, baking powder, and salt. PS: I sift it, but if you don't have a sifter then just mix it well so all your salt isn't in once place because then you end up with one cookie that is very salty. Ick.

Add the flour mixture to the butter mixture, a little at a time. Add, stir, add, stir, etc. Make sure all of the flour is mixed in. Scrape the sides and the bottom with a big rubber spatula. Flour likes to hide at the bottom of your bowl. If you don't mind messy hands, use them to mix it up.

Split the dough in half. Roll each half into a big ball and flatten into a disc. Wrap them in plastic and put in the fridge for a few hours or overnight. I always wait until the next day.

Preheat oven to 325 degrees Fahrenheit.

Prepare your surface: I always put down parchment paper and then flour it up. Then I top the dough with more flour and squash it flat before I roll it out with the rolling pin. Roll until the dough is about ¼-inch thick.

Prepare your cookie sheet: If you want to be a real baker, you really need Silpats. But they are expensive. So parchment is cheaper. Lay the parchment over the cookie sheet, all the way to the edges.

Use whatever cookie cutters you have to cut out shapes and put them on a cookie sheet lined with parchment. Beware! This is the part of cookie baking that is frustrating and will likely make you eat raw cookie dough because you get mad! But don't eat it! It's bad for you, raw eggs and stuff.

Sometimes, if you are lucky, you can pinch the cookie cutter together a little and it keeps the dough in it so you can move it quickly to the cookie sheet and release it there. If that doesn't work then use a floured spatula to carefully lift the raw cookies.

Anyway, lay out the cookies about an inch apart. Maybe more depending on the size. But really, sometimes your first batch ends up in the trash because cookies bake too close together so you end up with a cookie sheet that looks like a mess of dough. Like you wanted hearts and you end up with big puffy apple shapes.

Toss your cookie dough scraps into the bowl and refrigerate the dough you aren't using until you need it. Just remember—dough is easier to work with when it's a little colder.

Bake for about 10 minutes, but probably more like 15. You should check them at 10 minutes because it really depends on your oven or if you live up high in the mountains, etc. Watch carefully. The cookies should be golden around the edges. If they turn darker, don't panic, they will still taste good. But if they turn really, really dark then feed them to the trash can.

Let them sit on the cookie sheet for a few minutes before you transfer them to a rack.

When they are cool you can decorate them with either a tub of store-bought frosting, or you can be a real baker and make royal icing **(recipe follows)**. But then, who doesn't love a tub of store-bought frosting?

Store your cookies in an airtight container. In the fridge or freezer is really the best.

INGREDIENTS:

3   cups powdered sugar
(Real bakers call this confectioners' sugar.)
Have more ready in case you need it to make thicker icing,
which you want for piping.

1/4   cup warm water

1   tablespoon light corn syrup

1/4   teaspoon vanilla extract. Depending on what flavor you
want your icing to be, you can use almond (which tastes
like cherry), lemon, orange, or peppermint extract.

PREPARATION:

*Stir liquid ingredients together until corn syrup and extract have dissolved.

*Place powdered sugar into a separate bowl, and add the liquid ingredients.

*Beat with an electric mixer on low until smooth, and until you get the consistency you want. (If you want to use it for piping lines and adding details, you'll need thicker icing, so add extra powdered sugar a spoonful at a time. If you want to use it for flooding, add more water, but if you add liquid food coloring that will thin out the icing, too, so add that first.)

*Work quickly to get the icing into a piping bag. It can dry fast so keep it covered if you aren't using it right away. It can be stored for a week in a covered container in the fridge.

*If you aren't piping, you can spoon it on, too.

*Add sprinkles if you wish.

Acknowledgments

· ·

Thanks to the teachers, librarians and booksellers who put books into my younger hands, and for putting *this* book into someone's hands.

To my agent, Sarah Davies: From the second we met at SCBWI, you pushed me. I *adore* and fear you, and can listen to you talk all day! Your eyes, your questions, your digging, cutting and shaping made this book 1,000 times better and I'm in debt to you! I can only pay you back in cake pops for life. They make for good fairy wands.

To my editor, Dan Ehrenhaft, you're responsible for many happy tears. There's no better home for Kara and her story. Your love for this story and your guidance, kindness and affirmations have made this a sugary sweet experience. Thanks to Bronwen Hruska, Meredith Barnes, Rachel Kowal, Janine Agro and *everyone* at Soho Press. I hope I can meet you all someday. You've made this girl's *lifelong dream* come true!

Thanks to my critique girls: Greenhouse sisters Ashley Elston and Wendy Howell Mills; Tracey Neithercott, Bridgette Booth, Karen B. Schwartz, and beautiful Raynbow Gignilliat—rest in peace; you'll always be our Revising Queen. Most of all I thank you, Kelly Jensen, for pushing to make this sharp and pointy, and for reading my first chapters a gazillion times.

To my sister, Tara Stivers, who shares my love of writing YA, and who understands heart-palpitating words like "I got a partial!" like no one else in our family can.

I'm indebted to SCBWI Western WA and their annual writer conferences. (Thanks to Mandy Hubbard for introducing my sister and me to this conference and letting us sit at the Cool Kids table that year!) Thanks to my SCBWI WWA writer pals, my Blueboarders, The Fearless Fifteeners and The Fall Fifteeners: writing is solitary, but I *never* feel alone.

Thanks to my first creative writing teacher at Highline Community College for putting my work in the campus publication. You were the first one to love something I wrote.

To my friends and family, especially my brothers, and my parents, Julie and Ray Beatty, and the late Michael Grogan, for encouraging my imagination and always keeping me stocked with books, paper and ink.

To my husband, Blair, for supporting and encouraging me, and not complaining when I make dinners that are good for three nights. XO

To Keeley and Jack, you are my heart. Watch out for each other.